Peter Kay's
Phoenix
Nights

Dedicated to Michael Kay,
Gordon Bramwell and Pat Leonard

Thanks to
Natalie Jerome, Gordon Wise and everyone at Pan Macmillan,
Danielle Lux, Iain Morris, Kevin Lygo, Cheryl Taylor, Mark Herbert,
John Rushton, Henry Klejdys, Andy Hibbert, Jim Holloway,
John Wood and all the staff at the Soundhouse in Manchester

Special thanks to Susan, Deirdre, Edith, Julie, Mark,
Adam and Alex Kay, Lucy Ansbro, Adele Fowler, Kathryn Lowrie,
Chris Greeney, Michael Connell, Paul Coleman, Toni Baker, Liz Gallacher,
Marie Irving-Murphy, Peter Hallworth and Phil McIntyre

Extra Special thanks to Dave Spikey, Neil Fitzmaurice and Patrick McGuinness

Peter Kay's Phoenix Nights

The Scripts
Series 1 and 2

4 BOOKS

First published 2003 by Channel 4 Books
an imprint of Pan Macmillan Ltd
Pan Macmillan, 20 New Wharf Road, London N1 9RR
Basingstoke and Oxford
Associated companies throughout the world
www.panmacmillan.com

ISBN 0 7522 65229

Photography by Ken Loveday (Series 1) and Paul Cliff (Series 2)

Series 1
Written by Peter Kay, Dave Spikey & Neil Fitzmaurice
Director Johnny Campell
Producers John Rushton & Mark Herbert
Executive Producer Phil McIntyre

Series 2
Written by Peter Kay, Dave Spikey & Neil Fitzmaurice
Director Peter Kay
Producer Henry Klejdys
Executive Producer Phil McIntyre

1 3 5 7 9 8 6 4 2

A CIP catalogue record for this book is available from the British Library.

Designed by seagulls
Printed by Bath Press

Channel Four and Peter Kay woulld like to state that the character of Keith Lard may have led some persons
to wrongly believe that the character was based on a Mr Keith Laird. We wish to make it clear this is not the case,
and would like to apologise to Mr Laird and his family for the distress caused. We have also agreed to make a
donation to the Fire Service Benevolent Fund and to Mr Laird's family for his and his family's personal distress.

Mr Laird's contribution to fire safety in Bolton is well documented
and his professionalism and personal integrity are not in any doubt.

**If you would llike more information on fire safety either contact your local fire station
or go to channel4.com/firesafety for a list of links to useful websites. This information has been
put together with the co-operation of both Greater Manchester County Fire Service and Keith Laird.**

Contents

Foreword 6

Foreword

I've been thinking about what to write for this foreword for the last few hours or so, whether to write it as myself or as Brian Potter. I've decided to write it as myself. All Brian would do anyway is moan a lot and mention that the Phoenix is open six nights a week with coach parties and charities welcome.

Phoenix Nights was born out of *That Peter Kay Thing*, my first series, six slices of life set in Bolton and conceived as spoof documentary style. Extremely pleased with that series but also realising the restrictions of style I decided to jump ship and turn faction into fiction.

I'd always loved clubland, the escape of it all, car alarms and razor wire outside, line dancing and a Neil Diamond tribute act inside. I also knew that clubland was in bad shape, I kept seeing them boarded up round the north of England.

Dave Spikey and myself started to visit a few clubs armed with a Dictaphone, a ball-point pen microphone from the Spy Shop in Manchester hidden in my leather jacket (it was July). We'd chat to the club owners at great length about the way the club was run and what plans they had to get the punters through the door. We found that they all had a few things in common, grand dreams, no money and a rival club down the road that they were obviously pissing on from a great height. We knew we had comedy gold, all we had to do now was mine it.

We hired an office in Bolton Business Centre, asked Neil Fitzmaurice to join us once again and began writing a series that would become *Phoenix Nights*. Other title suggestions included 'Out Of Order' and 'On Its Arse' but we didn't fancy handing the critics any ammunition. My old school friend Patrick McGuinness would occasionally wander in between shifts at the Leisure Centre and throw us some comedy gems such as 'a dwarf fight, Robot Wars and Max and Paddy driving the Asian Elders'.

We wrote the series quite quickly, in two months in fact and we knew that if we could pull it off we had a winner. But we never wanted to take the piss out of Brian and the others, we wanted it to be affectionate. I've never been a subscriber to the comedy of hate, I wanted to create an atmosphere similar to *Only Fools and Horses*. No matter how much you knew Brian Potter was an underhand, devious crook you couldn't help but feel sorry for him and his collection of loyal misfits.

We continued the second year with a second series which was harder now because of the high standard we'd set ourselves on the first but in other ways it was easier, too, because we knew the characters. The pressure was on, but to our surprise we pulled it off again.

This book is a collection of the full original scripts. I hope you enjoy them as much we enjoyed writing them. I never would have believed that one day the work we did over those two summers would eventually be published. I suppose it's every writer's dream and a personal triumph for me as I never passed my English GCSE (fuck you, Mrs Dutson).

I don't know if the Phoenix will ever rise again, only time will tell. But until then don't forget to live the dream, and thank the Lord for spell check.

Peter Kay

Series 1

Episode 1

PART ONE

1. EXT. MAIN ROAD. DAY
We hear CHORLEY FM on the soundtrack.

PAUL LE ROY
    You're listening to Chorley FM. I'm
    Paul Le Roy, coming in your ears,
    and here's Yazz, and she's going up.
    The Phoenix Club in Bolton has its
    grand reopening tonight with chart-
    topping folk band Half a Shilling and
    TV's own Roy 'It's the way I tell
    them' Walker will be cutting the
    ribbon at seven thirty. Tickets are
    fifteen pounds each and that
    includes supper and bingo.

*BRIAN POTTER is riding on his shop-
mobility. Traffic building up behind him.
Behind him we see a man scrubbing painted
graffiti off a gable-end wall: 'ROGER
HALLIWELL SHAGGED MY WIFE' – he looks
around nervously and scrubs.*

BRIAN turns into the club car park.

CUT TO

2. EXT. CAR PARK. DAY
*Reveal on club. KENNY SNR and YOUNG
KENNY are on the roof installing fairy
lights. KENNY SNR hears BRIAN on the
radio, pulls out his mobile and dials.*

KENNY SNR
    Hello.

BRIAN   Hello.

KENNY   Hey, you've just been on the radio.

BRIAN   Have we? Did they mention the ticket prices?

KENNY SNR
    Yeah, they did. Where are you?

We cut back to BRIAN.

BRIAN   I'm behind you. I'm coming in now. Get me chair ready.

KENNY SNR
    Kenny, get his chair ready, he's on his way now.

YOUNG KENNY climbs down ladder and goes into club.

BRIAN rolls out of shot, then pulls up and stops.

KENNY SNR
    Hey, what d'you think?

YOUNG KENNY comes out of the club with BRIAN's wheelchair.

BRIAN   You need more bulbs than that. Think Las Vegas.

KENNY SNR
    Las Vegas?

BRIAN   A couple missing there.

KENNY SNR
    Where?

BRIAN   Right in corner, at the back there. They want them to see it for miles around. Opening night tonight.

CUT TO

3. INT. CLUB FOYER. DAY

In mid-decoration, there are pots of paint and dustsheets everywhere. There is a poster on the wall advertising the opening night. There is a model of a disabled boy and guide-dog moneybox in the corridor. BRIAN goes out of his way during the conversation to pat it on the head.

BRIAN   I can't ... I can't hear no banging. Where's Rafferty?

YOUNG KENNY
    He's on his dinner.

BRIAN   Dinner? It's half past ten in the bloody morning. Look at all this: it's a disgrace. All this ... We've got VIPs coming tonight. That Pennine Suite should be finished.

BRIAN looks up at the religious banner hanging from the ceiling: 'CH _ _ CH'? What's missing – 'UR'?

BRIAN   (cont.) Where is she?

YOUNG KENNY
    Who?

BRIAN   Holy Mary.

CUT TO

4. INT. JOCKEY WILSON SUITE. DAY

HOLY MARY is sitting on her own, blowing up religious balloons with helium. BRIAN comes over with a banner in his hand and throws it down onto the table. Photo of Jockey Wilson in action on the wall.

BRIAN   What are all these about?

HOLY MARY
          Well, you said banners.

BRIAN   I said ... don't wind me up, not today; get 'em down.

HOLY MARY
          (GIGGLES) What, here?

BRIAN   (READING BALLOON) 'Make it right, see the light'. Pop 'em or sling 'em or something. It's a club, not a mosque.

HOLY MARY
          Aah, Brian, they're not doing any harm.

BRIAN   (WHEELING HIMSELF OFF) Tell that to Cat Stevens – we'll be serving holy tonic water next.

HOLY MARY
          (SUCKS IN HELIUM) God loves you, Brian.

BRIAN   Does he? He's a funny way of showing it.

CUT TO

5. INT. GALAXY LOUNGE. DAY

BRIAN wheels himself behind the bar. We see only the top of his head. He gets a glass and reaches for the optics, but they have been raised up and are too high.

BRIAN   Rafferty! I'll ... I'll bloody kill him.

MARION enters from kitchen. BRIAN looks for something to use as a drinking glass. He sees a big vase at the end of the bar with about thirty or so flowers in it (one for each table and thirty little vases lined up by the side of it). He reaches up and takes out all the flowers.

MARION Oh, you're here. Nice of you to pop in. That phone's not stopped.

BRIAN   Mmmmm.

MARION I've enough to do as it is without being your secretary ...

BRIAN hands her the flowers. She starts to put them into the individual vases.

MARION (cont.) Mayor's office have confirmed, local papers are coming down. Eric's sending a fruit machine, damaged pasties are here at two, Roy Walker'll be here at six and pot washer won't work.

BRIAN   Where is he, lazy sod?

MARION Motor's playing up and you better
            sort it, 'cause you can think again if
            you think I'm using these …

She holds up her hands to him and shows
him her painted nails.

MARION (Cont.) … seventeen quid these …
            each.

She turns and goes back through the door.

BRIAN   Where's the Saint?

MARION Where d'you think?

CUT TO

6. INT. GENTS' TOILETS. DAY

JERRY St CLAIR, the compere, is on the
toilet. He is reading a pamphlet 'COLON
CARE' (ENDORSED BY BOB CAROLGEES).
He reads a few of the lines, then he raises
himself up and looks over his shoulder down
into the toilet. We hear BRIAN come in.

BRIAN   Jerry?

JERRY   What?

BRIAN   How long are you gonna be?

JERRY   How long's a piece of string?

BRIAN   What string?

JERRY   It's a saying.

BRIAN   Balls to that. Have you phoned the
            band?

JERRY   No, not yet. Look, Brian, I've had
            some bad reports. Jon Picard at the
            Vulcan had 'em las' week and it was
            nearly a riot.

BRIAN   A riot with Half a Shilling? They're
            a folk band – they're not The Who.
            They've had a song in the charts,
            flat caps and clogs – this lot will lap
            it up. And anyway, they've been
            booked for months.

JERRY   No, I've got a bad feeling.

BRIAN   It'll be your arse. Now get 'em rung.

JERRY   And we should have had a support
            for fifteen quid a ticket.

BRIAN   They've got enough. Free bingo and
            a pasty-and-pea supper. What more
            do they want?

JERRY   I'm not sure.

BRIAN   Well *I* am. Come on, stop crapping,
            get crackin' – we've work to do.
            Avanti!

CUT TO

7. EXT. CAR PARK. DAY

BRIAN argues with a DELIVERY MAN.
YOUNG KENNY is there. Das Boot fruit
machine is delivered. THE CAPTAIN
hovers around.

DELIVERY MAN
    It's the last one on the van.

BRIAN   I don't care if it's the *Last of the Mohicans*, I ordered *The Matrix*, I didn't order *Das Boot*.

DELIVERY MAN
    (TRYING TO SELL IT) It was a classic film.

BRIAN   Well, you take it, then. Stick it in your front room, impress your friends.

DELIVERY MAN
    I don't gamble.

BRIAN   And neither do I. I don't gamble. That my friend there's a gamble. Where's Eric? I want to speak to the organist, not the monkey grinder.

DELIVERY MAN
    He's busy.

THE CAPTAIN
    What door do you want me on tonight?

BRIAN   He's busy? I'm busy ...
    (TO CAPTAIN) What?

THE CAPTAIN
    What door do you want me on tonight?

BRIAN   Not now, Captain, get in.

DELIVERY MAN
    I'll give you a fortnight's free trial.

In the background we see ten or so builders walking across the car park. RAFFERTY is leading at the front. The other men are carrying oil lamps, traffic cones and a bag of yeast.

BRIAN   Make it a month.

DELIVERY MAN nods.

BRIAN   (cont.) Right, stick it in the Pennine Suite ... Oh, from one clown to another ... (SHOUTING) Where the hell have you been?

RAFFERTY
    Getting supplies.

BRIAN   What for, your gut? Ay – you'll work your dinner, I'll see to that. I don't know if you've heard, but we open tonight.

RAFFERTY
    Look, don't worry – it'll all be sorted.

BRIAN   I'd like to agree, but I'm not as feng shui as you. Now get the rest of the bloody Village People, get it inside and get glossing. Hey, Kenny, get me Zantac. I'm filling up here.

KENNY   What?

BRIAN   And me, get me an' all. Come on, up and at 'um, Pennine Suite, dickhead.

CUT TO

8. INT. BACKSTAGE/DRESSING ROOM. DAY

JERRY is rummaging around. LES goes past with his suit carrier.

LES   Hi, Jerry.

JERRY   Les, Les, have you seen bingo machine?

LES   No, have you seen Alan?

JERRY   Why, has he got it?

LES   No, he's not—

JERRY   What's up?

LES   (WORRIED) He should be here by now.

JERRY   Where is he?

LES   (SECRETLY) He's driving, long-haul, from Stranraer.

JERRY   Stranraer? In Scotland? Does Potter know? He'll do his bloody nut. Who's gonna do keyboards for my opening number?

LES   He'll be here ... he won't let us down.

A dopey-looking lad carrying a box of cds comes backstage.

SPENCER All right.

LES   All right, Spencer lad, did you find it all right?

SPENCER Er, just about.

LES   Jerry – Spencer, Spencer – Jerry, he's one of the lads from the youth club; he's going to do the disco for us tonight.

SPENCER All right, Jerry.

JERRY   All right.

JERRY   Are you having a sale, son, 'cause we've not got a CD player.

CUT TO

9. EXT. CAR PARK. DAY

MAX and PADDY (the club bouncers) are busy outside the club.

MAX   So he jumped on me back, I slipped me jacket off, he went down, I went in with me boot.

PADDY   Nowt wrong with that.

MAX   (DEMONSTRATES) ... quick scissor kick to the temple. Goodnight, my friend.

PADDY puts the ladder down.

PADDY   You see, that's why I don't go to parents' evenings, they get me angry.

MAX   I know what you mean.

PADDY   Come on, up you go.

MAX   Up *you* go, I'm not going up there.

PADDY   Why not?

MAX   Two words. Falklands.

PADDY   Come on.

CUT TO

10. INT. GALAXY LOUNGE. DAY

*JERRY is rehearsing 'NEW YORK, NEW
YORK'. He has TWO BUILDERS doing the
backing for him on stage. LES is on the
drums. As JERRY is singing we cut to
another part of the room where SPENCER is*
*setting up the DJ equipment. KENNY SNR
holds up two records, 'CHART ENCOUNTERS'
and 'THE SNOWMAN'.*

JERRY   (SINGING) I wanna be a part of it,
        Phoenix, Phoenix …

THE CAPTAIN
        What door do you want me on
        tonight?

BRIAN   Sod off. Whoa, whoa, whoa, whoa,
        whoa. Sweet baby Jesus and the
        orphans! What the hell's going on?
        Are my eyes dreaming, Jerry, or
        have you got two of my builders
        singing 'Acapulco'?

JERRY   I'm rehearsing, aren't I. It's me new opening for tonight.

BRIAN   What opening? There's not going to be an opening, not with the pissing Lighthouse Family up there singing instead of grafting. Get down, the pair of you ... Where's Alan? (PAUSE) Well, Leslie?

LES   (MUMBLING) Stranraer.

BRIAN   Where?

LES   Stranraer.

BRIAN   (LOSES IT) Stranraer? In Scotland? Today! Stranraer. Oh, me angina. You're killing me. Do you want to sing at me funeral, lads, because it's coming?

CUT TO

11. EXT. HARD SHOULDER. DAY
Articulated lorry, broken down. An A.R.C. 24-hour MECHANIC is close under the bonnet. ALAN's mobile rings. We cut to a close-up. It reads 'IRONSIDE' on the screen. He presses it off.

CUT TO

12. INT. GALAXY LOUNGE. DAY
We hear the voice on BRIAN's mobile: 'The mobile phone you have dialled is not responding. Please try again later.'

BRIAN   Not responding. He probably can't get a signal in Stranraer!

CUT TO

13. EXT. HARD SHOULDER. DAY
ALAN looks at his phone.

CUT TO

14. INT. GALAXY LOUNGE. DAY
BRIAN hangs up.

BRIAN   Balls to him! Can we close the circus and open the club? (TO YOUNG KENNY) You—

MARION   (INTERRUPTING) Brian, the man from the brewery's here.

BRIAN   Young Kenny, give these to Max and Paddy – headsets, so they've got to wear 'em, no buts. (TO JERRY) Anything else you want to tell me?

JERRY   I think somebody's nicked the bingo machine.

SPENCER Let's get ready to rumble.

BRIAN   Leslie. Can I have a word?

CUT TO

15. EXT. CAR PARK. DAY
MAX is up the ladders and PADDY is holding them. They're putting up banners.

MAX   You holding these or what?

PADDY   Shut up. Stop moaning.

PADDY searches round for a banner. MAX looks down on his head.

MAX   Chuck us an 'ammer.

PADDY   Here.

MAX   You going bald?

PADDY   No.

MAX   I can see your head through your hair.

PADDY   It's always been like that.

MAX   Since when?

PADDY   Since forever? Me hair, it's very fine.

MAX   It's thin, I don't know about fine, it's thin.

PADDY   It's not thin, it's not thin, all right?

MAX   Not thin, it's anorexic.

PADDY   (SHAKES THE LADDERS) Oy, shut it.

MAX   Whoa, dickhead.

YOUNG KENNY
          (COMES OVER) Here, here, these are for tonight. Brian said you've got to wear them.

PADDY   What are they?

YOUNG KENNY
          Headsets.

MAX   Headsets?

PADDY   Sets? For your head?

CUT TO

16. INT. GALAXY LOUNGE. DAY

BRIAN is looking at the brochures and talking to the BREWERY REP. THE CAPTAIN is still hovering with his door tin.

BREWERY REP
          See, it's all down here. Grand gala opening of the Phoenix Club.

BRIAN   Yeah, very good.

BREWERY REP
          Smithills Brewery.

BRIAN   Who's Brain?

BREWERY REP
          Brain?

BRIAN   Brain Potter. Brain Potter at the front and Brain Potter at the back. Disgrace.

BREWERY REP
          Where on earth does it say that?

BRIAN opens the brochure and inside there is a pop-up model of a club (not The Phoenix).

BREWERY REP
Pop-up.

BRIAN   Pop-up.

BREWERY REP
Aye.

BRIAN   What club's that? Whose club's that?
That's not my club, son.

BREWERY REP
Da da!

BRIAN   Who the hell's that? Who's that
supposed to be?

BREWERY REP
It's you.

BRIAN   Get it off. Get it off now!

YOUNG KENNY walks up to BRIAN and the
BREWERY MAN and throws down the
headsets.

YOUNG KENNY
Stick 'em up your arse.

CUT TO

17. EXT. CAR PARK. DAY
MAX and PADDY are still putting up the
banners. MAX is up ladders.

MAX   I know why you won't wear them
headsets.

PADDY   Why?

MAX   You don't want to mess up your
hair ... (LAUGHS) What hair you've
got left.

PADDY   Don't.

MAX   Baldy – baldy bouncer.

PADDY   Leave it.

MAX   Baldy, baldy bouncer, baldy, baldy
bouncer.

PADDY   (SHOUTING) Leave it.

PADDY pushes the ladders. MAX falls
through a window at the side of him.

CUT TO

18. INT. GALAXY LOUNGE. DAY
BRIAN is still arguing with the BREWERY
REP. He has YOUNG KENNY cutting off the
pop-up Brian potters with a pair of scissors
and dropping them into a bucket.

BRIAN   That's it ... every last one of them.

We hear a loud crash from the Pennine Suite.

BRIAN   (cont.) Shine a light, what were that?

CUT TO

19. INT. PENNINE SUITE. DAY
MAX is lying on the floor, glass around him.
BRIAN enters with the others. PADDY enters
a second later, panting. The BUILDERS attach
various items to the ceiling. A megaphone, oil
lamps, traffic cones. BRIAN looks up.

PADDY   Max? Is he all right? Has he fell?

MAX   Jesus Christ. Help me, will you?

BRIAN   Shut up, you girl.

MAX   Help me, will you?

BRIAN   Look at my window.

END OF PART ONE

PART TWO

20. EXT. CAR PARK. NIGHT

*The opening of the club is about to take place.
There are two sections outside the club – VIPs
and others. LES is looking up the road for
ALAN. PADDY is on the main entrance wearing
a headset. MAX is on the fire-exit entrance,
also wearing a headset. We reveal that MAX
and PADDY are only a small distance apart.
A couple of WOMEN aren't happy.*

MAX	Whoa. Could you move back, please? Could you move back, please?
DOT	Fifteen quid a ticket, why can't we go round there?
MAX	'Cause it's for VIPs only, that's why, love.

*Somebody pushes from behind and the crowd
surges forward.*

MOIRA	Oh, hey, it's all wrong this. We're penned in here like cows.
PADDY	(VOICE IN HEADSET) Punch her in the face.

CUT TO

21. EXT. CAR PARK. NIGHT

BRIAN	Right, Roy, would you just like to get under the ribbon?

*There is a countdown from ten. ROY WALKER
cuts the ribbon with a pair of children's paper
scissors. A trace of lights roll around the club
and the lights come on. Applause.*

BRIAN	Look at the light, look at the light. Oy, love, look at the light. Ladies and gentlemen and Roy, welcome to the Phoenix Club. If you'd like to make

your way through to Pennine Suite,
canapés will be served forthwith.

PADDY	Eyeball, eyeball, I think I've got myself a convoy here. Ten-four, rubber dick.

CUT TO

22. EXT. CAR PARK. NIGHT

We cut to MAX as he responds.

MAX	Aye, less of the rubber dick, baldy. (LAUGHS)

*In contrast, MAX is watching some of the
more ELDERLY LADIES entering the club
through the fire door.*

*We cut back to PADDY as THE GIRLS
approach him. He speaks into the headset.*

THE CAPTAIN

      Hold it. Whoa, whoa, whoa, whoa –
what's going on here? Thirty pence
apiece – and don't forget the raffle.

YOUNG KENNY

      Is Alan here?

BRIAN	Phone Alan, tell him if he's not here in half an hour he'll be playing his organ down the bloody job club. D'you hear me?

CUT TO

23. EXT. CAR PARK. NIGHT
We cut back to PADDY.

PADDY   Evening, ladies. No concealed weapons, I hope. In you go. There you go. That's it – in you pop. That's the one. Lordy, lordy, I wouldn't mind hanging out of that.

CUT TO

24. INT. FOYER. NIGHT
The VIPs have been stopped at the door by THE CAPTAIN using his walking stick as a makeshift turnstile. ROY WALKER at the front.

BRIAN   Ay, what's going on here? Can you move? Can I get through? What's going on, Captain?

THE CAPTAIN
    Who's signing this lot in?

BRIAN   That's TV's own Roy Walker, that. (TO ROY) Go on through, Roy. Go through, Roy. Go on. Go through. Can you get through?

CUT TO

25. INT. GALAXY LOUNGE. NIGHT
The room is busy. We can hear music but can't see the DISC JOCKEY.

SPENCER Let's get ready to rumble. All right, coming up now, a classic hit: Aled Jones singing that 'Walking in the Air' song. Classic. Here we go.

Song by ALED JONES.

SPENCER (Cont.) There we go. Walking in the air. Listen to his high voice. (SINGING) Walking in the air.

CUT TO

26. INT. PENNINE SUITE. NIGHT
Canapés are being passed round. BRIAN is with ROY, vase in hand, picking his nose.

BRIAN   Sorry about the smell of gloss and paint.

ROY   It's all right.

BRIAN   We've just had it all tarted up and that, you know.

ROY   Nice. It's nice.

BRIAN   Do you like it?

ROY   Yeah. Very nice.

BRIAN   So how's TV going? All right?

ROY   All right. All right, you know. Can't complain.

BRIAN   Is *Catchphrase* coming back?

ROY   No, I don't do that any more.

BRIAN   Do you not?

ROY   No, no, no.

BRIAN   I see, so you've pissed on your Mr
        Chips.

ROY gives BRIAN a look and turns away.
BRIAN notices white gloss on the back of
ROY's jacket.

CUT TO

27. EXT. CAR PARK. NIGHT
PADDY is standing on the door.

MAX   (ON HEADSET) Patrick, can you
        hear me now?

PADDY   Yeah.

MAX   (ON HEADSET) Hang on. Can you
        hear me now?

We cut to see MAX walking backwards
across the car park with his hands
outstretched.

PADDY   Hear you? I can see you, you dick.

MAX   (ON HEADSET) Can you hear me
        now?

PADDY   Yeah, you'll have to go further away
        than that – they're dear, these, you
        know.

MAX   (ON HEADSET) Can you hear me
        now?

CUT TO

28. INT. GALAXY LOUNGE. NIGHT
ALED JONES.

JERRY chats to his public.

JERRY   Oh, hey up, all right Billy lad – I like
        your glasses, son. An' the glamour
        girls are in. Look at these two. All
        right, Moira, love? How's your
        Ronnie? Is he still in hospital?

MOIRA   No.

JERRY   Oh that's good news.

MOIRA   He's dead.

JERRY smiles and nods and walks on.

SPENCER So there we go. That was Aled Jones
and that classic hit 'Walking in the Air' when
he was actually flying. That's a complete
misnomer in every consumable way. Now here
we go now with Paul Hardcastle's antiwar
song 'Nineteen'. N-n-n-n-n nineteen.

CUT TO

29. INT. PENNINE SUITE. NIGHT

BRIAN   (TO KENNY SNR) Would you look at
        the time! We should have started by
        now ... Is Alan here yet?

KENNY SNR
        No ... but the band are.

BRIAN Right, good lad. Go and find out where Alan is.

KENNY SNR
    Right.

KENNY SNR exits.

MARY is hovering, waiting for ROY to take off his jacket.

BRIAN Roy?

ROY Yeah.

BRIAN You w-w-warm?

ROY Yes.

BRIAN Phew. It's warm in here, isn't it?

ROY No, I'm fine. Fine.

BRIAN Are you sure?

ROY Yes, fine, thanks very much indeed.

BRIAN Slip your jacket off.

ROY No, I'm really fine.

BRIAN You'll not feel benefit when you get outside, you'll be shivering.

ROY No, honestly, I'm fine.

BRIAN Sure?

ROY Thanks for asking, yeah.

BRIAN Really?

ROY Yeah.

CUT TO

30. EXT. CAR PARK. NIGHT
ALAN's lorry pulls into the car park and alongside the club.

CUT TO

31. INT. PENNINE SUITE. NIGHT
BRIAN is talking to ROY.

BRIAN Do you ... Do you like the club? Like the room and that.

ROY Yeah, yeah, yeah ... I like it. I like it. I like the way ... I like the way you've got the er ...

BRIAN Say what you see, Roy, say what you see. (LAUGHS)

CUT TO

32. INT. BACKSTAGE/GALAXY LOUNGE. NIGHT

JERRY Ladies and gentlemen, it is my privilege and my pleasure to welcome you, one and all, to the gala opening night of ... the Phoenix Club.

APPLAUSE.

JERRY A very special occasion indeed and because of that tonight there'll be no bingo.

There is a huge moan and boo from the AUDIENCE.

JERRY Without further ado, will you welcome on stage the best backing in clubland – it is Les Alanos.

APPLAUSE.

JERRY   Ladies and gentlemen, welcome to the stage, your host with the most, your compere without compare, your very own Jerry 'The Saint' St Clair.

APPLAUSE.

The lights go up. LES ALANOS play THE SAINT theme then into 'NEW YORK, NEW YORK'. JERRY sings a few lines and then there is a loud bang and the club is plunged into darkness.

The AUDIENCE aren't happy and are starting to boo and hiss. JERRY tries to calm them down.

BRIAN   Jerry, Jerry, the bloody power's gone.

CUT TO

33. EXT. CAR PARK. NIGHT
PADDY is on the door. We can hear MAX on his headset.

MAX   Can you hear me, now? Paddy? Can you hear me now?

PADDY   Yeah, where are you?

MAX   (OUT OF VISION) I'm here, look! I'm on the bus! I'm on the bus. Look, I'm here. Hey, look, I'm on the bus. Hooray. Look, I'm on the bus. Hooray.

A bus goes past, lit up with people on it. MAX is waving from the top deck. PADDY laughs and gives him the V sign.

CUT TO

34. INT. GALAXY LOUNGE. NIGHT
We cut to the AUDIENCE lit with oil lamps and candles. Some people have lighters. We cut to show a couple of people racing cardboard. BRIAN potters down the table, blowing them with straws.

MARION   There you go. Look, it reminds you of war, doesn't it?

CUT TO

35. INT. BACKSTAGE. NIGHT
BRIAN and JERRY are looking at the generator. JERRY has an oil lamp.

JERRY   No, that's the upstairs toilet.

BRIAN   What's going on? What's the damage?

JERRY   The damage is I got a shock right down me arm.

BRIAN   Shut up, you girl. Where's Les and Alan? They should be here ...

SPENCER   (WORKED UP) Hey, it's pitch black out there. Me decks aren't working. It's ridiculous. It's unprofessional, this is. You can stick your disco.

BRIAN   D'you believe that?

CUT TO

36. INT. GALAXY LOUNGE. NIGHT
AUDIENCE SHOT: MARION and HOLY MARY are still dishing out oil lamps.

CUT TO

37. INT. BACKSTAGE. NIGHT

JERRY   Will you pack that in?

BRIAN   I'm trying these.

JERRY   Is he trying to kill me? Look.

BRIAN   Is it that one? That one anything?

JERRY   No.

BRIAN   That one. That one. Right.

LES and ALAN come back with a man called RAY VON.

LES   Brian, this is Ray Von.

BRIAN   What?

LES   Ray Von.

BRIAN   Ray who?

RAY VON Von. As in 'Rave on'.

BRIAN   Is he a turn?

LES   No, he's a spark. (TO RAY) Tell him what you've just told us.

RAY VON Well, you've seriously overloaded your main circuit ... you've far too many bulbs on that roof.

BRIAN   I said that, I said that ... Now can you fix that?

RAY VON I doubt it, I wouldn't even know where to begin, to be honest.

BRIAN   I'll pay yer.

RAY VON Right, I'll get the gear out me van.

BRIAN   Right, I said that, I said too many bulbs.

JERRY   You never said a word.

BRIAN   Why do you speak to me all the time while I'm saying things?

MIKE FIDDLER
         (THICK ACCENT) Are wi 'aving a three-day week in here or what?

BRIAN   Who's that?

MIKE FIDDLER
         It's as black as owt, owt there.

BRIAN hasn't a clue who he is.

JERRY   I don't think you'll be going on at all, mate, we've had a power cut.

MIKE FIDDLER
         Ney, ney lad, we daren't need 'lectric: we're a folk band.

BRIAN   Can you speak English? You're sending me over the edge.

MIKE FIDDLER
         (DROPS ACCENT COMPLETELY) We're acoustic, unplugged, we don't need electric.

BRIAN   They're acoustic, bang them straight. Get them straight on – they're acoustic, Jerry.

JERRY   But I've no microphone.

CUT TO

38. INT. GALAXY LOUNGE. NIGHT
JERRY is on stage in darkness talking through a megaphone.

JERRY   Ladies and gentlemen, there's an old saying in show business: 'The show must go on.' So that's what we're going to do. So will you welcome on stage your own, your very own, Half a Shilling.

APPLAUSE

MIKE FIDDLER
            How's tha dowing?

(The AUDIENCE reply 'WIS DOIN' FINE')

MIKE FIDDLER
            (COUNTS INTO SONG) One, two, three, four.

DEBRA QUINN enters.

DEBRA   Brian Potter? Debra Quinn, *Bolton Independent Leader*. How're you doin'?

BRIAN   All right, love?

DEBRA   Have you got a problem with your electrics?

BRIAN   Oh, no – it's all part of the show. These boys insist on it.

Cut to KENNY SNR chatting to ROY WALKER at the back.

KENNY SNR
            So there I was on the Centre Court – I'd not even been seeded.

The power comes back on. ROY and KENNY SNR react.

BRIAN   Back on now.

CUT TO

39. INT. BACKSTAGE. NIGHT
Knock on door, RAY comes in.

RAY VON Should be right now.

LES   Well done, son.

CUT TO

40. INT. GALAXY LOUNGE. NIGHT

KENNY SNR
            You know, I think it's really great the way you keep up that Irish accent when you're not on the telly.

ROY WALKER
            Well, I am Irish, you know.

KENNY SNR
            Are you?

ROY WALKER

    Aye.

KENNY SNR

    Oh, I thought you were just pissing
    around like that Gerry Adams.

ROY WALKER

    No. He's Irish as well, you know.

KENNY SNR

    Is he?

ROY WALKER

    Aye.

KENNY SNR

    Oh. Fair play to him.

CUT TO

41. INT. KITCHEN. NIGHT

*HOLY MARY is scrubbing ROY WALKER's
jacket. She pours on some turps. As she
turns it inside out she notices the label:
'PROPERTY OF SOUTHERN TELEVISION'.*

CUT TO

42. INT. CHINESE CHIP SHOP. NIGHT

*RICE AND EASY. MAX is ordering. Man in
queue wearing karate outfit.*

CHINESE MAN

    Salt and vinegar?

MAX   (INTO HEADSET) Patrick, do you
    want salt and vinegar, cock?

PADDY   (VIA HEADSET) Oh yeah ... and
    plenty of tomato sauce.

MAX   Yeah, and plenty of tomato sauce,
    please.

CHINESE MAN

    Ah, tomato sauce.

*The man just wraps PADDY's meal up. MAX
just stares at him confused.*

CHINESE MAN

    There you go. Who's next please?

MAN   Can I have a lightly battered, please?

CHINESE MAN

    Right. Lightly battered. OK. Fine.

CUT TO

43. INT. GALAXY LOUNGE. NIGHT

*BRIAN is still chatting to the REPORTER,
who is scribbling in shorthand.*

DEBRA   So, Brian, your first club flooded,
    your second club burnt down.

BRIAN   Correct.

DEBRA   And now you've rebuilt this. Why?

BRIAN   Third time lucky, I suppose. (HE
    LAUGHS ALONE)

DEBRA   So do you think there's a future for
    clubs like this?

BRIAN   Oh, clubland will never die. It'll
    never die. Always as popular as
    ever.

DEBRA   But how do you intend to compete
    with the more established clubs in
    the area, like the Banana Grove?

BRIAN   The Banana Grove ... Den Perry?
    Have you met him?

DEBRA   No.

BRIAN Den of Iniquity, we call him. Lap dancing on a Sabbath, little kiddies running around. It's a disgrace. The secret to running a successful club is to cater for the family. Nothing offensive, nothing blue, like these lads, Donna.

DEBRA (SHE CORRECTS HIM) Debra.

BRIAN Whatever.

We cut back to HALF A SHILLING on stage

MIKE FIDDLER
How's tha dowin?

AUDIENCE AND BRIAN
Wis doin' fine (BRIAN LAUGHS)

MIKE FIDDLER (cont.)
This next song's about the time I asked me mum and dad for a pair of white Holy Communion shoes. Times are 'ard in our 'ouse. Me dad used t'work shifts to buy uz those shooz. Anyroad, he ordered them and when they come back they weren't white at all, they were black, so he said send the buggers back. Er, one ... two ... three ...

(SONG)
Send the buggers back,
Oh, send the buggers back.
These aren't the ones I wanted, son,
I'm sending them straight back.
I only wanted white ones;
They've sent us bloody black.
I'm going to stick the lid back on
And send the buggers back.
My father worked hard all his life
Down t'pit and tannery.
He laboured every hour God sent
From June to January.
He saved his pennies in a jar ...

BRIAN (OVER SONG) See, nothing offensive, nothing blue.

DEBRA (OVER SONG) No, just racist.

DEBRA scribbles down the lyrics. BRIAN listens.

SONG (cont.)
To buy me Sunday shoes
'N' when they sent black instead of white
He blew a bloody fuse.
He shouted,
Send the buggers back.
Oh, send the buggers back.

BRIAN Get 'em off, get 'em off the stage ... Kenny, get 'em off ... Marion, Marion get 'em off the stage.

SONG (cont.)
These aren't the ones I wanted, son,
I'm sending them straight back.
I only wanted white ones;
They've sent us bloody black.
I'm going to stick the lid back on
And send the buggers back.

CUT TO

44. EXT. CAR PARK. NIGHT
KENNY SNR leans out of the door to PADDY.

KENNY SNR
Security!

PADDY (INTO HEADSET) Max, Max, get back here quick – it's kicking off.

CUT TO

45. EXT. HIGH STREET. NIGHT
MAX hears PADDY's message and starts to run with the chips under his arm.

CUT TO

46. INT. GALAXY LOUNGE. NIGHT
HALF A SHILLING sing. The AUDIENCE sing along. BRIAN, shocked, just sits helpless in his chair.

BRIAN   Get 'em off. Get 'em off the stage.

PADDY grabs MIKE FIDDLER from behind and drags him off the stage. JERRY runs on.

JERRY   There you go, Les. Half a Shilling –
let's hear it for the chart-toppers
Half a Shilling.

LES ALANOS sing and dance the night away. PADDY battles.

JERRY   (SINGING) ... back to where I should
have been.
Altogether now – here we go –
(chorus):
Just want to dance the night away ...
We can't hear you – come on, now.

CUT TO

47. EXT. HIGH STREET. NIGHT
MAX, running, misses the bus. He is knackered.

CUT TO

48. INT. CLUB FOYER. NIGHT
The night is over. KENNY SNR is in the corridor helping ROY WALKER on with his jacket. He is drunk and singing 'SEND THE BUGGERS BACK'.

ROY WALKER
        Send the buggers back, send the
        buggers back.

KENNY SNR
        You're an officer and a gentleman,
        Roy.

ROY smells his jacket.

ROY WALKER
        (LAUGHING) Hey, Kenny, can you
        smell turps?

KENNY SNR
        Listen. I'll ring you about that
        feature film. It's between you and
        Nick Nolte.

We cut back to BRIAN as he talks to RAY VON.

BRIAN   Well, you bailed us out the shit
tonight. Is that what you do? You're
a spark, are you?

RAY VON No, no, actually I'm a DJ.

BRIAN   Are you?

RAY VON Yeah. Electrics is just summat I do,
you know.

BRIAN   Have you got bookings, a residency?

RAY VON No ... no ... I've been out the game
for a while, you know.

BRIAN   Why don't you, er ... get a job here,
work here, climb on here? I don't
think Jive Jive Bunny'll be coming
back, whatever his name were.

RAY VON Really?

BRIAN   Oh, aye.

RAY VON Oh, cheers, thank you very much,
Mr Potter.

BRIAN   It's OK. I don't think the
equipment's up to much but ...

RAY VON Don't worry about that. I'll soon sort that out. I build all me own gear, you know, light systems, sound systems …

BRIAN Do you? You couldn't have a look at our pot washer, could you?

CUT TO

49. EXT. CAR PARK. NIGHT

BRIAN Come on, I wanna get back. I've got immersion on.

JERRY Well, how do you think it went?

BRIAN How do I think it went?

JERRY Yeah.

BRIAN It couldn't have gone better – a power cut and a singalong with Combat 18. I can't wait for tomorrow's papers. 'New Club in Racist Riot'. It'll ruin us, this.

JERRY Give over. The band had nothing to do with us.

BRIAN You booked 'em.

JERRY Me!

BRIAN The only good bit to come out of tonight is Ray Beam or whatever he's called – I'll tell you, he's solid gold, that lad. We've struck gold. Oh, oh and you – Alan Stranraer Johnson. Today of all days – driving.

CUT TO

50. EXT. CAR PARK. NIGHT
We cut to MAX, who has finally arrived. He is shattered. He runs the last few yards

and trips, *sending the food everywhere.*
He stands up and pulls on the wire he fell
over. All the lights go off.

CUT TO

51. EXT. CAR PARK. NIGHT

BRIAN   What's he doin'?

PADDY   He's brought the chips. He's brought
         'um and he's dropped 'um.

BRIAN   I don't know why I pay you two
         good money ay.

PADDY   Hey, look at this.

BRIAN   Get it up, will yer?

PADDY   Is it tomato sauce?

BRIAN   You act like bloody children.

MAX   What's this wire here? What's this
         bastard wire here.

MAX pulls on wire, lights go out.

BRIAN   The power's gone again.

JERRY   Bloody hell.

BRIAN   That's twice now. Where's that wire
         go? The lamppost – the bloody club's
         wired to the lamppost. Who's done
         that? Has Ray Von done that?
         Where's he learnt that?

LES   He'll have got it off the Waltzers –
         he used to work on the fairs,
         didn't he?

ALAN   Yes, he did. He did.

BRIAN	He's a gyppo? Oh my God. We're cursed. He'll be tarmacking the car park next and selling us pegs. Where's he pitched?
TOBY	Don't worry about it, that was all years ago. He's changed, hasn't he ...
ALAN	... since he got out of prison.
BRIAN	Prison? Prison?
ALAN	Do you not remember him?
BRIAN	I do not remember him.
ALAN	He used to go out with – what's her name? Tracy Burns ...
BRIAN	Tracy who?
ALAN	Tracy Burns.
BRIAN	I don't know no Tracy Burns.
LES	You do know Tracy Burns: she won that Junior Talentrek that year.
ALAN	Didn't she do that thing with the hula-hoops?
LES	That's it.
ALAN	Remember that?
BRIAN	(THINKING) Oh, young Tracy. (LAUGHS) I've not seen her for donkeys' years.
LES	I know, he killed her.

CUT TO

END CREDITS

52. GALAXY LOUNGE. NIGHT
BRIAN and Co. are auditioning.

A man is strapped to a revolving wheel singing 'STARMAN' (to a backing tape) and playing a guitar. Another man comes in firing a space gun.

BRIAN   Next!

STARMAN
    What?

BRIAN   Next!

STARMAN
    What? I can't hear you.

BRIAN   Here you are.

BRIAN writes next on a piece of paper and holds it up for the act to read. He starts to rotate, so that he can read it as he spins.

THE END

Episode 2

PART ONE

1. INT. GALAXY LOUNGE. NIGHT

JERRY on stage (backed by LES ALANOS) is finishing 'PERFECT 10'. There is a handful of people in the room.

JERRY   (LOOKING AT HIS WATCH) Thank you very much. Perfect ten there, and we're ten perfect minutes away from tonight's 'Open the Box', where the jackpot still stands at a big thirty-three pounds. So to take you to there I'll leave you in the very capable hands of your brand-new resident DJ, Mr Raaay Von.

RAY VON   Yeah, that's right. Ta Jezzer. My name is Ray Von, so let's R-R-R-Ray Von!

We hear a loud rave tune with plenty of bass. RAY VON has two rotating police lights and one either side of his equipment and a set of council traffic lights.

We cut to the ELDERLY AUDIENCE, far from happy with the noise. A few of them get up to leave. BRIAN is sitting at the back. He's not happy as he wheels himself over to RAY VON.

RAY starts the smoke machine.

BRIAN   (TO RAY) Excuse me. Hey, hey, could you lower it, son?

RAY VON (BUSY MIXING) What?

BRIAN   (NERVOUS) It's banging.

RAY VON Cheers! (INTO MIC) Come on, reach for the lasers!

BRIAN   Have you not got a nice foxtrot? Bit of Kenny G?

Smoke fires out under BRIAN's wheelchair. BRIAN reacts.

BRIAN   (OF SMOKE) Errr … What's that?

RAY VON Smoke machine.

RAY takes his finger off the button, but it's jammed.

BRIAN   Turn that off!

RAY VON It's jammed.

BRIAN   Turn that off. Hey, what's that?

Smoke spills out into the room. The smoke gets thick, very quickly.

BRIAN   (cont.) Oh … Too much.

CUT TO

2. EXT. CLUB. NIGHT
The ELDERLY REGULARS are evacuating the building because of the smoke, coughing as they leave.

CUT TO

3. INT. GALAXY LOUNGE. NIGHT
PEOPLE leaving in droves.

BRIAN   Jerry?

JERRY   Brian, Brian, where are ya?

BRIAN   Turn it off, turn it off, there's too much smoke.

JERRY waves his hands through the fog and slaps BRIAN hard on the side of the face.

BRIAN   Where is it, where are you? Turn this thing off.

BRIAN turns. From his POV we see RAY's arm raised about to swing a lump hammer at what seems like BRIAN. He pushes BRIAN back and smashes the smoke console. We see BRIAN's reaction of horror.

RAY VON Sorted!

CUT TO

OPENING CREDITS

CUT TO

4. INT. GALAXY LOUNGE. NIGHT
MARION and HOLY MARY are wiping condensation off the walls with towels.

We cut to PADDY. He's with THE CAPTAIN, who's slumped in the corner, pint in hand, fag in mouth.

PADDY   (SHOUTING) Come on, Captain, home time. I want to lock up. Captain, time's time, cock. Ship ahoy!

THE CAPTAIN's fag falls out of his mouth.

PADDY   (cont.) Shit!

CUT TO

5. INT. GALAXY LOUNGE. NIGHT
PEOPLE gather around THE CAPTAIN. JERRY is testing his pulse.

BRIAN   Well?

JERRY   He's dead, Brian.

BRIAN   Oh my God. He can't be dead. He can't be … Who's going to do the bloody door now?

LES   Captain?

BRIAN   Who's going to do door?

LES   Captain. Come on, Captain, lad, wake up.

JERRY   He can't hear you. It's one of the conditions of being dead.

PADDY   (TO KENNY. SHOCKED) I've never seen a dead body before.

KENNY   I've seen hundreds, me. I used to bag 'em up in Nam.

BRIAN   Oh, we're going to swing for this ... we'll swing for this. This'll finish us, this ...

JERRY   We didn't kill him.

BRIAN   We didn't kill him, no, but Smokey friggin' Robinson did over there. He's a psycho. How many more is he going to notch up?

JERRY   (CHECKING) I think he's had an asthma attack ...

LES   I'm not surprised with all this smoke.

ALAN   He was bad with angina an' all.

KENNY SNR
    Ay, he was, he was.

BRIAN   He was, he was asthmatic ...

KENNY SNR
    He was.

BRIAN   He was asthmatic ... Put him in the Pennine Suite.

JERRY   Why?

BRIAN   Why? Because in here's murder. Next door's natural causes. Go on, stick him in there.

KENNY SNR
    Good thinking, yeah.

THE CAPTAIN drops his teeth. The others jump back scared.

JERRY   Whoa, whoa, whoa.

CUT TO

6. INT. PENNINE SUITE. DAY
THE CAPTAIN's funeral reception.
The majority of people are old. Ex-war veterans and family.

A buffet table has a coffin on it, lid on. Paper plate by the side with remains of buffet. MARION walks through shot and sweeps it into a bin liner.

There is a little dog by the side of the coffin, eating from a plate, with a blue washing line round his neck.

A group of FEMALE RELATIVES in the corner haggle over THE CAPTAIN's estate.

FEMALE RELATIVE

Well, I tell you what, I'm having his fridge freezer. Right. It's less than twelve months old, that.

FEMALE RELATIVE 2

Well, what about his dog?

FEMALE RELATIVE

I don't want the dog. Get it put down.

BRIAN and JERRY are at the back, eating buffet.

JERRY   Deaf Tony died yesterday.

BRIAN   He didn't?

JERRY   Fifty-six.

BRIAN   That's no age.

JERRY   Bin lorry reversed over him.

BRIAN   How's Eileen taken it?

JERRY   Oh, bad, and they didn't empty her bin. (LAUGHS) Empty her bin, do you get it?

BRIAN   Just remember where you are.

The RELATIVES continue to haggle in the corner.

FEMALE RELATIVE

If we spread his ashes, do we get money back on urn?

Reaction from other RELATIVES.

BRIAN is at the back eating buffet. LES and ALAN come over.

LES   Brian.

ALAN   All right, Brian.

BRIAN   Hello, Les; hello, Alan.

LES   I see, I see Ray Von's not turned up.

BRIAN   Good, I'm glad.

ALAN   He never batted an eyelid, did he?

LES   I bet he's comfortable around death, that lad – used to it, you see.

BRIAN   Did he really kill Tracy Burns?

LES   Oh, aye, do you not remember? It were in all the papers, weren't it?

BRIAN   Why's he not in prison, then?

ALAN   Technicalities, isn't it?

LES   Look at O J Simpson.

ALAN   Yes.

BRIAN   I'm gonna get rid of him, I am. I'm going to sack him.

LES   Oh aye, you can't do that. That were Tracy's mistake. She ended up in a wheelie bin.

ALAN   Well, her head did.

One of the WAR VETERANS stands to toast 'THE CAPTAIN'.

ELDERLY WAR VETERAN

A bit of respect, ladies and gentlemen, for the Captain. The Captain. I'll never forget the day we first met. D-Day it were, aye, D-Day. We were fourth off the landing craft up Sword Beach. Sixty yards up the

beach they got him, the bastards, but he kept on running. Blew his eyeball right out.

Cut to BRIAN eating a scotch egg.

ELDERLY WAR VETERAN (cont.)
>But I caught it, and do you know what? He turned round and said to me, he said, 'I thought you were supposed to keep an eye out for me.' (LAUGHTER) But that was the Captain, always a joker. The Captain.

They all toast THE CAPTAIN.

A BLOKE in the corner playing Das Boot machine hits the jackpot. Machine pays out –

lights and jingle, the German National Anthem, to the room's disgust.

BRIAN   Flick it off. Flick the thing off.

YOUNG KENNY goes over and flicks it off at the wall.

CUT TO

7. INT. JOCKEY WILSON SUITE. DAY
REGULARS are watching an obscure documentary about amoebae on the TV. HOLY MARY is cleaning glasses. A few REGULARS play snooker on a slanted table. They remove the triangle and the balls roll.

TELEVISION VOICE
>It's an amoeba, a single cell. And this is it feeding. An amoeba can change shape easily: by pushing its cell surface forward it engulfs its food. That's fine if you're a single-celled organism, but if you're just one …

TWO LADS enter wearing overalls. They look around, see the television, walk over and switch it off and unplug it.

LAD   Sorry, guys.

KENNY SNR
>(TO STANLEY) … and who should pop his head out of the next tent? Mr Robert De Niro.

LAD   You couldn't give us a lift, could you, mate?

KENNY SNR
>He loves Pwllheli. He was there with his family. He was doing another Deer Hunter in Rhyl. I absolutely hammered him at swingball.

The MAN nods at KENNY SNR and humours him. The TWO BOYS exit carrying the TV. Nobody bats an eyelid.

CUT TO

8. EXT. CITROËN. DAY
The TWO LADS are sitting inside the car. KENNY SNR runs out of the club.

KENNY SNR

> Whoa, whoa, whoa.

The LADS in the car look slightly shocked (they think they've been rumbled). KENNY SNR taps on the window.

KENNY SNR

> Wind the window down. Wind it down. Not as clever as you think, are you?

The DRIVER lowers the window. KENNY SNR hands them the remote control.

KENNY SNR

> You forgot this. Ay, nothing gets past these. (POINTS TO HIS EYES)

LAD   Right. Cheers, mate.

KENNY SNR

> See you, lads.

LAD   Nice one.

CUT TO

9. EXT. CAR PARK. DAY
The TWO LADS in the Citroën drive off and pass an American Cadillac car driven by YOUNG KENNY. BRIAN is in the back. KENNY SNR watches it drive on.

CUT TO

10. INT. JOCKEY WILSON SUITE. DAY
BRIAN tackles the others.

BRIAN   Just let me get this straight again. Two lads walk in off the street and take the television and you did nothing.

MARION We thought you'd arranged it.

BRIAN   Arranged what?

KENNY SNR

> Well, they were wearing overalls.

BRIAN   Oh, overalls. Oh, well, excuse me, then. Overalls. Oh, well, that was Jesus H. (HOLY MARY CROSSES HERSELF) That was a brand-new set, that. The world's gone mad.

MARION They were probably drug addicts.

BRIAN   In overalls … ? In overalls?

KENNY SNR

> (CHANGING SUBJECT) Where did you get that new motor from, Brian?

BRIAN   Somewhere.

KENNY SNR

> Must have cost a bob or two.

BRIAN   It must have. I traded in my Shopmobility.

KENNY SNR

> For a Cadillac?

BRIAN   If I'd have been on the ball, I'd have worn overalls and driven it out the showroom.

MAN	Oy, this snooker table is knackered? Are you getting it fixed or what?	ERIC	What d'you mean? What's up?
BRIAN	Has he not been yet, Eric?	BRIAN	What's up? I've got a deformed snooker table, a Nazi bandit that pays out in Deutschmarks and a flavoured-condom machine that's ten years out of date.
MARION	No, he hasn't.		
BRIAN	You should have told them to take that thing.		
KENNY SNR	They only had a Citroën.	ERIC	And?

BRIAN *gives him a look and points to be pushed by* YOUNG KENNY.

CUT TO

11. INT. BRIAN'S OFFICE. DAY

BRIAN is on the phone and fiddling with his new computer. On screen we see a three-dimensional floor plan of the club. As BRIAN chats, he dips a biscuit into a cup of tea.

VOICE ON PHONE
    Hello, Games Sans Frontières.

BRIAN   Eric, Brian.

ERIC   Brian. How's it going?

BRIAN   It's not going. It's still here and it's as crooked as you.

ERIC   And? Would you suck a ten-year-old banana?

BRIAN   No.

BRIAN   No, neither will they.

ERIC   I'll have to get me papers together …

BRIAN   You'll get nothing except your arse down here today for this snooker table before I nail you to it. (SLAMS DOWN PHONE) Shithead!

CUT TO

12. INT. JOCKEY WILSON SUITE. DAY

ERIC is at the club. The snooker table has been replaced with a Bucking Bronco. BRIAN and the others stare at it. ERIC has a slight facial twitch.

ERIC   Well? What do you think?

BRIAN   It's hard to find the words to describe it, Eric, really. Oh, I've found some. What the frig is it?

ERIC   This! This is what the punters want, Brian.

BRIAN   A mechanical bull?

ERIC   A bucking bronco!

BRIAN   Get rid of it. Get rid of it now.

ERIC   I cannot. The van's gone.

BRIAN   Oh.

ERIC   This is the future, Brian. Snooker's dead and buried.

TWO BLOKES stand in the room with their snooker cues in hand, looking confused.

BRIAN   I'm not convinced. Get rid of it.

ERIC   Trust me, Brian … Trust me. They'll all want one when they see yours.

BRIAN   Oh, ho. Where've I heard that before? Indoor golf? Foxy boxing? How quick we forget. I've just got shut of your six-foot Ker Plunk.

ERIC   Have a ride, see what you think. (DOUBLE TAKE ON BRIAN'S DISABILITY) I'll give you a week's free trial while I get your table fixed. Then she's got to go to the European Finals in 'Doosledorf'.

BRIAN   Doosledorf? Oh, good. You can take Das Fruit Machine back with you.

ERIC   I'll throw you in an aeroplane, one previous owner.

BRIAN   Who were it? John Denver?

ERIC   Come on, Brian, you'll not regret it. Give it a couple of days it'll be shitting money.

BRIAN   Well, if it's not, it had better learn how to shit snooker tables.

CUT TO

13. INT. GALAXY LOUNGE. DAY
The waltz ends. The PENSIONERS start to sit down.

JERRY   This is Jerry St Clair welcoming you to your afternoon session of bingo. Fifty pee a line, seven pound yer full house. Get your dobbers and your dabbers and your dibbers and your cards and we'll be ready to go. Here we …

RAY pulls his new home-made bingo machine to the front of the stage for JERRY. He flicks it on and it makes a hell of a noise. JERRY is shocked.

JERRY   (OFF MIC) What's that?

RAY VON   New bingo machine. I built it … guts of a hoover.

RAY switches it on.

JERRY   Can you flick it to upholstery? (INTO MIC) Eyes down, look in, for your first number.

CUT TO

14. INT. JOCKEY WILSON SUITE. DAY
We see an OLD LADY riding the aeroplane that ERIC left.

RAY enters the room. There is an ELDERLY MAN riding the bronco and the others are cheering him on. RAY smiles.

CUT TO

15. INT. GALAXY LOUNGE. DAY
JERRY is having problems with the bingo machine. The balls are blowing out of it. He reads them out and chases them across the stage.

JERRY   Four and nine, forty-nine.

AUDIENCE
        (ANGRY) We've had that.

JERRY   We've not had it, it's in me hand.
        I've just picked it up off the
        bloody floor. (SHOUTING) Ray,
        Ray, where's he gone? Bloody hell!
        Four and two ...

CUT TO

16. INT. JOCKEY WILSON SUITE. DAY

*RAY VON is compering (into a microphone)
and working the controls as a DIFFERENT
PENSIONER rides the bronco. The others
cheer him on. KENNY SNR is taking people's
money and writing down riders' names.
YOUNG KENNY is keeping a makeshift league
on the dartboard blackboard.*

RAY VON Let's hear it for Albert. Albert's a
        registered diabetic. Come on, the
        louder you scream, the faster the
        ride. Open rules, folks, come on.
        What else are you going to do with
        your afternoons? Come on, son,
        you're nearly at the pensioner
        record. Here we go. Come on.

*BRIAN enters the room and is startled by
what he sees. JERRY enters. He can't believe
what he sees either.*

JERRY   There he is.

BRIAN   Who?

JERRY   Ray Von.

BRIAN   Look at him. I think he thinks he's
        back on the Waltzers.

JERRY   Aye. Look at this lot, though. I've
        not seen them so excited since they
        printed that paedophile's address in
        the papers.

*An OLD MAN comes hurtling off the ride. He
hits the floor.*

BRIAN   Oh, shit, not another one.

*The room waits in anticipation. The OLD MAN
springs to his feet and the room cheers.*

RAY VON Let's get another victim up— Let's
get another contestant on the ride.
Just a little joke there from Ray.
Come on.

JERRY I say, you know what we should
have, don't you?

BRIAN St John's Ambulance?

JERRY A Wild West night ...

BRIAN D'you reckon?

JERRY I do indeed. What with that thing
there, get some of them cowboys in,
do a bit of that gun-slinging, get
some line dancing going.

BRIAN Line dancing?

JERRY Yeah.

BRIAN It's a bit old-hat.

JERRY I know Den Perry had it every week
and it was sold out, made a fortune

BRIAN Did he?

JERRY He did.

BRIAN I draw the line at lynching.

END OF PART ONE

PART TWO

17. EXT. CAR PARK. NIGHT
We hear 'RING OF FIRE' by JOHNNY CASH.
MAX and PADDY (in stetsons) are on the
door. PADDY is chewing a match. A group of
girls go past.

PADDY (TIPPING HIS HAT)
Howdy, ladies.

MAX (TIPPING HIS HAT TOO) Evenin'
y'all.

PADDY (ASIDE TO MAX) I wouldn't mind
riding that.

CUT TO

18. INT. JOCKEY WILSON SUITE. NIGHT
RAY VON, mic in one hand and the bronco
control in the other. KENNY SNR takes the
money and issues tickets to the CUSTOMERS
with their number on.

RAY VON Do you want to go faster?
Let's try the other way. Come on,
George. Come on. Here we go,
my friend.

GEORGE falls off.

RAY VON (Cont.) Absolutely brilliant,
George. Who's next? Who's next
in line?

CUT TO

19. INT. GALAXY LOUNGE. NIGHT

JERRY is introducing the cabaret act.

JERRY So, cowboys and cowgirls. We've got a very special treat for you now. So will you give a mighty Phoenix welcome to a fabulous act? It's Wild Bill and Trigger.

The AUDIENCE clap. WILD BILL enters through the side door.

WILD BILL
  I'm Wild Bill. Say hello to Trigger.

APPLAUSE: TRIGGER THE HORSE rides into the room

BRIAN (IN SHOCK) There is a horse in my cabaret suite.

CUT TO

20. EXT. CAR PARK. NIGHT

MAX At the end of the day a hat's the worst thing you can wear if you're going bald.

PADDY Don't start.

MAX I'm telling you, I'm telling you, you've either got to accept it or you've got to cover up.

PADDY Cover up? It's *you* that's going bald, not me.

MAX I lost most of my hair worrying about yours.

CUT TO

21. INT. GALAXY LOUNGE. NIGHT
TRIGGER is performing tricks.

WILD BILL
  What's he doing now? (PAUSE) He's digging for gold.

APPLAUSE

JERRY Well, what do you think?

BRIAN   There is a horse in my cabaret suite.

JERRY   I know, he's brilliant, isn't he?

YOUNG KENNY
     Is it real?

The HORSE shits on the floor.

BRIAN   Oh, it's real, my friend, it's real, you'd better believe it.

JERRY   I'll clean it up.

BRIAN   Thirty grand, that cork floor.

APPLAUSE

CUT TO

22. EXT. CAR PARK. NIGHT

MAX   Bruce Willis, Yul Brynner, Sean Connery ... Skin's in, man. Women – they love it, can't get enough of it. It's nothing to be ashamed of.

PADDY   I'm not ashamed 'cos I'm not going bald.

MAX   (DOESN'T HEAR HIM) Connery, Connery wants the best of both worlds, Connery. Did you see his wig in *The Rock*? It's amazing. Thick-set. He loves wearing them, Connery. *Never Say Never Again* – that were another. Can't get enough.

CUT TO

23. INT. GALAXY LOUNGE. DAY

*WILD BILL and TRIGGER are finishing to
tumultuous applause.*

JERRY   One more time. Wild Bill and Trigger.
We're going to take a short interval
now. Meanwhile I'm gonna leave you
with your own rootin' tootin'
shootin' DJ Mr Ray Von … Just let
me … Just let me clean that shit up.

RAY VON Rayvon y'all! Shabba!

CUT TO

24. EXT. CAR PARK. NIGHT

MAX   *Highlander* – wig. He had a wig in
*Highlander. Highlander II, The
Quickening* – wig. (THINKING) What
were that mad one called where he
got his cock out?

PADDY   *Zardoz?*

MAX   *Zardoz* – wig.

CUT TO

25. INT. GALAXY LOUNGE. NIGHT

RAY VON Here we go. Let's set the dance floor
on fire. DJ Ray Van Kleef. Here we
go. Let's check this one out. Check it
out. Yeah. It doesn't matter what it
is, garage, house, it doesn't matter.
It's all OK for DJ Ray. Come on.

*The Chuck Wagon (a serving hatch). HOLY
MARY is serving food. There's a blackboard
with a menu on it.*

CUSTOMER
   Can I have chips and black-eyed peas?

HOLY MARY
   Yes.

CUSTOMER
   Excuse me, love – what's in your
   snake-eyed pie?

HOLY MARY
   Chicken and mushroom.

CUSTOMER
   Er … Go on, then, I'll have two.

HOLY MARY
   Right, love. (SHOUTING) Two snakes,
   Marion.

RAY VON I want to see some more hides on
the dance floor. Come on.

*BRIAN and JERRY are at the back of the
room.*

BRIAN   What time's the gunfight?

JERRY   After supper. It should be good,
I've got the Keighley Confederates
against the Preston Posse.

BRIAN   You … you what? Lancashire
against Yorkshire? Bloody hell,
Jerry, you don't mix the counties.
I wondered why we had a gap. Ike
and Tina, Chalk and Cheese. They
don't go. You're asking for trouble.
It's gonna kick off.

JERRY   No it's not.

BRIAN   Oh it is.

JERRY   It's all part of the show … they do it
all the time, this.

BRIAN   It better be. Who's judging?

JERRY   Ray Von.

BRIAN   Oh my God! Don't give him a gun ...
We'll be knee deep in bodies.

CUT TO

26. EXT. CAR PARK. NIGHT

MAX   *The Hunt for Red October* – wig.
The Avengers – wig.

PADDY   No, no, no, he were bald in *The
Avengers*. Think on.

MAX   He was, he was ... But it were a
flop, though, weren't it. No wig, no
hit – shit.

CUT TO

27. INT. GALAXY LOUNGE. NIGHT
*BRIAN and JERRY are at the back. WILD
BILL comes over with TRIGGER.*

WILD BILL
   Brian Potter.

BRIAN   Colin Bibby. I thought it were you.
How are you? I've not seen you for
donkey's years. I hope your money's
not gone up. How are you keeping?
Last time I saw you, Barracuda
Club, eh, you were in a double act
with what's her name?

WILD BILL
   Mini Ha-ha!

BRIAN   Mini Ha-ha eh? Not laughing now, is
she? Lost a leg to diabetes, poor cow.

WILD BILL

    Anyway I've got Trigger now.

BRIAN   Yeah, you have. Eh, she's a beauty, yeah. (NOTICES ITS PENIS) Sorry, 'he'. Christ he nearly had me eye out – bloody hell!

WILD BILL

    Would you mind if I put him in that other room over there? It's pissing down outside.

BRIAN   (LAUGHING) It's been pissing down in here and shitting on forty grand's worth of cork floor. Can you balls, eh! No, you can't. Forget it. Look at that, eh, get it away from me.

BRIAN exits.

WILD BILL

    (TO JERRY) He doesn't change, does he?

JERRY   No! Stick him in the Pennine Suite. He'll never know.

WILD BILL

    Right.

CUT TO

28. INT. PENNINE SUITE. NIGHT
WILD BILL ties TRIGGER to a bar rail. He gives him a toffee and exits.

WILD BILL

    Good boy. Good boy.

CUT TO

29. INT. GALAXY LOUNGE. NIGHT
The COWBOY CLUBS are getting ready for the gunfight. RAY is setting up his special homemade scoreboard.

JERRY   (BLOWS INTO MICROPHONE) Evening all. Hello, ladies and gentlemen. Welcome back, pardners. Welcome back, pardners, to *Gunfight at the Phoenix Corral*, with me Deputy St Clair. Eh, look at that, eh. And tonight we've got the Keighley Confederates (BIG CHEER) against the Preston Posse (BIG CHEER). So, without further ado, can we have the first two gunslingers on their marks?

MAN   Come on, Yorkshire.

JERRY   Draw!

They fire.

CUT TO

30 EXT. CAR PARK. NIGHT
MAX and PADDY react to sound of gunshot.

CUT TO

31. INT. PENNINE SUITE. NIGHT
TRIGGER walks forward, his reigns drop free and he wonders over to the bar.

TRIGGER knocks one of the beer taps with his head. Then gets underneath and drinks the lager.

CUT TO

32. INT. GALAXY LOUNGE. DAY
We're midway through the gunfight. The TWO GUNFIGHTERS stand apart (one of them looks like Elvis). They are eyeing each other up. LES ALANOS are backing with a country-music medley of cowboy shows.

JERRY   So let's hear it for the undefeated world champion, a very good friend

They both draw. Fire. There's a beat. JERRY turns to RAY.

JERRY   Ray ...?

RAY looks at him blankly.

JERRY   Lancashire

YORKSHIRE Boo, as it was obviously them.

CUT TO

33. INT. PENNINE SUITE. NIGHT
TRIGGER is still drinking from the lager tap.

CUT TO

34. INT. GALAXY LOUNGE. NIGHT
The atmosphere is mounting. Two NEW GUNFIGHTERS are up.

JERRY   And ... Fire!

They both draw and fire.

JERRY   Lancashire! Lancashire again. That's three in a row. Three in a row. Come on, come on, come on. Three in a row. (CHANTS TO YORKSHIRE)

JERRY (SINGING)
Sing when you're winning, you only sing when you're winning! You only sing when you're winning.

JERRY   Aye, Yorkshire, you're losing. (LAUGHTER) And next up for the Keighley Confederates we've got Georgia Jed. Where is he? Where's Georgia Jed? Stand up, son.

We cut to GEORGIA JED, who is small.

JERRY   (cont.) Oh, he is stood up. Here he comes, the nine-stone cowboy.

of mine, Cisco Sid. (APPLAUSE) And on my left over here we have (LAUGHS) – Christ, I've died and gone to Memphis. (TURNS ROUND AND PUTS ON SUNGLASSES) Who've we got here? It's Silverado Presley (APPLAUSE). Come on, son, crack a smile. Look at them glasses. He's a welder during the day, lads, he's a welder. Did you know, a welder? Look at this. (HOLDS UP HIS MEDALLION – ELVIS ISN'T IMPRESSED) Is that gold or is it chocolate? Is it? Is it chocolate, is it?

LAUGHTER

JERRY   (WHISPERS IN HIS EAR) It's very good, this, son, so keep it up. They love it. Come on, come on, here we go anyway, on your marks, on your marks. Lancashire, are you ready?

SID   Ready.

JERRY   Yorkshire, are you ready?

SILVERADO
(ELVIS STYLE) Uh-huh. (LAUGHTER)

JERRY   Draw!

KENNY SNR *runs into the room and goes over to* BRIAN *and* YOUNG KENNY *at the back.*

KENNY SNR

Brian! There's a horse in the Jockey Wilson Suite.

BRIAN   Yeah, right, whatever.

KENNY SNR

There is. Come on quick.

KENNY *exits.* BRIAN *and the others follow him.*

JERRY   Come on, let's hear it now.
(*SINGING*)
I wish I was a pixie, away, away,
In Pixieland I'll make my stand;
I'll live and die a pixie ...

(TURNS TO JED) Are you all right, Jed? Have we got a box?

JED *isn't amused either.*

CUT TO

35. INT. JOCKEY WILSON SUITE. NIGHT
TRIGGER's *pissed and moving around uneasily.* MEN *move out of his way.*

KENNY SNR

There you are, I told you.

BRIAN   Get off.

YOUNG KENNY

What's up with it?

BRIAN   What's up with it? It's pissed, that's what's up with it. Get Colin Bibby. Let go of me.

KENNY SNR

How do you know?

BRIAN   How do I know? I know a pissed horse when I see one ... Get it a kebab.

CUT TO

36. INT. GALAXY LOUNGE. NIGHT
Jerry is reading out the résumé of the GUNSLINGER.

JERRY   So, Jed, what do you want to be when you grow up ... Taller? Taller, eh? (LAUGHS) No, because he was born on the cusp of Leo and Capricorn ... Which makes him a leprechaun if I'm right. Am I right? (LAUGHS) Do you get it, Jed? Come on, where's he gone? Oh, there he is. Here we go. It says he's forty-seven and single. There's a surprise. D'you think he's probably one of them bandits? You know what I mean, lads. Rode into town, shot up the sheriff.

GEORGIA JED *punches him in the stomach.* JERRY *topples over into the bales of hay. Next thing, chairs start flying and a fight between both teams breaks out. They charge towards each other across the room.*

CUT TO

37. INT. JOCKEY WILSON SUITE. NIGHT
TRIGGER has approached the bucking bronco and he raises himself up in an effort to mount it. We cut to BRIAN's, KENNY SNR's and YOUNG KENNY's shocked reactions.

BRIAN   Oh my God. What's he doing? (TO KENNY SNR) Kenny, pull it off.

KENNY SNR
    You what? I'm not pulling off a horse

We track along their reactions as they watch TRIGGER. We pan down to BRIAN, who's lowest.

BRIAN   We've not got a licence for this. Kenny, get the mop.

WILD BILL runs into the room.

WILD BILL
    You'd better get in there. All hell's breaking loose! (REACTS TO TRIGGER) Who's taught him that?

CUT TO

38. INT. GALAXY LOUNGE. NIGHT
The place is in uproar. A fight scene from a classic western. JERRY, winded, is crawling across the stage. LES ALANOS, both sitting low down, are playing Dixie. Tables are being turned over, guns are being fired, punches are being thrown. SILVERADO PRESLEY dives off a table into the action.

CUT TO

39. EXT. CAR PARK. NIGHT
MAX and PADDY outside are oblivious to the fight inside.

PADDY   I thought it were Yul Brynner.

MAX   No, this is Guns of Seven. It's Coburn, this. He's in the saloon ...

PADDY   That's right, yeah.

MAX   ... he picks the chair up, the bloke ducks, he chucks it straight through the window.

PADDY   Bang, yeah.

A chair comes through the window of the Galaxy Lounge. They look at each other and run inside.

CUT TO

40. INT. GALAXY LOUNGE. NIGHT
The fight continues. A KEIGHLEY MAN is standing on a table waving a huge flag. A PRESTON MAN on the opposite side is playing a 'charge' on a bugle. MARION and HOLY MARY are throwing griddles. MAX and PADDY enter.

PADDY   They've got guns ... They've got guns.

We cut to a wide shot of the chaos. MAX and PADDY panic and run out of the Galaxy Lounge.

CUT TO

41. EXT. CAR PARK. NIGHT
The POLICE are loading COWBOYS into the back of a van. ELVIS is escorted out handcuffed, past MAX and PADDY.

MAX   Get 'em out. Come on. Get 'em out. Come on. Elvis has left the building.

We cut to BRIAN and JERRY.

BRIAN   Forty-five grand, that cork floor, destroyed by him. He's one …

JERRY   (CLUTCHING STOMACH) I think I've ruptured an artery, Brian.

BRIAN   What? Good. I'm glad. Wild West? It's been bloody wild, that's for sure.

JERRY   I'll say. I know why Den Perry stopped having them.

BRIAN   What?

JERRY   Well, it was like this every night, kicking off. They were like animals.

BRIAN   Oh, *now* you tell me!

WILD BILL comes out behind BRIAN and JERRY.

WILD BILL
      You! He's in there and he's pissed out of his mind and he's got a corporate in Torquay tomorrow.

BRIAN   Well, he'll have to go back on the wagon. (LAUGHS ALONE)

BRIAN   (WATCHING POLICE LOADING COWBOYS INTO BACK OF VAN) Chuck the key away.

CUT TO

END CREDITS

42. INT. GALAXY LOUNGE. DAY
BRIAN AND CO. are auditioning a Houdini-type act. The ESCAPOLOGIST is inside the sack. There is a lot of groaning and rolling around going on on the stage.

ESCAPOLOGIST
      Hold on, any minute now. This is me. Seeing is believing.

BRIAN   Whose keys are those?

JERRY   I don't know.

ESCAPOLOGIST
      Big finish.

BRIAN   (TO ESCAPOLOGIST) Are these your keys?

ESCAPOLOGIST
      What?

BRIAN   Next.

ESCAPOLOGIST
      Oh, fu—

THE END

Episode 3

PART ONE

1. EXT. HOUSING ESTATE. DAY

Close up of YOUNG KENNY as he pins up an advert for 'CLINTON BAPTISTE – PSYCHIC'.

We hear CHORLEY FM on the soundtrack.

PAUL LE ROY

> This is Chorley FM coming in your ears.

'COME UP (AND MAKE ME SMILE)' by STEVE HARLEY AND COCKNEY REBEL is playing.

A TRAFFIC COP approaches YOUNG KENNY on his bike, lights flashing. He pulls up by the side of YOUNG KENNY.

YOUNG KENNY

> (OFFERING POSTER) Do you want one of these for the station?

CUT TO

2. INT. BRIAN'S OFFICE. DAY

RAY is showing BRIAN how to work his computer. Artwork for the psychic poster is on screen. YOUNG KENNY enters with an armful of posters.

BRIAN   What happened?

YOUNG KENNY

> The police stopped me again.

BRIAN   Right!

CUT TO

3. EXT. ROAD. DAY

YOUNG KENNY has covered up a road sign with an old hospital blanket and is writing, 'PHOENIX CLUB – 2 MILES. TONIGHT PSYKICK 8 O'CLOCK' in red paint.

We cut to an interior shot of BRIAN's car. BRIAN is sitting in the back (denim cap, sunglasses).

BRIAN (OUT OF WINDOW) Hurry up. Come on. Hurry up. You're spelling wrong, you're spelling it wrong. 'Pyskick'? What's a 'pyskick'? It's supposed to be 'Psychic'. Tit!

CUT TO

OPENING CREDITS

CUT TO

4. INT. JOCKEY WILSON SUITE. DAY
MAX, PADDY, MARION, HOLY MARY and KENNY SNR are watching an ENGINEER as he fits Sky Digital. There is a huge wide-screen TV sitting where the TV used to sit.

MAX That's it. Put it on now. Let's have a look.

The ENGINEER switches it on to a unanimous cheer. He gives the remote to MAX, who flicks through the channels.

PADDY Put the porn on.

HOLY MARY
Hey.

KENNY SNR
(LOOKING AT HIS WATCH) There'll be no porn on at this time.

HOLY MARY switches to a religious channel.

MAX You can get that off!

CUT TO

5. INT. BRIAN'S OFFICE. DAY

RAY is continuing to teach BRIAN. He is showing him how to scan and print. He's just printed out a poster of Superman (with BRIAN's head) saying 'NO UNDER-AGE DRINKING' in a speech bubble. The poster for the psychic is also on BRIAN's desk.

RAY VON See, now you can print that to any size you like.

BRIAN Emmm. (LOOKING AT PICTURE) Amazing what they can do. Technology.

RAY VON It's easy as well, you know. All I do is cut your head off, drag it round.

BRIAN What?

RAY VON demonstrates.

BRIAN Ahhh ...

RAY VON And you can drop it wherever you want.

BRIAN Yeah ...

He pastes it on top of a black athlete jumping hurdles. BRIAN just stares at it.

CUT TO

6. INT. JOCKEY WILSON SUITE. DAY

CROWD watching television get annoyed with MARION when she goes in front of screen.

MAX Will you get out of the way?

MARION Ay, if you think you're congregating in here every day you can think again. This is for regulars.

MAX We are regulars.

MARION You're staff and you're not on 'til seven. Now get out and get a life.

MAX We've got a life. We've just not got Sky.

CUT

7. INT. BRIAN'S OFFICE. DAY

RAY VON prints out another picture: a man holding a huge scythe. BRIAN's head is superimposed on the figure's face. Underneath, it reads, 'TAKE YOUR GLASSES BACK TO THE BAR OR ELSE'.

RAY VON Look at the blades, look. Look at that one. Go right through bone, that.

BRIAN (ANXIOUS) Yeah ... Very good ... Where did you get that picture from?

RAY VON Downloaded it – I got it off the Net.

BRIAN   Do you like that sort of thing …
do you?

RAY VON Emmm.

BRIAN   (NERVOUS) Is that what gets you
going? Murders? Do you like
murders?

RAY VON Yeah. Fascinated by it, me … yeah.
Look at this, though. Hannibal
Potter.

They laugh.

*RAY VON has superimposed a Hannibal
Lecter mask on a photo of BRIAN. It reads
'SORRY NO HOT FOOD'.*

BRIAN laughs uncomfortably.

JERRY   (LEANING AROUND THE DOOR) Are
we goin' to this meeting or what?

BRIAN   Yes let's … let's go now.

CUT TO

8. INT. GALAXY LOUNGE. DAY
*JERRY is wheeling BRIAN through the club.
Newspaper on BRIAN's knee.*

BRIAN   (LOOKING AT HIS WATCH) Imagine
calling an affiliates' meeting for this
time in the morning.

JERRY   Yeah, I know.

BRIAN   Bloody Den Perry, bighead.

LES   (COMES OVER) Can I have a word?

BRIAN   We're late, Leslie.

LES   You know this drama group that
me and Alan run down at the
youth club?

BRIAN   No.

LES   You do … Well we've got a big show
coming up soon and—

JERRY   What show are you doing?

LES   *Karate Kid – The Musical …*

BRIAN   And?

LES   It's just that the room that we've
been rehearsing in has had to be
fumigated.

BRIAN   And you want to know if you can
use one of mine?

LES   Yeah. It'll only be for a couple
of days …

BRIAN   That's what they said to Terry
Waite.

JERRY   Well, this room's free …

BRIAN   Big mouth.

CUT TO

9. INT. JOCKEY WILSON SUITE/
CORRIDOR/GALAXY LOUNGE. DAY

JERRY wheels BRIAN into the Jockey Wilson Suite. They're all watching CRACKER in French.

BRIAN sees the big screen.

BRIAN   Weh hey. Oh look at that, now that's wide-screen. Cinerama, comin' at ya. That's fantastic. Special, that, isn't it? I didn't know Cracker was French. It's brilliant. We'll be selling popcorn soon.

PADDY   (OUT OF EARSHOT) We will be when they put the blueys on.

MARION   Aye, Brian. The psychic phoned. Said he wanted to know what time he was on.

BRIAN   If he's any good he'll know already. Oh, whoa … Where's me dartboard gone? (TO DART PLAYERS) Don't throw them in there: it's Anaglypta, that – twelve quid a roll, son. It's like living in a ghetto. Every bloody week.

The MEN playing darts shrug and we reveal that they're throwing darts into a makeshift dartboard scrawled on the wall in chalk.

BRIAN   (cont.) Kenny, I think we'll have that bull mastiff if it's not been nicked.

KENNY   Right.

BRIAN   How they getting in?

LES   It'll be kids with nothing better to do.

BRIAN   Amen to that. Probably one of your lot – and you're teaching them karate.

LES   It's not ours – ours are good kids. Look, can we have this room or not?

BRIAN   If it was up to me, Leslie …

LES   It is!

BRIAN   No, you can't. What's in it for me?

LES   Nothing.

BRIAN   Nothing. Well they can sod off, sponging off the state. They want to go out and get a job. Jobs won't come looking for them. When I was their age …

BRIAN glances into the Galaxy Suite. ALAN and the young GROUP OF KIDS are already sitting inside.

BRIAN   (cont.) H'yer, y'alright? (TO LES) Make sure they get some pop and crisps, Leslie. Avanti, Jerry. (JERRY PUSHES HIM OFF) And check 'em for dartboards.

CUT TO

10. INT. BANANA GROVE. DAY

The room is full of COMMITTEE MEN and CLUB OWNERS. DEN PERRY is already addressing. BRIAN and JERRY are sitting at the back.

DEN PERRY
(INTO MIC) Like I say, she has got a cock, so you have been warned. Now as I'm sure you'll all know, we here at the Banana Grove are thrilled to be hosting the heats for this year's

Talent Trek and no doubt that'll go for the grand final as well, so I must say it's about time somebody decent had it. If you'd like some posters, they're out by the Tropicana Suite, just near the toilets ... And speaking of shithouses I'd like to welcome back Mr Brian Potter from the newly refurbished Phoenix Club ... Killed many pensioners this week Brian? (LAUGHTER) If you like your folk music with just a touch of racism, Brian's your man.

LAUGHTER

BRIAN   Fat pig. (SOMEBODY HANDS BRIAN A FLYER) Oh, I don't believe it, look who's on.

JERRY   Who?

BRIAN   Keith Lard. You know Keith Lard. He got done for interfering with dogs.

JERRY   Oh, that's him, that's him.

BRIAN   It was in all the newspapers and in court ...

JERRY   Yeah. He got off, though, didn't he?

BRIAN   Hmmm, you wanna try getting an Alsatian to testify. Where is he?

DEN PERRY
    Er ... I'd like to now unleash our guest speaker today, Mr Keith Lard. Here to discuss the very important matter: fire safety in the workplace ... Would you care to take the lead, Keith? He's a good lad, this ... His bark's worse than his bite. Sorry ... Sorry, Keith – there you go, mate.

KEITH walks centre stage to his preset stall.

KEITH   (BLOWING INTO MIC) Fire! Smoke kills in seconds, fire kills in minutes and there's no smoke without fire. Do you know what my biggest fear is?

DEN PERRY
    (OUT OF SHOT) Rabies!

LAUGHTER

KEITH   No. (HOLDING UP FLYER) Ignorance!

LAUGHTER

KEITH   (TO MAN LAUGHING) Have you ever smelt burning flesh, son?

MAN   Yeah.

KEITH doesn't know what to say.

KEITH   (OF DOLL) This is Veronica.

VOICE FROM AUDIENCE
    She's a bit of a dog.

LAUGHTER

CUT TO

11. INT. JOCKEY WILSON SUITE. DAY
They are reluctantly watching Armchair
Super Store Shopping Channel. There is an
advert for SPRAY MAINE, a hair product.

PRESENTER 1
>You spray on the affected area.

PRESENTER 2
>Right.

PRESENTER 1
>Wow, now look at that: you can see
>that going to work already ... What's
>happening ...

MAX   This is shite.

PADDY   You can turn this crap off.

HOLY MARY
>No, we're having it on.

MARION No, actually it stays on.

HOLY MARY
>Armchair Super Store.

MARION We like it.

MAX   I hate this home shopping bollocks.

PRESENTER 1
>And, hey presto, you get a beautiful
>full head of hair.

PRESENTER 2
>Wow! Incredible! Look at that. Now
>that's what I call ready for action.

PRESENTER 1
>And Spray Maine's available in
>many different colours: brown,
>black, dark brown and silver.

KENNY SNR
>Hey, there you go: assorted colours,
>Paddy.

PADDY   (TO MAX) Who else have you told,
>big mouth?

MAX   I haven't told anybody. They've got
>eyes, they can see your problem.

PRESENTER
>... in the comfort of your own
>armchair. Don't delay, call today.

CUT TO

12. INT. BANANA GROVE. DAY
KEITH scribbles a diagram of a club on an
overhead projector. It starts to resemble
a dog.

KEITH   If it were my ideal club, lads and lasses, I'd draw the basic club, I'd build the ... the car park would be there, I'd have a fire exit here, fire exit here ...

BRIAN   Is he drawing a dog?

KEITH   A back entrance there.

BRIAN   That's a dog he's drawing ... He's drawing a dog. He's drawing a dog. He's obsessed.

People mutter generally among themselves about how the drawing looks like a dog.

KEITH   Round the back, see the things outside it – what I'd do, I'd QQC the situation. Quickly, calmly ... Can I have your attention, please?

KEITH realises that they are not listening and fires an air horn. The men jump. A MAN walking back from the bar with a tray of drinks drops them on the floor.

MAN   You prick!

KEITH   Life or burn? Take your pick.

CUT TO

13. INT. JOCKEY WILSON SUITE. DAY
They're still watching the Armchair Super Store Channel and are starting to become intrigued.

PRESENTER 1
    For many men, Gary, sex is a frustrating hobby.

PRESENTER 2
    Yeah, like playing snooker with a rope.

FORCED LAUGH

PRESENTER 1
    Exactly. Well, modern technology combined with an ancient herbal remedy from South America has combined to create Piagra.

PRESENTER 2
    It's a chewing gum.

PRESENTER 1
    It is a chewing gum. Now its juices, when mixed with saliva, enhances and maximises sexual performance for up to six hours.

PRESENTER 2
    Wow! Hard times are coming. Does it come in a flavour?

PRESENTER 1
    It does. Aniseed, spearmint and liddement.

CUT TO

14. INT. BANANA GROVE. DAY
KEITH is on stage.

KEITH   Dead! You're all dead. It's that easy. (GETS OUT PIECE OF PAPER) I'll leave you with this. A friend of mine sent me from America – a very shocking headline: 'Fire inferno wrecks lives'. It's not for the squeamish if you want to cover your ears. 'To my surprise, one hundred storeys high, that's how high fire can get, that people get loose who are trying to get down from the roof. Folks were screaming, out of control, pandemonium. It was so devastating when the boogie' – which must be the American term

for 'fire', I think – 'started to grow.
Someone was quoted as saying,
"Burn, baby, burn, disco inferno.
Burn, baby, burn, burn that mother
down." Another child orphaned. Sick
minds we're dealing with.'

CUT TO

15. INT. JOCKEY WILSON SUITE. DAY

*PADDY is on the payphone (which clearly
has an 'OUT OF ORDER' sign on it).
Armchair Super Store Channel is playing in
the background.*

PADDY   419 – 876672 ... have you er ... got
           aniseed flavour? Max, Max.

MAX   What?

PADDY   Do you want some of this Piagra?

*MAX is watching Armchair Super Store
Channel – an advert for a sophisticated
diver's watch with a powerful light.*

MAX   Do I balls. I don't need it, me.

PRESENTER 1
        It's a piece of history, it's history on
        your wrist. What I would like to call
        'wristory'.

PADDY   No, no, no – it's not for me.

CUT TO

16. INT. BANANA GROVE. DAY

*JERRY bumps into DEN PERRY on the way
to the toilets.*

JERRY   Den.

DEN PERRY
        Oh, Jerry. Hey, I see you booked that
        psychic I told you about.

JERRY   Yeah. He's on tonight, yeah.

DEN PERRY
        Pure gold, that boy, pure gold. You
        won't go far wrong with him. Does a
        lot of work overseas. Shifted many
        tickets?

JERRY   (PROUD) Aye, we've sold out, yeah.
          It should be good.

DEN PERRY
        Ding dong.

*We cut back to BRIAN. KEITH LARD comes
over.*

KEITH   Brian Potter. I hope you were taking
         all that in. We don't want this new
         club of yours ravaged by fire. What
         is it? The ... em ...

BRIAN   The Phoenix.

KEITH   The Phoenix, that's right. I'm off
         down there now. You're first down
         for inspection.

BRIAN   Well, we've just had that done.
         I've got a bloke who does that.
         We had it done the other week.

KEITH   Dave Sherland? (BRIAN NODS)
         He's been suspended ... allegations
         of bribery.

BRIAN   Bribery?

KEITH   You know … backhanders. Some club owners, they … they'll stop at nothing to make money, even if it includes risking the lives of the customers. I'll see you down there directly.

DEN PERRY comes up behind them both.

DEN PERRY
> I'd watch yourself down there if I were you, Keith. Dog rough. (TO BRIAN) All right, Brian?

BRIAN   (GIVES DEN THE FINGER, WITHOUT LOOKING UP AT HIM) Den.

DEN PERRY
> (TO KEITH) Dog rough.

END OF PART ONE

PART TWO

17. INT. JERRY'S CAR, MAIN ROAD. DAY
JERRY is driving. BRIAN is in the passenger seat.

JERRY   Pack it in. They're on stop.

BRIAN   There not, they're on green. Come on, hurry up.

JERRY   Me, hurry up. I was waiting for you.

BRIAN   I'm disabled, Jerry. I can't slide through the window like Daisy Duke. Come on, get your foot down – we've got to get back to the club before Keith Lard.

JERRY   Why? Everything's all right. We've got a licence.

BRIAN   We've a colour photocopy and Christ knows what else.

JERRY   Who are you ringing?

BRIAN   The club. I've got to warn them.

JERRY   You can't. The phone's out of order.

CUT TO

18. INT. JOCKEY WILSON SUITE. DAY
MAX is on the payphone 'OUT OF ORDER' sign still on it. We see that PADDY is watching an advert for a diver's watch.

MAX   The Diver's Watch. Nineteen ninety-five. The one with the light. The Diver's Watch.

PRESENTER 1
> Look at that. That is a powerful light.

CUT TO

19. INT. JERRY'S CAR, MAIN ROAD. DAY
BRIAN and JERRY are still on the main road.

JERRY   Well, I'm doing thirty as it is.

BRIAN   Where are your balls, man? Floor it.

BRIAN pushes JERRY's foot down onto the accelerator peddle.

JERRY   Brian, pack it in. No.

BRIAN   Go on.

JERRY   I can't.

BRIAN   Get round here.

CUT TO

20. EXT. PHOENIX CLUB CAR PARK. DAY
KEITH LARD arrives and takes bag out of boot.

CUT TO

21. INT. JERRY'S CAR, MAIN ROAD. DAY
JERRY isn't happy. We hear a police siren.

BRIAN   Oh, no.

JERRY   What?

BRIAN   Look. Police.

JERRY   Oh. Ignore him. Ignore him. He doesn't want ... Oh, he does.

BRIAN   Swines, they are. They clamped me outside the gym last week. Can we not shake him?

CUT TO

22. INT. JOCKEY WILSON SUITE. DAY
KEITH knocks and enters. They're all watching the big screen.

KEITH   If I was a fire I wouldn't knock!

CUT TO

23. INT. JERRY'S CAR, MAIN ROAD. DAY
BRIAN and JERRY are in the car as the POLICEMAN approaches.

JERRY   What are you doing?

BRIAN   (BREATHING HEAVILY) I'm faking an attack. Just go with it.

MOTORCYCLE COP
         What's the rush, gents?

JERRY   It's me dad ... he's having an attack.

BRIAN   Who's there? Who's there? All I can see is a bright light. Should I walk towards the light, Jerry, or away from it?

JERRY   He needs his medication ...

BRIAN   Is that one of our glorious boys in blue? They do a grand job.

MOTORCYCLE COP
         Where are you off to?

JERRY   We're going to hospital.

MOTORCYCLE COP
         Follow me.

The POLICEMAN leaves. BRIAN stops faking his attack.

BRIAN   'Dad'?

CUT TO

24. INT. PENNINE SUITE. DAY
Aerobics class. Ten to fifteen WOMEN doing aerobics to 'SUMMER OF '69' by BRYAN ADAMS. HOLY MARY is one of the women. EDIE is next to her. She spots KEITH.

AEROBICS INSTRUCTOR
     Are you with us, Pat?

EDIE   Hey, look: there's Renee Lard's lad.

HOLY MARY
     Where?

EDIE   There ...

KEITH   (TURNS DOWN CASSETTE PLAYER)
     Too loud, this.

AEROBICS INSTRUCTOR
     Up, good, strain. Let's see those
     stretches.

EDIE   Hey, I never told you, did I?

AEROBICS INSTRUCTOR
     Up.

EDIE   Me and Pauline went on a power
     walk last week. We saw a car with
     its engine running and it was still
     running when we got back. And I
     thought, Well that's dead weird, that.
     I mean, what if someone's tried to
     do themselves in? You know. Suicide.
     So I went over for a look but the
     windows were all steamed up. Then
     Pauline shouts, 'Hey, there's a man
     on back seat with a dog on his knee.'
     When I looked, it were young Keith
     with a spaniel across his lap.

HOLY MARY
     A Spaniard?

ANOTHER WOMAN
     He's been done for that before.

HOLY MARY
     Yeah, but he got off, didn't he?

EDIE   He was getting off then, and all.

CUT TO

25. EXT. MAIN ROAD. DAY
*MOTORCYCLE TRAFFIC COP. JERRY's car
follows behind.*

CUT TO

26. INT. PENNINE SUITE. DAY
*We cut to show KEITH. He's taking coats off
the fire extinguisher in the corner. He then
looks at KENNY SNR, shakes his head and
writes it down on his checklist.*

KEITH   Is there a fire extinguisher under
     here? (OF COATS) Get them off.

KENNY SNR
     Yeah. When I was in Mexico with
     the giant redwoods – have you ever
     seen them?

KEITH   Not a coat hook.

KENNY SNR
     When they go up, you know about it.
     Chucking kiddies out the windows.
     We were catching them, me and Red
     Da Der – have you ever been to
     Mexico?

KEITH is in the corner of the room by the curtains. He pulls a cord and the curtains part, to reveal a set of heavily padlocked double fire doors.

KEITH   Aah. Padlocked. A fire door. Do you know … d'you know the Mexican for 'Let us out'? Let us out, we're burning – aaaaaah.

KENNY SNR
    Déjenos hacia fuera, nos estamos quemando – aaaaaah.

CUT TO

27. EXT. BRIDGE. DAY
We look down on TRAFFIC COP leading JERRY's car at high speed.

The road forks left and right.

BRIAN   Fork off.

JERRY   What?

BRIAN   Fork off. Here.

JERRY   No, Brian, No, no. I can't no.

BRIAN   There you go. Lost him.

CUT TO

28. INT. GALAXY SUITE. DAY
The Karate Kid rehearsals. The KIDS are sitting on the floor in skeleton costumes made from bin bags. LES is on stage with a small bonsai tree.

LES   This is the bonsai, the little tree of life. Focus on its power, focus on its strength.

KEITH walks over. Puts a lighter to the bonsai tree and it bursts into flames.

KEITH   Focus on the fact it's highly flammable.

LES lunges for KEITH but the fire alarm goes off.

CUT TO

29. EXT. CAR PARK. DAY
We cut to everybody outside. AEROBICS LADIES, KARATE KIDS. KEITH is fire-taping the front doors.

CUT TO

30. INT./EXT. JERRY'S CAR/CLUB CAR PARK. DAY
We cut to a POV shot of the scene from the interior of JERRY's car.

JERRY   Oh no! Look who it is.

BRIAN   What's he doing? He can't do that …

The car stops. BRIAN opens the door and shouts to KEITH.

KEITH   Closed until further notice.

FEMALE VOICE
    He's here now – look.

BRIAN   Oy, what you doing? You can't do that!

KEITH   (WALKING TO HIS ESTATE) I can and I have, Potter.

BRIAN   Why?

KEITH   Why? A serious breach of fire regulations. You're closed till further notice.

BRIAN   Oh no, no, no. We're full tonight. We're full.

KEITH drives off.

CUT TO

31. INT. JOCKEY WILSON SUITE. DAY

Everybody is gathered. JERRY and BRIAN are sitting at a table. BRIAN is drinking from his vase. Armchair Super Store is on the big screen. The others are glued.

JERRY   Well, what are we going to do?

BRIAN   I don't know, Jerry. I do not know. We need that licence for tonight. Can you flick that thing off. We're in the shit here.

MAX and PADDY begrudgingly turn off the big screen.

LES   Can we not reason with him?

BRIAN   Keith Lard? You're joking. He's power-mad, Leslie. He wants to destroy us. He's got it in for me.

MAX   If you want, me and Paddy could have a chat to him ...

PADDY   ... and bite his ears off.

KENNY SNR
    I'm very friendly with the SAS.

BRIAN   (SHOUTING) But, you see, you're not, Kenny.

HOLY MARY
    (TO BRIAN) Why don't we fight fire with fire?

BRIAN just gives her a confused look.

BRIAN   Eh?

HOLY MARY
    John, Chapter 8, Verse 7.

BRIAN   What?

HOLY MARY
    Let him who is without sin cast the first stone.

BRIAN   Is it me, or has everybody gone mad?

MARION   (TO HOLY MARY) Tell him what you told me.

BRIAN   Tell him what?

HOLY MARY
    Well, Edie said that Keith Lard ...

CUT TO

32. INT. BRIAN'S OFFICE DAY

BRIAN is on the phone. He is holding the creased flyer of KEITH LARD.

KEITH   Hello.

BRIAN   Keith Lard? Brian Potter. You'd better get back here. You've made a big mistake, and between me and you, Keith, I think it's gonna cost you your job.

KEITH   I don't make mistakes, Pott—

BRIAN hangs up.

JERRY   Well, do you think he'll come back?

BRIAN   Well, if he knows what's good for him, Jerry.

CUT TO

33. EXT. CAR PARK. DAY
KEITH LARD's estate pulls into the car park and screeches to a halt.

CUT TO

34. INT. BRIAN'S OFFICE. DAY
BRIAN at his desk. KEITH standing in front. RAY is there.

KEITH   Well, Potter, what d'you want?

BRIAN   Sit down.

KEITH   I won't bother, I'm not going to be here that long ...

BRIAN   Fair enough, just give us a licence and go.

KEITH   It's not as simple as that, Potter.

BRIAN   We've done everything on the list. We need that licence for tonight.

KEITH   Too little, too late. This isn't about a list, Potter, this is about your attitude. Your shoddy attitude towards fire safety.

BRIAN   If I had a wet nose and a waggy tail you'd give me one ...

KEITH   You're a disease, Potter, and I'm the cure.

BRIAN   You're the disease, Dogtanian. Word has it you're back on the prowl.

KEITH   What do you mean?

BRIAN   What do I mean? You know what I mean. There's been sightings of cars, of you on back seats – with dogs.

KEITH   I wondered how long it'd take. I wondered how long it'd take you to dig up the past. Not guilty. Don't you read the papers, Potter? Lack of proof. Where's your proof? (SILENCE) You see, you've nothing.

BRIAN throws him a file.

KEITH   (cont.) What's this?

KEITH takes out a photograph and looks at it. We cut to a close-up to see KEITH LARD naked on a bed (in high heels) with an Airedale dog masking his genitals.

BRIAN   Man and beast in perfect harmony. They've managed to capture a look of excitement rarely seen on an Airedale.

KEITH   That's not me ...

BRIAN   I know, but it's amazing what you can to do with computers and access to t'Internet and the right pictures. In't that right, Ray?

RAY VON Oh, yeah.

KEITH   You'll never get away with this.
         No ... no one will believe it.

BRIAN   I don't know, Keith. If you throw
         enough shit, some sticks. Three
         hundred of those dumped in the
         right places and you know what
         people will say: there's no smoke
         without fire.

BRIAN holds up KEITH's flyer.

He laughs, quite proud of the gag.

We cut to a reaction shot of KEITH.

CUT TO

35. INT. FOYER. DAY
*We see a shot of The Psychic Night poster
with 'SOLD OUT' across it.*

CUT TO

36. INT. GALAXY LOUNGE. NIGHT
*The room is packed and ready for the
PSYCHIC.*

*The lights go down. Smoke starts to fill the
stage. A very light wash of blues/ greens
hits the stage. We hear a VOICE OF GOD.*

VOICE OF GOD
         Hundreds of years ago when man
         walked the planet, he had no real
         means of communication. In time,
         man developed a phenomenon which
         has never been fully understood by
         the psychic community – this
         phenomenon is Clinton Baptiste!

*There is a huge thunderclap. The AUDIENCE
applaud. A SMALL MAN enters through the
smoke. He walks forward.*

CLINTON Y'alright?

*The AUDIENCE applaud. Clinton sits on a
stool.*

CLINTON (cont.) Now, I'm getting a voice, the
         spirits are very strong tonight, very
         strong ... Hey ... I'm getting the
         name, I'm getting the name John.
         Is there a John in the audience?

*We hear a handful of PEOPLE say 'YEAH'.
We cut to Brian. He gives JERRY a look.*

CUT TO

37. EXT. CAR PARK. NIGHT
MAX and PADDY are on the door.

MAX   How's that Piagra?

PADDY   It's all right. Shit for bubbles.

MAX   They're great, these. What flavour
         did you get?

PADDY   Aniseed.

MAX   Has it kicked in yet?

PADDY   I can't tell.

MAX   You should have got yourself a diver's watch. Look at this.

PADDY   Ay, it's not the kind of diving I'll be doing. Eh …

TWO GIRLS approach.

PADDY   (cont.) Evening, girls. D'you want to have a look into me crystal balls?

MAX   See me glowing.

GIRL   What's that smell? What're you chewing?

PADDY   Right. In you go.

GIRL   It stinks.

The GIRLS enter the club.

PADDY   Yeah. Get in.

MAX   (SHINING THE WATCH LIGHT) Can you see where you're going? It's half-six in Japan.

CUT TO

38. INT. GALAXY LOUNGE. NIGHT
CLINTON BAPTISTE is in the AUDIENCE with a hand-mic talking to one of the JOHNS.

CLINTON   Your mother, John. She were quite young when she died, am I right?

JOHN   Ninety-three.

CLINTON   Yeah, but she were young in herself, though. She were young at heart. And she seemed to slow down a lot towards the end, am I right?

JOHN   Yeah.

CLINTON   This is your partner, correct? Now I think there's something you want to tell her, am I right?

JOHN   No.

CLINTON   I think there is. Something you wanted to get off your chest you may be a bit ashamed of. Don't you think you should tell her, John? Before you both get hurt?

JOHN   Nothing. There's nothing.

JOHN'S WIFE
   What is it?

JOHN   (TO CLINTON) Hey, mouth!

CLINTON moves on.

CUT TO

39. INT. CAR PARK. NIGHT
PADDY is still chewing and reading a porn magazine.

PADDY   Dave likes to see me holding what?

MAX   Anything?

PADDY   Nothing. Not a pulse. Come on,
son, let's have you. (TAPS HIS
GENITALS)

CUT TO

40. INT. GALAXY LOUNGE. NIGHT

*CLINTON is handing a tissue to a woman
in tears.*

CLINTON Don't worry, love, you'll still be able
to visit.

The AUDIENCE react. CLINTON moves on.

CLINTON (cont.) Now, I'm feeling it very
strongly over here.

CLINTON sees a necklace with an 'S' on it.

CLINTON (cont.) Now what's your name, love?
Don't tell me. It's Su-sa-sha-so?

SONIA   (SAYS IT WITH CLINTON) Sonia.

CLINTON Sonia, Sonia. Now, Sonia, love,
you've not been very well, have you,
love? Am I right?

SONIA   No. (POINTING) Debbie's been ill.

CLINTON Debbie, Debbie's been ... You have,
haven't you, love? You've been very
poorly and it's not been easy, has it?

CLINTON And it is terminal, isn't it?

DEBBIE No, no.

*CLINTON just gives her a knowing look and
walks off. The others comfort her. The
AUDIENCE react.*

CLINTON Right. Hands up who can't have
children.

BRIAN and JERRY are both in shock.

CUT TO

41. EXT. CAR PARK. NIGHT

*MAX and PADDY. Members of the
AUDIENCE are leaving.*

MAX   Shit. I'm out of oxygen.

JOHN'S WIFE
    I bloody well know there's
something going on. (SHOUTING)
Well tell me what's going on.

JOHN   Nothing. All right. (TO MAX AND
PADDY) It's wrong what he's doing
in there. He's just offending people.

JOHN'S WIFE
    Bloody tell me what's going on.

MAX   Stay back. Domestic. Don't get
involved, son.

CUT TO

42. INT. GALAXY LOUNGE. NIGHT

*CLINTON is standing in front of a COUPLE OF
MEN. BRIAN isn't happy.*

CLINTON You've got to be cruel to be kind.
Aye, don't shoot the messenger. I'm
only telling you what the spirits are
telling me. Now I'm getting the word
'nonce'!

*We hear the scrape of chairs as TERRY
lunges for CLINTON.*

CUT TO

43. INT. FOYER. NIGHT
BRIAN is seeing people out.

BRIAN   Thank you very much. Goodnight,
        God bless.

FEMALE AUDIENCE MEMBER
        Goodnight.

JERRY   Goodnight.

MALE AUDIENCE MEMBER
        We're not coming here again.

BRIAN   Where the bloody hell did you get
        him from?

JERRY   He came highly recommended.

BRIAN   By who?

JERRY   Den Perry.

BRIAN   Den Perry. Jerry Jerry Perry,
        Jerry Perry Perry. He wants us
        shut down, man. (TO CLINTON)
        Ho ho, thank you, thank you, good
        buddy. Thank you for upsetting

my customers customers. I've just
had to refund ...

CLINTON How long did I do?

BRIAN   Too long.

JERRY   You did fifteen minutes.

CLINTON Really? I don't usually last longer
         than ten. It's them, they can't
         handle the truth.

BRIAN   You ... Some bloody psychic. You
        didn't see that coming, did you?

CLINTON Look, can I have my money?

BRIAN   Can you have ... can you have ...?
        Can you read minds? Can you read
        minds? Read this.

BRIAN puts his hands to his head.

CLINTON Hey. You can walk.

BRIAN   Get out of it. Get out. Get off.

*We cut to see the TRAFFIC COP from earlier
come into the club.*

*BRIAN and JERRY start to act the fake
attack again.*

JERRY   Dad! Oh not again, no, no, no.

BRIAN   Where are we, Jerry? This isn't the
        hospital, son?

POLICEMAN
        Another attack sir? (READING)
        Must be me you're allergic to, eh?
        OK. I've brought your prescription.
        Three points and a two-hundred-
        pound fine, to be taken immediately.

*BRIAN looks at the fine and hands it to
JERRY.*

BRIAN   Jerry.

CUT TO

END CREDITS

44. INT. GALAXY LOUNGE. DAY

*BRIAN AND CO. Are auditioning a
JUGGLER. He is juggling balls. He drops one,
smiles nervously, turns to a props table and
turns back with three plates. He juggles. He
drops one. It smashes. He smiles nervously,
kicks the debris away. He turns back to the
props table.*

The PANEL are not impressed.

*We cut back to the JUGGLER. He turns
around with three flaming torches.*

*We cut to BRIAN and the others. They all
run – except BRIAN: he quickly wheels
himself away.*

BRIAN   *(OVER HIS SHOULDER) Next!*

THE END

Episode 4

PART ONE

**1. INT./EXT. BRIAN'S
BEDROOM/TELEPHONE BOX. NIGHT**
*BRIAN is asleep. The telephone rings. Half
asleep, he reaches for the phone. He puts the
bedside lamp on and puts on his glasses.*

BRIAN   What?

MAX   (VO) (PUTTING ON A VOICE) Hello.
Could I speak to Mr Potter, please?

BRIAN   Speaking.

MAX   (VO) Mr Potter from the Phoenix
Club?

BRIAN   Yeah. Who's this? It's half-three in
the pissing morning.

MAX   (VO) It's … It's Mixu Patalinen.

BRIAN   Who?

MAX   (VO) Bolton Coroner's Office. I'm
afraid your club has burnt down.

BRIAN   What? Oh God, no, oh no, not again.

MAX   (VO) I'm afraid we've found a body,
Mr Potter.

BRAIN   A body? Oh God, no. Jerry, oh Jerry,
the compere, he was last to lock up.
Oh, Jerry, Jerry, Jerry. Nineteen
years, Jerry … Nineteen years …
No goodbyes.

MAX (VO) All we need to know Mr Potter …
did he have false teeth?

PADDY stifles a laugh.

BRIAN   Did he what? False teeth? How the
pissin' hell should I know if he had
false teeth? Who is this?

*We hear a giggle. MAX and PADDY can't
contain their laughter.*

BRIAN   Hey, I know who you are. Who are
you?

The phone goes dead.

PADDY   (LAUGHING) Mixu Pataliner.

CUT TO

2. INT. BRIAN'S BEDROOM. NIGHT

BRIAN   You're sick animals. Laughing at death, half past three in the bloody morning. The bloody world's gone mad.

BRIAN turns the light off and lies down.

The phone rings again. Light goes on quickly. BRIAN reaches for it.

BRIAN   Who is this? Hello.

SERGEANT PATTERSON (VO)
          Mr Potter?

BRIAN   Who is this?

SERGEANT PATTERSON (VO)
          This is Sergeant Patterson. I'm ringing regarding a break-in at your club.

BRIAN   Oh, a break in now, is it? Eh? Who's broke in? Bloody fire brigade. It had

burnt down a minute ago, you sick bastards.

SERGEANT PATTERSON (VO)
          I beg your pardon.

BRIAN   Do you. Well cop for this.

BRIAN puts the phone under the blankets and farts down the receiver.

BRIAN   (cont.) Goodnight.

BRIAN hangs up.

CUT TO

3. EXT. CAR PARK. NIGHT
BRIAN is in his brewery dressing gown and pyjamas. YOUNG KENNY is pushing him. He is talking to SERGEANT PATTERSON. A blue light is flashing.

BRIAN   Well, thanks again for coming down, Sergeant Patterson. I appreciate it.

SERGEANT PATTERSON
          Not at all, Mr Potter. Like I said, I can't understand anyone stealing beer crates.

BRIAN   Yeah, yeah. It'll be young bulls sniffing crack ... They'll go straight up their nose, them beer crates. Bloody filth.

SERGEANT PATTERSON leaves.

BRIAN   (cont.) See yer.

CUT TO

OPENING CREDITS

CUT TO

4. INT. GALAXY LOUNGE. NIGHT

The singles night – quarter full (mainly blokes). LES and ALAN are by the door, dressed up. LES takes off his wedding ring. MAX and PADDY enter. They're in their work clothes.

RAY VON is doing the disco. Song ends.

RAY VON That was 'Lonely This Christmas'. It's singles night tonight here at the Phoenix Club, where you could meet the love of your life.

PADDY   Oh, we're living *la vida* tonight.

RAY VON There are people here to suit all tastes – and, speaking of taste, the flavoured-condom machine is restocked and ready for action. OK, we're going to move straight along now with the fantastic Mr Eric Carmen, and he's 'All By Himself.' Aaaah. I bet you've cried yourself to sleep many a night with this one, Shabba.

MAX   (LOOKING AROUND) Where are all the women?

RAY leaves the disco and goes to the bar to join his GIRLFRIEND. He passes a man sitting by himself looking fed up and pats him on the back as he goes past.

BRIAN is at the other end of the room with KENNY SNR.

KENNY SNR
            So I woke up, rolled over, guess who's lying next to me. Bonnie Langford.

BRIAN   (IGNORES KENNY SNR) Look at that lot ... they're like pigs on heat.

KENNY SNR
            Nearly broke her back.

The lads are watching the female talent.

PADDY   No wonder they're all single: they're all hanging.

MAX   Who let the dogs out?

JERRY goes past.

JERRY   Evening, boys.

BOYS   Hello. Hi, Jerry.

JERRY   On your own?

MAX   (BREATHES IN) What have you got on? (SMELLS) You stink.

JERRY   Summat you can't afford.

PADDY   What? Fabreze?

They laugh.

JERRY   Who said that? Oh, sorry, Paddy. I didn't see you there with lights bouncing off your head.

LAUGHTER

We cut back to BRIAN and KENNY SNR.

BRIAN   Who's that with Ray Von?

We cut to show RAY chatting to a GIRL by the bar.

KENNY SNR
    Dunno.

BRIAN   She's dicing with death. I'd better go and warn her, or they'll be dragging her out the canal Monday.

We cut back to MAX, PADDY, LES and ALAN.

ALAN   You know, song lyrics make good chat-up lines, don't they? You know, like 'Heaven must be missing an angel' or 'If I said you had a beautiful body would you hold it against me?' You know, stuff like that.

MAX   I don't know who you are, but you're a real dead ringer for love ... Who sang that?

PADDY   Meatloaf.

LES   Everywhere you go you always take the weather with you.

ALAN/MAX/PADDY
    No.

BRIAN wheels himself up to RAY VON and his GIRL.

BRIAN   (TO RAY, NERVOUS) Hey, Ray.

RAY VON Hello, Mr Potter.

BRIAN   Aye, you've tapped off quick.

RAY VON This is my girlfriend, Mr Potter, Tracy ... D'you fancy a beer?

BRIAN   No, ta. Beer's not my cup of tea ... I'll have a drop of Teacher's though. (HANDS HIM VASE)

RAY turns away. BRIAN wheels himself closer.

BRIAN   (cont.) Tracy! His last one were called Tracy. It must be a name thing ... run while you can.

TRACY   What are you on about?

BRIAN   Just get out of here. DJ Death, the Yorkshire Rapper ... You don't know what happened to Tracy Burns? (WHISPERS)

TRACY   I *am* Tracy Burns.

BRIAN   What?

TRACY   I'm Tracy Burns.

BRIAN (LOOKING) You're Tracy ... You're Trac— You're Tracy Burns, your Tracy Burns, you're alive, alive here in the flesh, all grown up ... and breathing. I didn't recognise you without your hula-hoop ... (REALISATION) ... Ah, excuse me while I go and sack me backing band.

BRIAN reverses in embarrassment. Three-point turn. He goes over a WOMAN's foot. She makes a noise.

BRIAN Well, if you'd move! I don't know if you've noticed but I'm ...

BRIAN turns around and realises that she's hurt.

BRIAN (cont.) ... in a rush. What have you done? Have I run over your foot?

BEVERLY No it's ... I'm all right ... I'm fine ... honestly.

BRIAN (FLUSTERED) It's this wheelchair, love. It's like a shopping trolley: it has a mind of it's own. You've spilt your drink down yer—

BEVERLY It's all right.

BRIAN Do you want another one? Get another one ... it'll numb the pain. You've dropped your brolly now. Marion, drink for this lady. What d'you want, love?

BEVERLEY I'll just have a Coke.

BRIAN A Coke?

BEVERLEY Yes.

BRIAN Is that all? A Coke? Do you want something else?

BEVERLEY A Tia Maria ...

BRIAN A Tia Maria ...

BEVERLEY Yes. A double, please.

BRIAN Double. (BRIAN MOTIONS FOR A SINGLE). It's on me.

The LADS at the bar all look round.

BRIAN (cont.) Are you with somebody? Are you on your own?

BEVERLEY It's a singles night.

BRIAN Oh, aye. Isn't it just? I should know: I organised it.

BEVERLEY Oh, d'you work here?

BRIAN Sometimes, yes. I own it. All this. I'm the manager – Brian.

BEVERLEY Beverley.

BRIAN No, Brian. (LAUGHS)

Cut back to MAX, PADDY, LES and ALAN.

PADDY   (DRINKS UP) Do you want a drink?

MAX   I'll have a lemonade.

PADDY   Lemonade?

PADDY   (TO ALAN AND LES) You?

ALAN   (HOLDS UP GLASS) One of them.

LES   You, hey, she's too young for you.

PADDY   Hey. If there's grass on the pitch ...

MAX gives him a look.

ALAN   Hey, I see Ironsides trapped off
here.

Others laugh.

MAX   Go on, Brian.

*We cut to BRIAN and BEVERLY from a
distance. They are sitting at the table in mid-
conversation.*

*RAY VON is doing the disco. It's a bit later in
the evening. TRACY is standing by his side.*

RAY VON OK, we're going to slow things right
down now as we enter the erection
section. That's right, if you've met
somebody tonight, get them on the
dance floor. If you haven't, what
are you still here for? (OFF MIC)
You losers.

*ALAN is slow-dancing with a WOMAN.
We reveal that she is smoking when they
turn around. Tips ash down the back of
his shirt.*

*We see LES approach a WOMAN, tries a
chat-up line but is rebuffed. He then walks*

PADDY   I don't think I'm going to get my end
away tonight.

MAX   You're addicted to sex.

PADDY   I am. It's an illness. Michael Douglas
had it.

MAX   You are, and you know you're going
to be single for a long time.

PADDY   Like you?

MAX   That's different, that's through choice.

PADDY   Yeah. Theirs.

*PADDY notices HOLY MARY'S DAUGHTER
behind the bar.*

PADDY   Who is that behind bar?

LES   That's Mary, that ... Holy Mary's
youngest.

PADDY   I never knew she had kids.

LES   Yeah, she's two. Mary and Joseph,
Joe's doing a B-Tech in joinery down
at the college.

over to ANOTHER LADY and sits a chair
distance apart. She turns and he awkwardly
smiles at her.

LES   I'm horny! Horny, horny, horny.

LADY   Piss off.

LES   Right. (HE PICKS HIS PINT UP AND
          WALKS AWAY)

PADDY is chatting to MARY over the bar.
She is obviously flirting with him.

MAX   (CALLS OVER) Go on, that's it,
          Patrick.

PADDY throws a salute to MAX. MAX turns
back towards the dance floor. Watching the
couples, he stands on his own. KENNY SNR
comes over.

KENNY SNR
          All right?

MAX   OK, Kenny, lad. How's it hanging?

KENNY SNR
          It's nearly hanging off. I've just had
          three of them round the back.

MAX walks off, shaking his head.

We cut back to PADDY and MARY. HOLY
MARY isn't impressed.

HOLY MARY
          (TO MARY) Shouldn't you be
          collecting glasses, Mary?

PADDY   Listen, what're you doing after
          work?

CUT TO

5. INT. GALAXY LOUNGE. LATER IN THE EVENING

BRIAN is talking to BEVERLEY. They're the
last to leave.

BRIAN   Fruit machine. Pinned me up against
          serving hatch. I were in a coma
          until new year. When I woke up I'd
          lost my club, I'd lost my legs, I'd lost
          my will to live ... You can't go back,
          you can't go back. This ...

The lights flicker on in the Galaxy Lounge.

BEVERLEY
          I think they want us to leave.

BRIAN   I think they do – I've got to lock up.

BEVERLEY
          I've really enjoyed tonight.

BRIAN   Yeah. I don't get chance to go out
          much. Makes a nice change, you
          know, running this place.

BEVERLEY
          We could go out ... sometime, if you
          wanted.

BRIAN   Who, us?

BEVERLEY
          Yes.

BRIAN   Oh, aye, I'd like that ...

BEVERLEY
          We can do that if you like.

BRIAN   I'd like that very much.

BEVERLEY
          Great. Lovely.

BRIAN   Yeah.

CUT TO

6. EXT. PUBLIC PARK. DAY
BEVERLEY is pushing BRIAN in his wheelchair. He's feeding the ducks.

CUT TO

7. INT. BOWLING ALLEY. DAY
BEVERLEY is wheeling BRIAN on a run-up towards the bowling aisle. She pushes him a bit too hard and lets him go, sending him down the aisle. BRIAN has the bowl in his hands. He just lets it drop and it rolls into the side. BEVERLEY looks embarrassed.

CUT TO

8. EXT. FOREST. DAY
BRIAN and BEVERLEY are paint-balling. Twigs and camouflage in his wheels. We see BRIAN, gun in hands. Paint hits his chest. BEVERLEY is firing again and again.

CUT TO

9. INT. RESTAURANT. NIGHT
BRIAN and BEVERLY are having a romantic meal. A LADY comes up selling roses.

LADY   Flower for the lady?

BRIAN   Fuck off.

The LADY leaves. BRIAN carries on eating.

CUT TO

10. INT. GALAXY LOUNGE. NIGHT

Half full. 'Jerryoke'. BRIAN is singing on
stage: 'WIND BENEATH MY WHEELS'. He
doesn't know the words and occasionally has
to look to the monitor. He gestures to
BEVERLY, who is sitting on her own and
genuinely moved.

BRIAN   Thank you very much. That's for
            Beverly over there. Thank you.

JERRY   Brian Potter, ladies and gentlemen,
            your very own, your very own Brian
            Potter.

END OF PART ONE

PART TWO

11. INT. MAIN CORRIDOR. DAY

BRIAN's in the corridor, he's singing 'WIND
BENEATH MY WINGS'. He pats his 'disabled
boy' on the head and as an afterthought puts
a few coppers into his slot.

CUT TO

12. INT. GENTS' TOILET. DAY

BRIAN enters and sees the condom machine
on the floor.

BRIAN   Jerry?

JERRY   Yeah.

BRIAN   Who's done this?

JERRY   Don't know.

BRIAN   Who's knocked all this off here?
            Vandals! It wants screwing in that.
            Christ, my eyes are burning.

JERRY   It's not my fault. I've not been the
            same since that cowboy punched me.
            It's murder. Are you regular, Brian?

BRIAN   Like a Kennedy funeral. You could
            set your watch by my arse.

JERRY strains.

BRIAN   (cont.) Big night tonight.

JERRY   Yeah, yeah. Bucket Bingo, it should
            be good.

BRIAN   No, I'm talking about me and
            Beverley.

JERRY   Oh?

BRIAN   I'm taking her back to *chez* Potter.
            We're going to have a meal.

JERRY   A meal? I didn't know you could
            cook.

BRIAN   Oh, aye. There's a lot you didn't
            know about me. We'll have a meal
            for two and then the world's your
            lobster. I was thinking of giving her
            a pearl necklace.

JERRY   Does she know?

The toilet flushes and JERRY comes out. He
was in the cubicle behind BRIAN.

BRIAN   I was gonna surprise her.

JERRY   I think you might just do that.

BRIAN   Jerry?

The hand dryer comes on. JERRY carries on talking. BRIAN reacts, shocked at what he can hear, but we can't hear. JERRY makes hand gestures. The dryer stops.

JERRY   (cont.) ... covered in piss.

BRIAN stares at him, shocked. swallows.

CUT TO

13. INT. BRIAN'S LOUNGE. NIGHT

BEVERLEY
   Thanks again for this present. You shouldn't have, you know. It must have cost a fortune.

BRIAN   (OFFERS HER CHOCOLATES) They were me mother's, them, and they're no use to me, and she would have wanted you to have them.

BEVERLEY
   You must miss her a lot.

BRIAN   She's not dead. Lives up Stitch Mi Lane ... Toblerone?

BRIAN smashes it on the table to break off a piece.

BEVERLEY
   Erm, no, no, thanks. If I eat anything else I'll burst.

BRIAN   I know. Lovely meal that, weren't it? It's a cracker, that burger bar. They do the lot, kebabs, burgers ... Blue Nun? (REACHES FOR BOTTLE) Drop of Blue Nun?

BEVERLEY
   Er ...

BRIAN   Top up? Go on.

JERRY   Yeah?

BRIAN   What d'you do, Jerry.

JERRY   I'm a compere.

BRIAN   No, what d'you do?

JERRY   What d'you mean?

BRIAN   You know ... women ... tactics ... manoeuvres.

JERRY   (WASHING HANDS) Well you and Jean must at some point. I mean for goodness sake.

BRIAN   Me and Jean?

JERRY   Yeah.

BRIAN   No ... no.

JERRY   Never?

BRIAN   Well, once or twice, but I'm not a machine. That was years ago. Beverley's different, Jerry. She's a modern woman, I can tell.

JERRY   Well, I'll tell you this. Don't rush. I had a girl once, I rushed, big mistake ...

BEVERLEY

Yes, go on ... go on, then, I will.

BRIAN   You only live once.

BEVERLEY

I've got to go though soon 'cos I've got an early start tomorrow.

BRIAN   Have you?

BEVERLEY

Yeah.

BRIAN   You've not seen me jukebox yet. You can't go without seeing me jukebox. Look at that ... Motown Special. I got that ... It's a cracker, in't it?

BEVERLEY

It's great.

BRIAN   I got that from the States. America. Hmmm, brilliant, that. There's only a few of them in the world. D'you like Motown?

BEVERLEY

Lovely, yeah.

BRIAN   You can't whack it. Have you got any change? It's five for a pound.

BEVERLEY

(SEARCHES IN HER BAG) Er, yeah, I think I have, actually. Hang on.

Jump cut – BRIAN drops a coin into the slot. We hear the opening to 'LET'S GET IT ON', by MARVIN GAYE.

BRIAN   (SINGING) Baby ... Oh yes 26B, a bit of Marvin. He knew the score. (SINGING) 'I've been feeling fine, baby, got to hold back the feeling for so long ...'

BEVERLEY

Do you never get lonely?

BRIAN   No. Not with Marvin, anyway. (SINGING) 'Like I feel, baby ... Oh, come on, oooh.' Have you ever been to America?

BEVERLEY

No.

BRIAN   Me and Jerry went when the Neptune burnt down couple of years ago. Oh, yeah, we had a marvellous two weeks. Jerry got the shits! Lovely time. I've got a video of it somewhere – it's on the floor down there ... Just whack it in. I've set it.

BEVERLEY

Where?

BRIAN   Jerry did it with his camcorder. It's there on top of *Flashdance* ...(SINGING) 'We're all sensitive people ... So much to give ... I love you, sugar ...'

The video comes on. BEVERLY sits down on the couch.

BRIAN   This is it here, look. There you go.
Last night, this – they had a big
firework display.

BEVERLEY
Have you always lived on your own?

BRIAN   (CONTINUES TO SING) No. I were
with Jean for many years – worst
luck. Here we are, look at this. Look
at these rockets. Stand well back,
they'll blow your head off. In't it
marvellous what they can do? Look.

*BRIAN turns to BEVERLEY. He leans
forward and they kiss. They're silhouetted
against the fireworks on screen. The camera
rises as they kiss, and they're both lowered
out of shot. After a few seconds, sash scrolls
up the screen and a pornographic film
comes on.*

TV VOICE Splash your cream right in her
headlights.

BRIAN   Where's the remote? Where's the
remote? Knock it off. It's Jerry's
tape, this. It's Jerry's. Knock it off!

CUT TO

14. INT. BED SHOWROOM. DAY
*BRIAN is lying on a bed. We slow-zoom out
of an extreme close-up. It seems as though
BRIAN has just had sex with BEVERLEY.*

BRIAN   Oooh, it's wonderful. Feels great. Oh
it's been years since I felt like this.

*We pull out slowly to reveal JERRY lying
next to him on the other side of the bed.*

JERRY   I told you you'd like it if you gave it
a try.

BRIAN   Is it orthopaedic? Is it orthopaedic,
this, love?

SHOP ASSISTANT
It is, and can you take your feet off,
please?

*Later, JERRY is pushing BRIAN through
the shop.*

JERRY   So, a waterbed, eh?

BRIAN   That's right.

JERRY   You're splashing out, aren't you?

BRIAN Emm.

JERRY Splashing out. D'you geddit?

BRIAN Do you begrudge me a bit of happiness, Jerry?

JERRY No. It's just ... well it was only a kiss.

BRIAN Oho. It was more than a kiss. It was a connection.

JERRY Don't get carried away.

BRIAN No, it's too late for that. She's started a fire in Potter's heart. You see, Jerry, I always thought that love was only true in fairy tales, meant for someone else but not for me. It's been twelve years. He thinks he's in for life you know ...

JERRY Who?

BRIAN (POINTS TO HIS PENIS) Him! He's up for parole soon. If he gets out I want him coming home in style.

CUT TO

15. INT. BRIAN'S CONSERVATORY. DAY

BRIAN and BEVERLEY are sitting up at a table in a conservatory. BRIAN raises a novelty cup with a naked woman pictured it on to his mouth and drinks. Then he takes a bite of his food, leaving a crumb on the side of his mouth.

BRIAN Listen, Beverley. Erm. I'm not very good with words, I was ... I was wondering if ...

BEVERLEY
Shh.

BEVERLEY puts her finger to his lips and shushes him. She holds it there and then brushes the crumb from his lip. We stay on a close-up of BRIAN, showing his awkwardness.

CUT TO

16. INT. BRIAN'S STAIRS. NIGHT
BRIAN is riding the stairlift. BEVERLEY is holding his hand. He moves up slowly. She waits and moves up two steps at a time. Silence, except for the hum of the motor.

BRIAN It won't be long now. Just you wait ... things I'm gonna do to you.

CUT TO

17. INT. BRIAN'S BEDROOM. NIGHT
BEVERLEY is bouncing on the edge of the bed.

BRIAN (EXCITED) Climb on.

BEVERLEY and BRIAN are both lying on the king-size waterbed.

BRIAN   (LAUGHS) There, feel it.

BEVERLEY
    Yeah.

BRIAN   It's water, that.

BEVERLEY
    It feels weird. I've never been on a
    waterbed before.

BRIAN   Aaaah. Maybe I've found me sea
    legs ... Whoops, steady! Listen:
    before we crack on there's
    something I want to ask you.

BEVERLEY touches his arm.

BEVERLEY
    No, actually ... I wanted to talk to
    you, actually.

BRIAN   Now let's say cheese.

*He pulls out a polaroid camera from under
the bed and takes a photograph of them
both.*

BEVERLEY
    Brian, there's something I really
    want to—

BRIAN   It'll be a good one, that.

BEVERLEY
    Yeah. Brian, listen. I said I need to
    talk to you about something and it's
    not easy.

BRIAN   Good 'un, that. It'll be a good 'un,
    that.

BEVERLEY
    Will you listen?

BRIAN   Me and you, that.

BEVERLEY
    Brian, please.

BRIAN   What?

BEVERLEY
    I'm not the person that you think
    I am.

BRIAN   You're not a bloke, are yer?

BEVERLEY
    No.

BRIAN   You didn't used to be?

BEVERLEY
    No. Brian.

BRIAN   Like Hayley?

BEVERLEY
    No, I've never been a bloke.

BRIAN   Thank God for that.

BEVERLEY
    And you ... you never ran over my
    foot that night in the club.

BRIAN   What?

BEVERLEY
    I work for the DSS, Brian. They sent
    me to investigate you for fraudulent
    disability claims.

BRIAN   What?

BEVERLEY
    Just ... just hear me out, will yer? I
    know ... I know what you're
    thinking, right, but it's not like that.
    I never expected any of this. I never
    expected any of this to happen.
    Never. You know, I've never felt like

this about anybody. That's why I wanted to tell you, you know, I wanted to tell you the truth, 'cos I can't keep lying to you any more.

BRIAN   From the beginning ... All this time? Turn away. Turn away. Look over there. I don't want to look at yer. Turn away.

BEVERLEY
        Brian.

BRIAN   Go on.

We cut to BEVERLEY. She has her back turned.

BEVERLEY
        Brian, it's my job, you know. I ... I've got no choice.

BRIAN   You know where the front door is. You'll understand if I don't see you out.

CUT TO

18. INT. BRIAN'S OFFICE. DAY
BRIAN is at his desk. He's opening a brown paper parcel. It reads 'BRIAN WINSTON POTTER' on the front and an address of the Phoenix Club with BEVERLEY's address on the back. He feels inside and pulls out his mother's pearl necklace, then looks at the photograph of himself and BEVERLEY on the waterbed.

JERRY (OUT OF SHOT)
        Brian?

BRIAN   Right.

BRIAN quickly slides them back inside and puts them in his desk drawer.

CUT TO

19. INT. JOCKEY WILSON SUITE. DAY
JERRY wheels BRIAN over to the notice board.

JERRY   So, you all right?

BRIAN   Yeah, I'm all right. Why wouldn't I be all right?

PADDY is on the telephone.

PADDY   (OOV) Seven three six four one nine.

BRIAN   This old heart of mine's been broke a thousand times, Jerry.

PADDY   (OOV) Six six seven two.

BRIAN   Patrick, I thought that phone were out of order.

PADDY   Knackered. (REPLACES THE RECEIVER) Hello?

JERRY   Still, must have been a shock. It must be painful.

BRIAN   (FALSE SMILE) Like watching you compere, Jerry.

JERRY   She's phoned again.

BRIAN   Hmm.

JERRY   That's twice now.

BRIAN   She'll stop.

They stop at the notice board and JERRY pins up an advert for the waterbed. It's one of RAY VON's computer designs. BRIAN in his wheelchair on a surfboard riding a giant wave. A speech bubble reads, 'AHOY THERE, KINGSIZE WATERBED FOR SALE'.

JERRY   There you go.

BRIAN   We never even christened it.

CUT TO

20. INT. GALAXY LOUNGE. DAY
JERRY is on the stage. He has switched on the stage lights and is checking the microphone by blowing into it. BRIAN's in front of the stage.

JERRY   (INTO MIC) Still, who'd have thought it? Fraudulent claims?

BRIAN   Whoa. Whoa.

JERRY   What?

BRIAN   Shouting around the world.

JERRY   I don't believe it, that's all.

BRIAN   Yeah. It's gone, all right. Forget about it. I've bigger fish to fry. No woman, no cry. Hmm. I'll worry about this place now. Put me energies into here. Get this year's Talent Trek and we're back in the fast lane. That's what's important.

JERRY has uncovered the drums and now he pulls a cover off the organ, but it's not there, just a pile of stacked crates.

JERRY   Oh, no.

BRIAN   What?

JERRY   I've found your missing beer crates, but they've nicked your organ.

BRIAN   Bastards.

CUT TO

END CREDITS

21. INT. GALAXY LOUNGE. DAY
Backing music 'NELLIE THE ELEPHANT'. We are on the build-up to the chorus. We cut to extreme close-up of what looks like an elephant face, eyes and trunk. We cut between the elephant and the reactions of BRIAN AND CO in close-up. They have a look of confusion and shock. The song climaxes into the chorus. We reveal (in a full-length shot) a MAN standing on a table wearing a long raincoat (held open) and shoes. He is wearing an elephant G string (his penis is in the trunk) and he is jumping up and down to the music.

ALL   Next!

THE END

Episode 5

PART ONE

1. EXT. CAR PARK. NIGHT

MAX and PADDY are on the door. JERRY's singing in the background.

PADDY   Prostitutes are rough in Amsterdam. The first one I went with made me wash me old man in the sink.

MAX   You took your dad?

PADDY GIVES MAX A LOOK

A minibus pulls into the car park. A GROUP OF DWARF BLOKES get out (in Bolton Wanderers tops), singing.

DWARVES   'Super super John, super John McGinley ...'

PADDY   Oh, oh. I hate match days. Look at this.

DWARF   (TO DRIVER) Cheers, Duggy.

DWARVES (SINGING) 'We're Bolton, we're barmy, we're on the march tonight ...'

MAX   (SQUINTING) How far away are they?

They come up to the club singing.

DWARVES (SINGING) 'We're Bolton, we're
        barmy, we're on the march tonight;
        we're Bolton, we're barmy we're on
        the piss tonight ...'

MAX   Whoa, whoa, whoa. Whoa. Whoa. Get
        back on the bus, you're not coming
        in.

DWARF   Aye, I'm getting married next
        week ...

MAX   You know, I don't care. You're not
        coming in. All right?

DWARF   Come on, let him in. It's his stag
        night.

DWARF   (GETTING WALLET OUT) Is it money
        you want? 'Cos we've got money.

MAX   We don't want your money. We don't
        want your money. Just get back on
        the bus.

*A couple get past MAX and PADDY and into
the club. The others cheer.*

CUT TO

2. INT. FOYER. NIGHT
*They run to the cigarette machine in the
corner. It says 'OUT OF ORDER'. They put
money in for cigarettes and nothing comes out.*

DWARF   (PUNCHES AND KICKS THE
        MACHINE) Aye, what's up with this?

PADDY   Can't you read?

MAX   Oy, tattoo. Get away from there.

DWARF   Who you calling 'tattoo', yer long
        streak of piss?

*MAX and PADDY move towards them. But
two jump on their backs. A bottle smashes. A
fight starts.*

CUT TO

3. INT. CORRIDOR/FOYER. NIGHT
*BRIAN pats his 'disabled boy' moneybox. He
hears the muffled commotion and opens the
door. MAX is on the floor choking. The
DWARVES are attacking MAX and PADDY.
PADDY has one in a headlock from behind.
One is hitting him in the face. Two are trying
to get their money back out of the machine. A*

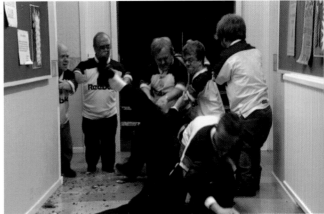

bottle smashes over PADDY's head. Brian
stares, takes a beat, then shuts the door.

CUT TO

OPENING CREDITS

CUT TO

4. EXT. HOSPITAL. DAY
Establishing shot of hospital.

CUT TO

5. INT. HOSPITAL WAITING ROOM. DAY
JERRY is sitting waiting for his endoscopy.
He is wearing a disposable gown and holding
a basket containing his clothes. Armchair
Super Store is on TV.

PRESENTER
> To have your car stolen, which
> happened to me a few months
> back – the scumbags! – ranks
> amongst the lowest of the low. Here
> with us now is John Lennon with
> the latest deterrent. What've you got
> for us, John?

JOHN LENNON
> I've got the answer to your dreams,
> Gary. There we go, the Invader 2000.

PRESENTER
> It's a car alarm?

JOHN LENNON
> Well it is, but the difference between
> this little beauty ...

NURSE   (CALLING) Mr Dignan?

JOHN LENNON
> ... and your other bog-standard
> security systems ...

NURSE   (CALLING) Jerry Dignan?

JERRY   Yes, sorry.

JOHN LENNON
> ... is that the Invader 2000 has the
> unique facility to record and
> personalise your alarm.

PRESENTER
> Wow!

CUT TO

6. INT. EXAMINATION ROOM. DAY
JERRY is on his side. He is wearing a
hospital gown with a split up the back. His
backside is visible. A FEMALE NURSE and a
DOCTOR are present.

DOCTOR So, Mr Dignan, do you know what's
going to happen?

JERRY   Well, sort of, yeah.

DOCTOR OK. If you'd just like to pull your
knees up for me.

JERRY   OK.

DOCTOR All right? That's lovely, thank you
very much. Now I'm just going to
introduce a camera into your back
passage.

JERRY   Introduce?

DOCTOR Oh, look at the state of that, eh? It's
filthy, Sheila. Can you give it a wipe?

NURSE   Yeah.

JERRY struggles to look around. The NURSE
is wiping the monitor. The DOCTOR inserts
the camera.

CUT TO

7. INT. JOCKEY WILSON SUITE. DAY
HOLY MARY and MARION are behind the bar washing glasses.

HOLY MARY
      She was with him again last night, Marion.

MARION Who?

HOLY MARY
      Our Mary, with that Patrick off the door. They didn't get back till one o'clock and then they was out on front doorstep saying 'night-night' till gone two.

MARION Have you said anything?

HOLY MARY
      Well, what can you say? I've prayed for her.

MARION He's not a bad lad, Paddy, but he likes his women.

HOLY MARY
      Well, my Mary's not a woman. She hasn't even finished her A levels yet. Come on, let's talk about summat else, anyway. Let's talk about summat else.

CUT TO

8. INT. EXAMINATION ROOM. DAY
JERRY is on his side, midway through the examination.

JERRY   Oooh, ahhh!

NURSE   Ah, is it painful?

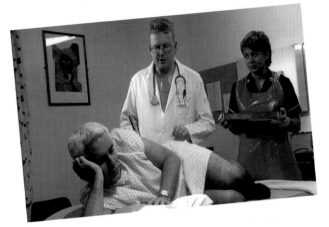

JERRY   Very.

NURSE   Ah, don't worry now, love, it won't be long. Here you are, have a look at this monitor here. It'll help take your mind off it.

She swings round the monitor and shows JERRY his bowels live in colour.

NURSE   Them's your bowels.

CUT TO

9. INT. BARBER'S SHOP. DAY
PADDY is sitting in the chair. EMU THE BARBER stands behind him. We see the reflection in the mirror. CHORLEY FM is on the radio. PAUL LE ROY Classic Eighties.

EMU   Hello, Paddy

PADDY Are you all right?

EMU   How's it going?

PADDY All right.

EMU   Well, what do you want?

PADDY Your opinion, really …

EMU   Eh?

PADDY   Am I going bald?

EMU   Eh?

PADDY   A bit thin on top. Just ... Just there.

We hear a banging on the glass. EMU and PADDY both look at the same time. We turn to reveal MAX and his brother TERRY smiling and pointing at PADDY through the window.

PADDY   Oh Christ, no!

MAX   What you doing, Paddy?

TERRY   Paddy.

MAX   What you doing?

MAX and TERRY enter the shop.

MAX   Aye.

TERRY   Aye, Paddy.

MAX   Aye, what's going on here? What you doing? Emu you've met our Terry.

TERRY   Hi, Emu.

EMU   Hi, Terry.

MAX   What's going on, then?

PADDY   What do you think?

MAX   You're throwing your money away ... Hey, Emu, I didn't know you did takeaways.

TERRY bends down and picks up some dead hair off the floor.

TERRY   (HOLDING HAIR) Hey, you should be putting it on, not taking if off.

PADDY   Get off.

MAX   Hey, hey.

They both laugh, including EMU. PADDY isn't amused.

RADIO VOICE
        You're listening to Chorley FM coming in your ears.

CUT TO

10. INT. JOCKEY WILSON SUITE. DAY
BRIAN is chatting to JERRY. JERRY is stirring his tea constantly.

BRIAN   I mean look at Sushi: he's only forty-two and he's coping.

JERRY   Sushi?

BRIAN   Roy Fish off the estate. (POINTS) He's had half his stomach out and a bag on his hip. He still goes jogging.

JERRY   (SARCASTIC) Oh, thanks.

BRIAN   (SHOUTING) Jesus! I'm only trying to cheer you up, man. You're A-one, you know, you're … you're a bloody hypodermic, Jerry.

JERRY   What?

BRIAN   (STILL SHOUTING) Well, you are. 'I'm worried about this, I'm worried about that'. You wanna put yourself in my shoes. Stop stirring your tea, dickhead. I had dreams, Jerry, me. I wanted Frank Sinatra, I wanted Showaddywaddy. What have I got? Robot Wars and alternative friggin' comedy.

JERRY   (BURIES HIS HEAD IN HIS HANDS) Oh no, it's tonight, isn't it? Oh.

BRIAN   Yes, it's tonight. Yes it's tonight. It's another one of your dreams I've been strong-armed into. 'It'll get the students in: they love all that new comedy.' (WAVING HANDS) Where's Marion? Eh, do you know how many tickets we've sold? Marion? She's gone. She's seen the iceberg. Well it's not many, I can tell you that … And what've you called us? What've you called the finest cabaret lounge this side of Garstang?

JERRY   The Funny Farm.

BRIAN   (BRIAN JOINS IN) The Funny Farm, Jerry. The bloody Funny Farm – that's where they'll be taking me. That's where they'll be carting me off to 'cos Potter is pissing in the wind. And Den Perry and all the other boys are laughing at us, they're laughing at us, Jerry. So don't you, don't you go throwing a sickie tonight, boy! Don't you dare. You get up on that stage and you get your act together because I can't get up there. 'Cos I've got real problems. 'Cos I don't know if you've noticed Jerry but—

JERRY   Oh, shut up.

BRIAN   Oh, OK, all right, we'll play it that way, we'll play it that way, then. Now I know where I stand. Goodnight and God bless. If you want me I'll be in me office shaking off a migraine … Sorry, brain tumour.

CUT TO

11. INT. BARBER'S SHOP. DAY
TERRY is now getting his hair cut. MAX is standing by the side of him. Meanwhile, PADDY is sitting in the waiting area of the room thumbing through various magazines featuring hairstyles.

MAX   Are you coming down club tonight? They're having Robot Wars.

TERRY   Robot Wars at the club?

MAX   Yeah, Pennine Suite.

TERRY   Oh, like on telly?

MAX   Aye.

TERRY   He must be on his arse, Potter.

MAX   We've entered a robot.

TERRY   Who?

MAX   Me and 'The Hills Have Eyes'.
         (LAUGHS)

PADDY looks up, he isn't amused

TERRY   Bollocks ... Who's built it?

MAX   We have.

TERRY   You can't even change a plug.

MAX   I tell you. It's an all-out assault
         vehicle.

TERRY   (LAUGHING) Bollocks.

MAX   You want to see it. Isn't that right?
         Tell him, Patrick.

PADDY   (LOOKS UP AGAIN) It's a bitch.

TERRY   Bollocks ... How many gears has
         it got?

MAX   Plenty. That's how many.

TERRY   Where is it?

MAX   Er ... She is in the boot.

TERRY   Bollocks ... I've got to see this.

MAX   Yeah. Straight up.

CUT TO

12. EXT. BARBER'S SHOP. DAY
*MAX and PADDY are showing TERRY the
robot in the boot. POV from inside the boot
of them looking in.*

MAX   Aye ... There she is.

TERRY   You built that?

PADDY   Oh aye, yes.

TERRY   Bollocks.

PADDY   Oh no, we're living *la vida* with this.

TERRY   You haven't built that.

TERRY goes to handle the robot

PADDY/MAX
         Whoa, whoa hands off.

TERRY   What?

MAX   It'll take your hands off.

END OF PART ONE

PART TWO

13. EXT. CAR PARK. NIGHT

JERRY is chatting to MAX. 'THE FUNNY FARM' banner above.

JERRY   So, they said they'd be in touch. All I've got to do is wait, really.

MAX   Yeah.

JERRY   Play the old waiting game.

MAX   Yeah.

There is an embarrassing silence until PADDY comes out with two cups of tea.

PADDY   (TO MAX) There you go.

JERRY   Hello, Paddy.

PADDY   Jerry. You all right?

JERRY   Yeah. Well, I'd better get back inside. If any more comedians come just send them through.

JERRY exits.

MAX   Will do, Jerry, lad. (TAKES A DRINK) He's one of the good guys, Jerry.

PADDY   Oh, he's sound as a pound. (TAKES A DRINK) Is he still shitting blood?

CUT TO

14. INT. GALAXY LOUNGE. NIGHT

JERRY   This is the Funny Farm, ladies and gentlemen, the birth of merriment and laughter. Join in. Here we go.

JERRY sings 'SMILE'.

JERRY   (SINGING) 'Every silver lining has a cloud.
         And each piece of good fortune must be paid for by the pound ...'

CUT TO

15. EXT. CAR PARK. NIGHT

MAX and PADDY. A GROUP OF STUDENTS come up to the door.

STUDENT BOY
         I was really off my head, right? I didn't get in till three o'clock. I missed four tutorials.

The others laugh.

STUDENT GIRL
         Is this the Funny Farm?

PADDY   Fanny Farm?

STUDENT (LOOKING AT THE FLIER) The Funny Farm, yeah, the funny farm.

PADDY   Fanny?

MAX   (LOOKS AT FLIER) She means 'funny'. D'you mean 'Funny Farm'? Yes, this is the Funny Farm, yes, it is. Straight down there, door on your right.

STUDENT GIRL
Erm. Do you take NUS?

MAX   What?

STUDENT GIRL
Do you take NUS?

MAX   (SQUARING UP) I don't take none of that shit, love, and neither will you if you know what's good for you ... My body's a temple. Go on, get in. Coming in here with your bloody ha-ha hashish.

STUDENT BOY (OOV)
Ooo, well it certainly smells funny.

Other STUDENTS laugh.

STUDENT BOY 2 (OOV)
Hey, look at the wallpaper ... Cool.

PADDY   I hate students.

MAX   You hate students. That's rich: you're bloody courting one.

PADDY   No, I'm not.

MAX   Whatever.

CUT TO

16. INT. GALAXY LOUNGE. NIGHT
JERRY is singing.

JERRY   (SINGING) 'I don't know how it started but it won't go away ...'

He chats to the AUDIENCE during the instrumental break.

JERRY   Come in and sit down. Here we go. Welcome. My name's Jerry St Clair. It's my privilege and my pleasure to welcome you to a new night of comedy in alternative sty-lee. Oh, yes. The posse are here. So you'd better smile ... smile ... smile ...smile ... smile ... smile ...

CUT TO

17. INT. BACKSTAGE. NIGHT
BRIAN is briefing the COMICS.

BRIAN   Right, listen up, these are the rules. You get ... you get five minutes, ten if they're laughing. If they're not laughing and you're crap, you're off.

COMIC   Yeah, when do we get paid?

BRIAN   When do you get paid? When you make me laugh. Mouth! You're on first. Kenny, tell the Saint.

ANOTHER COMIC
Who's the Saint?

BRIAN   Who's the Saint? Him, trying to sing out there. Watch and learn: he's forgotten more than you lot know.

CUT TO

18. INT. GALAXY LOUNGE. NIGHT
JERRY continues to sing on stage.

JERRY   (SINGING) 'Your life's in a mess, you've been cut adrift, you've got to smile ...'

CUT TO

19. INT. BACKSTAGE. NIGHT
BRIAN continues to brief COMICS.

BRIAN   No filth, simple as. No smut, no swearing, no racism, right? No queer or lezzie stuff. We don't go there. It's a family club. There's a picture of Her Majesty the Queen out there and as far as you lot are concerned she may as well be sat on the front row. Do I make meself crystal?

COMICS   Yeah.

CUT TO

20. INT. GALAXY LOUNGE. NIGHT
We cut to the FIRST COMIC on stage, he is mid-rant.

COMIC 1   Is it me or do all pensioners stink of piss! (LAUGHTER) My grandmother, right, she can't even remember where the toilet is, and that's why she stinks of piss.

We cut to reveal the AUDIENCE's stunned reaction (predominantly pensioners). STUDENTS laugh.

CUT TO

21. INT. PENNINE SUITE. NIGHT
The room is set out for Robot Wars. RAY VON is wearing a black leather suit and sunglasses. RAY comes to the mic.

RAY VON   Welcome to Robot Wars. Tonight is about the survival of the fittest, where the last robot standing will be crowned tonight's winner and receive a jackpot prize of sixty-three pounds. Roboteers, are you ready?

CHILD   Yeah, ready.

We cut to reveal twelve or so people standing in the room.

CUT TO

22. EXT. CAR PARK. NIGHT
MARY approaches the club.

MAX   Ay up. Here's your latest flame now, Paddy.

MARY   Hiya.

PADDY   (PRETENDING HE DOESN'T KNOW HER) Hiya. You all right. It's Mary's daughter. Mary? You all right?

MARY   Yeah, are you?

MAX   Hello, Mary, how are you?

MARY   OK, thanks, are you?

PADDY   Are you going in?

MARY   Yeah, yeah.

PADDY   (ASIDE) Go on, in you go. Never mind, just, just go in.

MAX Mary's daughter. Who you trying to kid?

PAUSE

PADDY Do you want a brew?

MAX No.

PADDY Are you sure? You know, I've got a hell of a thirst on me.

MAX No, no.

PADDY I had gammon for me tea. Are you sure you don't want a brew?

MAX I've just had a brew.

PADDY Listen, I'm going and getting a brew.

MAX Yeah, you go and get a brew, Paddy. (PADDY LEAVES) Must think I'm bloody stupid.

CUT TO

23. INT. PENNINE SUITE. NIGHT

Robot Wars. RAY is standing with TWO OTHER MEN and a TEENAGER. YOUNG KENNY is working the music. RAY looks at a robot with sharp 'Jaws'-like teeth.

RAY VON I tell you, that fella needs a trip to the dentist.

We hear the theme from Buck Rogers. KENNY SNR pushes BRIAN to the middle of the virtually empty room.

RAY VON (DOWN MIC) OK, and here he is, everybody, here he is to get this rollerball rolling. Please welcome our very own Davros, Mr Brian Potter. Come on. Welcome to Robot Wars.

BRIAN I thought you said there were gonna be thirty.

RAY VON This is Team Chaos and this is The Cleaner.

BRIAN (EYEING UP SUSPICIOUSLY) Is that a robot, son, is it?

TEENAGER (INTO MIC) Actually the term is 'automaton'! The Cleaner's multidirectional. It's fitted with a twin whizzer-blade mechanism at the back and it's also got a trip-hammer device at the front.

BRIAN (SLIGHTLY OFF MIC) Have you ever kissed a girl?

CUT TO

24. INT. GALAXY LOUNGE. NIGHT

COMIC There's a lot of bitterness in my life, there's a lot of bitterness in my life, there's a lot of bitterness in my life, there's a lot of bitterness in my life. Da, di de di de di de dee de diddly dee, da, di de di de di de dee de diddly dee.

CUT TO

25. INT. BACKSTAGE. NIGHT

We cut to JERRY in the wings watching the act. ANOTHER ACT stands next to him.

JERRY Are you nervous, son?

MARTIN (NODS) Oh yeah ...

JERRY Do you work?

MARTIN Teacher.

JERRY Good lad, good lad.

MARTIN Do you?

JERRY I'm on sick at the moment, been really ill.

MARTIN Nothing serious?

JERRY They don't know. I'm waiting for test results you know. (BEAT) Playing the old waiting game. Still this alternative comedy, what do you make of it? All a bit weird, isn't it?

MARTIN nods.

CUT TO

26. INT. GALAXY LOUNGE. NIGHT

JERRY There you go, well done, well done, son. Mik Artistic, eh? Comedy in a rhyming style, eh? Les Alanos likes him, anyway. So just before we crack on, got an announcement for you here. Will the owner of the car with number plate G65 347 2173 45864 5191742X please move it because the number plate's blocking the fire exit. Hey. Right, so anyway, y'all posse. Now here we go with the

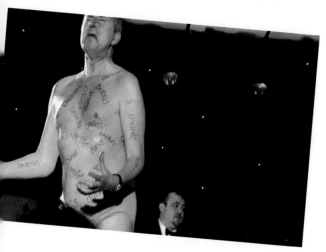

next act for yourselves, ladies and gentlemen here. Will you welcome all the way from over there, it's (LOOKS AT PAPER) Darius.

The COMIC JERRY's just been talking to in the wings runs on stage. He is naked apart from a pair of blue underpants. He has the name 'DARIUS' drawn all over his body.

The man runs around the stage confused, violently beating his fists on the side of his head. LES and ALAN watch shocked. We cut to BRIAN.

BRIAN Is this as bad as it gets, Kenny? Can we sink any lower than this?

KENNY SNR
  He taught me metalwork.

CUT TO

27. INT. CLUB CELLAR. NIGHT
POV MAX opens the door. PADDY and MARY kissing, quickly stop, turn and pretend that they weren't. MARY counts the bottles and fastens her blouse.

MAX Hey.

MARY Thirteen ... fourteen ... fifteen ...

PADDY What?

MAX Have you had yer brew?

PADDY Why?

MAX Come on, it's us, we're up next, it's us.

MARY still counting.

PADDY What?

MAX   Robot Wars – we're up against
         'Death by Chocolate'.

PADDY   Oh, we'll shit 'em.

CUT TO

28. INT. PENNINE SUITE. NIGHT

RAY VON That's 'Team Voodoo' with their
         robot 'Death by Chocolate'. And now,
         Robotians, their opponents, 'Team
         Double Trouble', and their robot,
         'Ass Kicker'.

*We hear the opening strains of 'TWO
TRIBES'. The smoke machine billows. The
fire doors open and a shaft of white light
pierces the room. Slowly 'Ass Kicker' enters,
it's clearly the biggest, strongest, most
heavily armed robot in the room. Behind it,
looking very proud, are MAX and PADDY in
sunglasses, who both carry control units.
There is a gasp of wonderment in the room.
We cut to 'Death By Chocolate', terrified.*

CUT TO

29. INT. GALAXY LOUNGE. NIGHT

JERRY (ENDING A GAG)
         So the king says, he says, 'No, yer
         pillock, I said ping-pong balls, not
         King Kong's balls.'

The AUDIENCE laugh.

STUDENT BOY
         You're shit. Get off.

JERRY   They spoilt a lovely set of teeth
         when they put a mouth in your
         arse, didn't they, eh?

STUDENT BOY
         What?

Silence. We cut to BRIAN.

JERRY (OOV)
         Anyway, ladies and gentlemen, on
         with the show …

BRIAN   He always ceases to amaze me,
         Kenny.

CUT TO

30. INT. PENNINE SUITE. NIGHT
*'Ass Kickers' is smashing 'Death By
Chocolate' to bits. MAX and PADDY are
loving every second of it.*

CUT TO

31. INT. GALAXY LOUNGE. NIGHT

COMIC   You spend a lifetime waiting for
         Godot, when three come along at
         once.

BRIAN   Tell us a joke we know.

CUT TO

32. INT. PENNINE SUITE. NIGHT
*'Ass Kicker' has now moved on to the other
robots. The others watch angrily.*

CUT TO

36. INT. PENNINE SUITE. NIGHT

RAY VON Let's hear it for our winners –
'Ass ...', 'Ass Kicker' ... Come on.

APPLAUSE.

RAY VON (cont.) Well, that's just about it for
Robot Wars. Thank you and
goodnight.

*We cut to a close-up of a YOUNG BOY as he
pulls part of his robot from the axe blade
that is attached to the front of 'Ass Kicker'.
The BOY is near to tears.*

CUT TO

37. INT. PENNINE SUITE. LATER
*We cut to MAX and PADDY as RAY hands
over their prize money.*

RAY VON There you go, my friend. The job's a
good 'un.

MAX   Whoa, whoa, whoa – what's this?

RAY VON It's your prize money.

MAX   Twenty quid. Where's his?

RAY VON It's between you.

MAX   We want more than that.

RAY VON Uh, I build it, you race it. We agreed.

MAX   We agreed a three-way split.

PADDY Typical gyppo, this ... I bet he were
like this on the dodgems.

MAX   Oh yes.

CUT TO

33. INT. GALAXY LOUNGE. NIGHT

JEFF BITCH
Good evening. Come on. My name's
Jeff Bitch, but you can just call me
Bitch. That's just the ladies, that is.
(LAUGHS) I'm a bitch. (SLAPS HIS
ARSE, HARD)

CUT TO

34. INT. PENNINE SUITE. NIGHT
'Ass Kicker' is destroying the other robots.

CUT TO

35. INT. GALAXY LOUNGE. NIGHT
JEFF BITCH is on stage.

JEFF BITCH
(SINGING AND PLAYING GUITAR,
BADLY) 'Tits, tits, I want tits. Come
on, get your tits out, ladies ...'

BRIAN   (IN SHOCK) Kenny, get me Zantac.

JERRY   (UNPLUGGING JEFF BITCH'S
GUITAR) There you go, Jeff Bitch,
ladies and gentlemen, there he goes.

RAY VON I spent weeks building that. I put all the graft in.

MAX (MENACING) And I'll put my boot in, flower, if you don't dip your hand in your pocket.

CUT TO

38. INT. GALAXY LOUNGE. NIGHT

JERRY Well, ladies and gentlemen, I've had a great night. This wasn't it, like, you know, but I've had a great night.

STUDENT BOY
Hey, granddad, your jokes are as old as you.

The OTHER STUDENTS laugh.

JERRY (TO STUDENT) So what are you into?

STUDENT BOY
Your mother.

JERRY (SERIOUS) My mother's dead.

STUDENT BOY
Did she hear your act?

There are a few giggles from the OTHER STUDENTS, then silence. We cut to BRIAN.

BRIAN (TO KENNY SNR) Get Max and Paddy.

We cut back to JERRY. He is resting his head on the microphone and sweating. LES and ALAN give each other a look. There is a slight feedback on the microphone.

JERRY I can't believe it, honestly, it's amazing. A hundred million sperm, you were the quickest. There's no justice, is there?

STUDENT BOY
At least I'm funny.

JERRY Sorry?

STUDENT I said at least—

JERRY I heard you, son. (STUDENT TRIES TO SPEAK) I'm just sorry. You want to save your breath for later on for blowing up your girlfriend. You know you lot make me sick. You think you know it all, don't you? You don't. When there's a knock at the door, why do dogs always think it's for them?

Behind BRIAN at the back of the club a MAN comes in. He looks around and watches from the back.

JERRY (cont.) What exactly did cured ham have? Why do kamikaze pilots wear crash helmets? I've no idea, have you? When they circumcised you, did they throw away the best bit?

(AUDIENCE LAUGH) Eh. It's funny, can you hear them? Listen, laughter, laughter. It's not coincidence that when I finish talking they laugh.

We cut to the MAN in the audience. He is laughing. He is watching the AUDIENCE laughing. The STUDENT isn't laughing, but the OTHER STUDENTS are.

JERRY (cont.) A bloke went to the doctor's. He'd got his steering wheel stuck down his underpants. The doctor says, 'That looks painful.' He said, 'It's driving me nuts.' Driving me nuts, eh? Come on, beam down planet comedy, son. I don't know where you are. Eh, listen: I'm a little teapot, short and stout, here's my handle, here's my – oh, me sugar bowl!

More laughter.

JERRY (cont.) I was in the butcher's. I said, 'Where's your assistant?' He said, 'I sacked him.' 'So why've you sacked him?' He said, 'He kept putting his willy in the bacon slicer.' I said, 'Oooh, what happened to your bacon slicer?' He said, 'I sacked her an' all. Sacked 'em both.'

Audience laugh.

JERRY (cont.) Listen, listen. They love it.

STUDENT BOY
        You're not funny.

JERRY What's your name, son? Any ideas?

STUDENT BOY
        Stu.

JERRY Stu? Short for 'stupid'.

Audience laughter.

JERRY Well, Stu, this might come as quite a surprise to you but …

JERRY jumps off stage and shouts at STU, who spills drink all over himself.

STUDENT You dick! This is a new top.

JERRY New top – are you taking the piss? You look like an extra from *Tenko*. Don't go out on bonfire night, eh, don't go out on bonfire night, they'll sling yer. You'll be on.

STU pushes JERRY.

BRIAN (SHOUTING) Ay, ay, ay … You push him, son, you push me.

LES   And me.

ALAN   (REMOVING HIS GLASSES) And me.

ALAN   And me.

MAX   And us.

KENNY SNR
        And me.

BRIAN Right, you lot, out. Before I knock you out. Sling it. Go on. You're not welcome. All of you leave.

STUDENT BOY
        I'm not going until I get a refund.

BRIAN (TO KENNY SNR) Kenny, you'd best make him a bed up.

STUDENT BOY
        I want my money back.

BRIAN I want to moon-walk, son, but life's
       a shithouse. Out.

STUDENT Leave it, Stu. I wouldn't come back
       here, anyway. Come on.

BRIAN Good. (CALLING AFTER THEM)
       You're not welcome. You're barred.

BRIAN gives them the V sign.

JERRY Come on, everybody here we go,
       come on. This is the one, this is the
       one. 'Bye Bye Baby'.

*LES ALANOS start to play the opening bars
to 'BYE BYE BABY'. JERRY gets back on
stage and starts to sing.*

MAX   Go on, get out. I warned you,
       didn't I?

CUT TO

39. INT. JERRY'S DRESSING ROOM. NIGHT
*JERRY is sitting wiping his head. There is a
knock on the door.*

JERRY Come in.

The MAN who arrived late at the back of the Galaxy Suite enters.

DUGGY HAYES
> Jerry? All right?

JERRY   Yeah, not so bad.

DUGGY HAYES
> Duggy Hayes. I work for Hayes and Marshall, the agency.

JERRY   Oh, right, Hayes and Marshall, yeah.

DUGGY HAYES
> I really enjoyed what you did tonight.

JERRY   Really?

DUGGY HAYES
> Yeah, I thought you handled the situation very well.

JERRY   Hey, you want to be in on Saturday night, cabaret night.

DUGGY HAYES
> No, no I don't. I like what I've seen already.

JERRY   That's very kind of you, sir.

DUGGY HAYES
> Look, em, we do cruises, we do the Caribbean, Mediterranean, Hull to Rotterdam. You're not bothered about getting your feet wet, are you?

JERRY   Oh, not at all Duggy, no.

DUGGY HAYES
> Give me a bell.

JERRY   Thanks. I will, Duggy.

DUGGY HAYES
> See you later.

JERRY   I might just do that.

CUT TO

END CREDITS

40. INT. GALAXY LOUNGE. DAY

BRIAN AND CO. are auditioning. They watch a very bad dancing act. THE PANEL cannot contain their laughter.

BRIAN is impressed with the act.

BRIAN   (TO LES) I used to be able to do that, you know.

LES laughs.

BRIAN   (cont.) I did, Leslie.

THE PANEL are getting even more hysterical.

BRIAN   They're booked. I like them. I think I'll book them.

They continue to dance.

BRIAN   (cont.) You're booked. We'll have yer.

THE END

Episode 6

PART ONE

1. INT/EXT. HOSPITAL. DAY

Big-band music – 'OPUS ONE' by TOMMY DORSEY. JERRY throws open a set of double doors and walks down the street with a gleeful sprint in his stride. He climbs over a railing and greets whoever he passes. Skips off up the street.

CUT TO

2. INT. MAIN CORRIDOR. DAY

BRIAN pats his disabled moneybox on the head.

BRIAN   Ho, ho, ho, Corfu for Christmas.

He goes into the Pennine Suite.

CUT TO

3. EXT. PARKLAND. DAY

We cut to JERRY as he runs across some parkland. Some LADS are playing football. JERRY heads the football (leaving a dirt mark on his forehead) into the goal. JERRY runs, arms outstretched. The KIDS stare at him.

CUT TO

4. INT. PENNINE SUITE. DAY

There is a BIG BAND practising. BRIAN sits and enjoys the music. It reaches its climax.

BRIAN   (CLAPPING) Aye. That's what we want. Fantastic, that. Must be thirsty work that. The bar's open next door if you want to have a drink. Go and help yourselves, be my guest.

BRIAN turns and sees a gap in the paintwork where the Das Boot fruit machine should sit.

BRIAN   (cont.) Bloody hell! Where's me fruit
         machine gone?

CUT TO

OPENING CREDITS

CUT TO

5. INT. JOCKEY WILSON SUITE. DAY
*Armchair Super Store TV is on the big
screen.*

PRESENTER
         And then you spray on the affected
         area.

PRESENTER 2
         Wow.

BRIAN switches off the set.

HOLY MARY
         I was enjoying that.

BRIAN   Well, you'll enjoy this even
         more. (TO ROOM) I have a
         special announcement to make …
         After hours of tremendous
         pressure and …

*BRIAN turns round as a REGULAR enters
room.*

BRIAN   (cont.) … listen, Tony, tremendous
         pressure and ruthless negotiation,
         I am proud to announce we got
         Talent Trek.

OTHERS   Hooray!

BRIAN   The grand final.

HOLY MARY
         Hallelujah! Praise the Lord!

BRIAN   Praise Brian Potter – it were me
         that got it.

HOLY MARY
         When is it?

BRIAN   Thursday.

MARION   Thursday? This Thursday?

BRIAN   Correct.

MARION   That's two days away.

BRIAN   I know, and that is why we've got to
         grab the cow by the horns and pull
         together. I want everything shit-
         shaped and Bristol fashion – and
         spread the word because the
         Phoenix is rising.

EVERYONE CHEERS.

CUT TO

6. INT. THEATRE/BRIAN'S OFFICE. DAY
INTERCUT BETWEEN BOTH LOCATIONS.

*LES is in a small theatre space with ALAN
and the YOUTH CLUB KIDS. Some of them*

are painting scenery. The rest are doing karate choreography with ALAN at the head. LES's mobile rings.

LES   Hello?

BRIAN   Les, it's Brian.

LES   Hello, Brian.

BRIAN   Are you all right? Listen, I've got some great news. We've got Talent Trek.

LES   You're joking! When?

BRIAN   Just now.

LES   No. When is it?

BRIAN   This Thursday.

LES   We can't do this Thursday, Brian. We've got ... we've got the big show.

BRIAN   What big show?

LES   *Karate Kid – The Musical* with the kids from the drama group.

BRIAN   Screw the Karate Kid, Leslie, I need my backing band.

LES   Brian, we can't let 'em down on this. They've been at it for months, you'll break their hearts. (THINKING) Can we not do it next week?

BRIAN   Yeah, yeah, you're right. Yeah, probably. Yeah, I'll give 'em a ring. Can they balls do it next week! They're not gonna shift the grand final so that you can frig about with kimonos down a church hall.

LES   Brian, we just can't do it, mate. I'm sorry.

BRIAN   Sorry, Leslie. This is the ... Right, then, right, well now, I know where I stand. Right, that's it. I think, I think I'll go and give Right Said Frank a ring.

LES   You can't do that.

BRIAN   Why?

LES   Well, they'll be busy.

BRIAN   Busy? Busy? They're a Right Said Fred tribute band. How the bloody hell are they going to be busy? Anyway, if they're any good, Leslie, they can have the job.

LES   What job?

BRIAN   Yours and Alan's – you're sacked.

BRIAN slams down the phone.

BRIAN   (cont.) Shithead.

CUT TO

7. EXT. CAR PARK. DAY

MAX is leaning on his Volvo. RAY is inside wiring in a new alarm system. PADDY's car pulls up alongside, stereo on loud. He parks, turns off the engine.

MAX   (TO RAY) Have you put it in?

RAY VON Yeah, I'm just doing it now. I'm pulling it through from the battery.

MAX   Good morning, Patrick. Wet enough for yer?

MAX   With Mary? Why?

PADDY   She's getting a bit too keen. Paddy
        likes to play the field, Paddy does.
        Have a kickabout, put a few in the
        net.

MAX   Two words Paddy. Own goal. You've
        got a cracker of one there. Don't
        blow it, son. D'you hear me?

*JERRY skips and dances past and into the
club, laughing as he goes*

PADDY   What's everybody on today?

CUT TO

8. INT. BRIAN'S OFFICE. DAY
*The door bursts open. JERRY comes in
(football imprint still on his head).*

BRIAN and JERRY are both laughing.

JERRY   Come on, come here.

*He goes straight over to BRIAN and kisses
him on the head.*

BRIAN   Get off me, yer girl.

PADDY   It's never wet enough for me, Max.
        (BEAT) What are you doing?

MAX   We're fitting an alarm.

RAY VON We?

MAX   Shut it. Yes, we. You all right?
        (SPIES AN ARMCHAIR SUPER
        STORE BOX ON THE BACK SEAT)
        Ay, what's in yer box?

PADDY taps his nose

MAX   (cont.) Cocaine?

PADDY   It's top secret.

YOUNG KENNY comes out of the club.

YOUNG KENNY
        Hey, lads, spread the word: the
        Phoenix is rising. The Phoenix is
        rising.

MAX   What is it, eh? A present for your
        girlfriend? Is it a present for Mary?

PADDY   I've not got her nothing. In fact I'm
        thinking of letting things cool down
        a bit.

They're both laughing.

BRIAN   You've heard, then.

JERRY   Oh, I've heard.

BRIAN   Aye? And?

JERRY   Irritable bowel syndrome. Spasms, just got spasms!

BRIAN   (CONFUSED) What?

JERRY   I'm A-one. They've give me the all-clear. I'm fit as a fiddle. Look at that, look at that, Brian. (DOES PRESS-UPS ON BRIAN'S DESK)

BRIAN   So you're all clear.

JERRY   Yeah.

BRIAN   Who've you told? Shut the door.

JERRY   I've not told anybody. I come straight here from the hospital. Oh, I tell you, in't life wonderful?

BRIAN   Yeah.

JERRY   Breathe it in, Brian. Come on, breathe with me. Just take a deep breath of life – it's wonderful. It's like ... it's like being born again. It's like having a new life.

BRIAN   It's always you, you, you!

JERRY   What?

BRIAN   Listen, I've got something to tell yer.

JERRY   What?

BRIAN   We've got Talent Trek.

JERRY   We've not. Ha, ha.

BRIAN   The grand final.

JERRY   (WHOOPING) Oh, what a day. What a ... How did you get that? I bet Den Perry weren't happy, were he?

BRIAN   Crying in his beer.

JERRY   When is it?

BRIAN   It's this Thursday.

JERRY   This Thursday?

BRIAN   Yeah.

JERRY   We'd better get a wriggle on ... Have you told Les and Alan we've got it?

BRIAN   Will you shut up! I've got to tell you something.

JERRY   What?

BRIAN   Just sit down.

JERRY   I'm all clear, me. Ha, ha. I'm all clear.

BRIAN   Yeah, I know, I know. Shut up and listen. Now I want you to know. It's not ... it's not easy for me to tell you this, Jerry. I want you to know I was under tremendous pressure at the time.

JERRY   What? What? What is it?

BRIAN   You're dying.

JERRY   I'm not ... what?

BRIAN   You're dying.

JERRY No, I've got the all-clear.

BRIAN I know you have, but I had to tell the committee something so we could get Talent Trek.

JERRY So you told them I were dying?

BRIAN I were desperate, Jerry. They asked me how you were and I said I didn't think you'd see Christmas. And that swung it. They loved it, they said it could be your swan song.

JERRY How could you say something like that?

BRIAN It just came out. I don't know ... But we've got Talent Trek, the grand final, from Den Perry, Jerry. This is the one, this is the light at the end of our tunnel.

JERRY But I'm all clear.

BRIAN Trust you to bloody ruin everything! I didn't know that, did I? And everyone thinks you're dying anyway. We had a collection for yer last—

JERRY But I'm all clear.

BRIAN I know you're all ... you're ... you're all clear, but we're not, are we? We're in the bloody red. Up to here with the bills. We're going tits up. We're in a Catch 21 situation, Jerry, and only you can get us out of it.

JERRY Me? How?

BRIAN Pretend you're dying.

JERRY But I'm all clear.

BRIAN I know you're all clear ... You keep telling all the world. Shut up. You know and I know but no one else needs to know, do they? Not till after Talent Trek.

CUT TO

9. EXT. CAR PARK. DAY
RAY, MAX and PADDY are still chatting.

MAX The difference between the Invader 2000 and your other bog-standard security systems is that you've got the facility to record and personalise your alarm.

RAY VON Right, she's ready.

MAX Eh?

RAY VON Do you want to give her a go?

MAX Is this it?

RAY VON Aye.

MAX Arming the Invader. Activate ... activate.

RAY VON You need to flick the switch.

MAX What?

RAY VON Flick the switch.

MAX Flicking the switch.

MAX flicks the switch and the sidelights flash on.

MAX See them. Lighting up now. See, it is now alarmed and any exterior force will trigger it.

MAX flicks the door handle. Nothing.
Gently rocks it. Nothing.

MAX   It's new. It'll need tweaking.

PADDY   Maybe if you—

PADDY boots the side of the car. The alarm
goes off. There is a siren tone and then we
hear:

TONE (MAX'S VOICE)
        Get back, you bastard … I'll break
        your legs.

MAX   That's me, that's my voice.

PADDY   And that is shit-hot.

MAX   And at a price you can afford.

TONE (MAX'S VOICE)
        Get back, you bastard … I'll break
        your legs.

CUT TO

10. INT. BRIAN'S OFFICE. DAY
BRIAN is still trying to talk JERRY round.
We can still hear MAX's car alarm outside.

BRIAN   Pretend you're dying.

JERRY   (THINKING) I can't … I can't do it.

BRIAN   If you can't do it for me, do it for
         the club. Do it for the Phoenix.

JERRY   I've been offered a cruise.

BRIAN   Oh … oh … I wondered why Duggy
         Hayes was sniffing around. Hey, hey.
         When's it sail?

JERRY   Next month.

BRIAN   Well, then, that's all the more
         reason to do it, if you're going
         away anyway. What've you got
         to lose?

JERRY   You're not bothered, are yer?

BRIAN   Oh, oh, I'm bothered, but I'm more
         bothered about this club, Jerry
         Dignan. We deserve this. We deserve
         the pot at the end of the rainbow. Do
         it, Jerry. Do this one thing. Be the
         hero. Go out in style.

END OF PART ONE

PART TWO

11. INT. GALAXY LOUNGE. NIGHT
We cut to RIGHT SAID FRANK tuning up on
stage. Both bald and wearing T-shirts with
muscles drawn on them. RIGHT SAID FRANK
replace 'LES ALANOS' with 'RIGHT SAID
FRANK' on drum front. One of them is on
keyboard, the other is on drums.

CUT TO

12. INT. BACKSTAGE. NIGHT
We cut backstage to JERRY and BRIAN. JERRY is nervously watching RIGHT SAID FRANK.

BRIAN   This is what we want, Jerry. Packed out. Grand final.

JERRY   (LOOKING ON STAGE) How many keyboards does he need, him? It's Talent Trek, this, not bloody Live Aid.

BRIAN   Shut up, yer girl. Look, Jerry, I've got something for you. (HANDS JERRY A BASEBALL CAP) I want you to wear this.

JERRY   Why?

BRIAN   Because it makes you look ill.

JERRY   No, I can't, Brian ... honest.

BRIAN   You can, Jerry, go on. Live the dream. Don't forget you're dying.

JERRY takes a deep breath and steps up on stage.

CUT TO

13. INT. GALAXY LOUNGE. NIGHT
RIGHT SAID FRANK go into 'SEASONS IN THE SUN'. JERRY is slightly confused. He has no choice but to sing.

JERRY   (SINGING) 'Goodbye my friends it's hard to die, when all the birds are singing in the sky; now that the spring is in the air, pretty girls are everywhere, I'll be there. Bye to you, my trusted friend ...'

FRANK hands JERRY a note. JERRY opens while he's singing. It reads 'COLLAPSE'. JERRY looks at BRIAN, who winks and gives him the thumbs-up.

JERRY   (cont.) (SINGING) '... we've known each other since we were nine or ten; together we climbed hills and trees, skinned our hearts and skinned our knees ...'

DEN PERRY enters with two of his cronies.

JERRY   (cont.) (SINGING) 'We had joy, we had fun, we had seasons in the sun, but the hills that we climbed were just seasons out of time. We had joy, we had fun, we had seasons in the sun, but the wine and the song like the seasons had all gone.

'We had joy we had fun we had seasons in the sun ...'

We cut to the back of the room. BRIAN rolls up to DEN PERRY, vase in hand.

BRIAN   Look what the cat's spat out. Den Perry. Have you come to see how it's done, Den?

DEN PERRY
        I never miss Talent Trek, Brian, you know that.

BRIAN   (ENJOYING THE MOMENT) You missed it this year. Must have come as a bit of a shock.

DEN PERRY
        I'll not lie to you, Brian: I was gutted when I heard. It's the golden goose, we all know that ...

BRIAN   Oooh, this is just the beginning, this is. You'd better get used to it.

DEN PERRY
        You've not lost the Potter touch. I'll give you that. I know when I've been beaten and there's no hard feelings. That's my word and you can put my word in the bank.

JERRY's speech is heard under BRIAN and DEN's conversation.

JERRY   Thank you. Thank you very much, ladies and gentlemen, and welcome to Talent Trek. It's lovely to see you all here tonight in the Phoenix tonight. So without further ado, ladies and gentlemen, let's get tonight's Talent Trek grand final under way. First up we've got a young lady who made the final last year. It took a lot to get her here and that's what she's going to be singing tonight ...

DEN PERRY
        Long live the Phoenix.

BRIAN   Long live the Phoenix, Dennis.

They shake hands. BRIAN obviously enjoys the praise. DEN raises his glass, BRIAN raises his vase.

BRIAN/DEN PERRY
(BOTH MUTTER SIMULTANEOUSLY)
Bastard.

We cut to JERRY on stage.

JERRY (cont.) ... will you welcome on stage
act number one – it's Michelle
(SHAKES FIST) Coffee, come on.

APPLAUSE

*MICHELLE COFFEE comes on stage and
starts singing. FRANK, of RIGHT SAID
FRANK, starts to upstage her by using
keyboard sound effects to demonstrate the
lyrics of the song. MICHELLE is not happy.*

CUT TO

14. INT. BACKSTAGE. NIGHT
We cut to JERRY backstage.

JERRY   (TO RAY) I told him, I told him
they'd be like this.

CUT TO

15. EXT. CHURCH HALL. NIGHT
*Establishing shot of poster for KARATE KID
– THE MUSICAL.*

CUT TO

16. INT. CHURCH HALL. NIGHT
*Small audience. The curtains open. Table
with bonsai tree on it. LES walks on stage.
DANIELSON wheels a BMX on stage with a
suitcase hanging on the handlebars. There is
a cardboard sign on the stage with
'CALIFORNIA' written it.*

LES   My name is Mr Myagi from
Okinawa. This is the story of
Danielson, a young street punk from
New Jersey, who came to California
with a suitcase full of dreams and
left a Karate Kid.

A mobile goes off in the audience.

LES (cont.) Can you turn your mobile off
please, love?

CUT TO

17. INT. GALAXY LOUNGE. NIGHT
*SINGING BUILDERS are on stage singing
'BRIDGE TO YOUR HEART'.*

CUT TO

18. INT. BACKSTAGE. NIGHT
RIGHT SAID FRANK come backstage.

FRANK   (TO JERRY) Just nipping for a fag, Jerry.

JERRY   Good.

They exit through the fire door. RAY watches them go and closes the door behind them.

CUT TO

19. INT. GENTS' TOILETS. NIGHT
PADDY is wearing a visor and spraying his hair with 'SPRAY MAINE'.

PADDY   In for a penny.

CUT TO

20. INT. GALAXY LOUNGE. NIGHT
The SINGING BUILDERS continue their act.

CUT TO

21. INT. BACKSTAGE. NIGHT
RIGHT SAID FRANK knock on door. RAY lets them in and sees they're carrying a holdall. RAY is still suspicious.

The SINGING BUILDERS finish their song.

JERRY (OOV) Well done. The Singing Builders. Well done, lads. The Singing Builders, fantastic.

CUT TO

22. INT. CHURCH HALL. NIGHT
LES is teaching DANIELSON. The OTHER YOUNG KIDS are silhouetted on stage. ALAN has a small keyboard hung round his neck.

ALL   (SINGING) 'Sand the decks, sand the decks ...' (CLAPS) 'Sand the decks, sand the decks ...' (CLAPS) 'Paint the fence, paint the fence ...' (CLAPS) 'Paint the fence, paint the fence (CLAPS). Wax off, wax off. Now you learn karate, kid.'

AUDIENCE APPLAUD.

CUT TO

23. INT. GENTS' TOILETS. NIGHT
PADDY has just finished using his Spray Maine. He has a huge head of hair, raised quite high.

MARY   Paddy?

PADDY   Yeah.

MARY   Paddy, are you in there?

PADDY   Yeah. Whoa, hang on, hang on.

PADDY throws Spray Maine can into bin.

PADDY   (cont.) Wait. (CHECKS HIS APPEARANCE) Right, come in.

MARY   Why've you been avoiding me?
What've you done to your hair?

PADDY   Why, what?

MARY   It looks all big.

PADDY   It's me hair. It grows really quick, it always has done. Do you like it?

CUT TO

24. INT. GALAXY LOUNGE. NIGHT
There's a VENTRILOQUIST monkey act on stage.

VENTRILOQUIST
    Friends may forsake me.

MONKEY What will you do, Daddy?

VENTRILOQUIST
    I just let them all forsake me. For I still have you …

MONKEY Who am I, Daddy?

VENTRILOQUIST
    Sonny boy.

AUDIENCE APPLAUD.

CUT TO

25. INT. BACKSTAGE. NIGHT

JERRY (OOV)
    There you go, then, ladies and gentlemen. Keep it going. Now, ladies and gentlemen, be prepared to be amazed by Miss Bonnie Le Muff.

AUDIENCE APPLAUD.

RIGHT SAID FRANK go out with the holdall.
RAY is still suspicious of RIGHT SAID
FRANK and goes to watch them.

CUT TO

26. EXT. CAR PARK. NIGHT
We cut to the car park and make out RIGHT
SAID FRANK robbing a car, loading items
into the bag. We see RAY's POV of RIGHT
SAID FRANK. He goes back inside to tell
JERRY and KENNY SNR.

CUT TO

27. INT. GALAXY LOUNGE. NIGHT
BONNIE LE MUFF is on stage twirling her
batons.

CUT TO

28. EXT. CAR PARK. NIGHT
RAY, KENNY SNR and JERRY all lean out of
the fire door and take a look.

JERRY   Shit! I knew this was gonna happen.
        What're we gonna do?

RAY VON (TO KENNY SNR) Kenny, you phone
        the police, we'll tackle them.

KENNY SNR exits.

JERRY   We? We won't – I'm ill, remember.
        Let the police sort this lot out. I'll go
        and tell Potter.

JERRY goes off.

RAY VON (ON HIS OWN) Right!

RAY heads towards RIGHT SAID FRANK.

CUT TO

29. INT. GALAXY LOUNGE. NIGHT
BONNIE LE MUFF continues on stage.

CUT TO

30. EXT. CAR PARK. NIGHT
RAY approaches RIGHT SAID FRANK.

RAY VON What you up to, boys?

They spin round.

FRANK   You made me jump then. (STARTLED)
        Get inside. You've seen nothing.

RAY VON I've seen enough.

RAY squares up to them. FRANK stands up,
tool in hand. RAY runs for him. They fight.

FRANK swings RAY into MAX's car. The
alarm goes off.

CUT TO

31. EXT. CLUB DOOR. NIGHT
MAX on the door. He hears the alarm:
'Get back, you bastard – I'll break your legs.'
He runs.

CUT TO

32. EXT. CAR PARK. NIGHT
RIGHT SAID FRANK continue to punch RAY.

CUT TO

33. INT. GENTS' TOILETS. NIGHT

PADDY is still in the toilets with MARY.

PADDY   What's up, eh?

MARY   I don't know ... It's just that ... Well you never seem to have the time for me ...

PADDY   (HEARS THE ALARM) Shh!

PADDY exits the toilets.

CUT TO

34. EXT. CAR PARK. NIGHT
RAY is still fighting RIGHT SAID FRANK. MAX approaches, backlit by the security light. It is still raining heavily.

MAX   All right, Ray? Need some help?

RAY VON   I wouldn't mind.

FRANK   What are you going to do, old man, on your own?

PADDY   (COMES OUT OF THE SHADOWS) He's not on his own.

MAX and PADDY walk towards them.

MAX   (TO PADDY) What have you done to yer hair?

PADDY   Nothing.

They get stuck in.

MAX   Are you wearing a wig?

PADDY   No.

MAX   Is that a wig?

PADDY   Will you shut up about my hair?

KENNY SNR pushes BRIAN out of the club and over to the fight.

BRIAN   Sweet baby James! Call the police.

KENNY SNR
  I've called them – they're on their way.

BRIAN   What are those?

RAY VON   Car stereos.

FRANK   (TO BRIAN) Tell them to get off me, Potter.

BRIAN   I knew you'd be like this. (SEES PADDY'S HAIR) Who's that – the Fonz?

JERRY runs over.

JERRY   I've called an interval but they're all getting a bit restless. (GIVES PADDY A LOOK) What we gonna do?

FRANK   Get off.

BRIAN   (TO RIGHT SAID FRANK) Shut up, you girl. (GETS OUT HIS MOBILE) We're going to have to beg, Jerry.

CUT TO

35. INT. CHURCH HALL/EXT CAR PARK. NIGHT
Karate Kid – The Musical. *LES and ALI (DANIELSON'S GIRLFRIEND) are on one side.*

The rest of the YOUTH GROUP are on the
other side. DANIELSON is about to win. He is
performing his crane kick.

ALAN   (TO KARATE STUDENT) Sweep the
        leg ... no mercy ... finish him.

LES   Danielson. Always the eyes.

LES's mobile goes off. Embarrassed, he goes
into the wings.

LES   What?

BRIAN   Hello, Leslie. It's Brian. Are you busy?

LES   What do you want?

BRIAN   How d'you fancy your old job back?
        Tonight?

CUT TO

JERRY   Ladies and gentlemen, will you
        welcome back, at very short notice,
        the best backing band in clubland –
        it's Les Alanos!

LES ALANOS come on stage, still in their
Karate Kid costumes. They climb on stage.

AUDIENCE APPLAUSE.

36. INT. GALAXY LOUNGE. NIGHT

JERRY is on stage.

JERRY   (Cont.) As you know, there can only be one winner, but getting to the final they're all winners, they're all winners ...

BRIAN comes from the back of the stage. He wheels himself to JERRY, carrying a gold envelope.

BRIAN   Whoa, whoa, whoa ... I have the results.

JERRY looks confused. He realises what BRIAN has come on stage for when he sees the envelope.

JERRY   It's Brian Potter, ladies and gentlemen, give him a round of applause.

APPLAUSE

BRIAN   Ladies and gentlemen, I have the results, but these are not the results of Talent Trek, ladies and gentlemen. I don't know if you've noticed that I'm disabled, ladies and gentlemen, I can't stand up here on this stage every night like this brave man can, singing and dancing for your entertainment. And those of you who know Jerry 'The Saint' St Clair will know he's not been a well man. Yes, it's been touch and go and he's had a couple of ... he's had some tests, ladies and gentlemen, and these ... these are the results of those tests, Jerry.

JERRY   I can't believe you're doing this.

He tries to grab the envelope.

BRIAN   (ON MIC) Drum roll please, Leslie.

We cut to TWO REGULARS in the audience.

DOT   A gold envelope.

MOIRA   Must be BUPA.

BRIAN opens the gold envelope.

BRIAN   It's an all-clear, ladies and
        gentlemen: Jerry's got an all-clear!
        Hit it, boys!

*The AUDIENCE applaud and cheer. LES
ALANOS play 'CELEBRATION'. We see DEN
PERRY's reaction.*

BRIAN   (SINGING)
        'There's a party going on right
          here.
        Jerry's better, he's got the all-clear.
        So bring your good times and your
          laughter too.
        We're gonna celebrate Jerry's all-
          clear with you.
        It's time to come together, it's up to
          you.
        Jerry's better.
        Everyone around the world, come
          on, clap along.
        Yahoo! It's a celebration. Celebrate
          good times, come on. Come on,
        Jerry. Live the dream.'

        Thank you very much. Thank you.
        Long live the Phoenix.

CUT TO

37. INT. GALAXY LOUNGE. NIGHT
*We dissolve into the same set but the lounge
is empty. HOLY MARY and YOUNG MARY
are collecting glasses.*

CUT TO

38. INT. GENTS' TOILETS. NIGHT
*DEN PERRY is drying his hands. ANOTHER
MAN is having a pee.*

OLD MAN (TURNS ROUND AND DOES HIS
        FLIES) It's a cracking little club,
        in't it?

DEN PERRY (TO MIRROR)
        Oh yeah, a crackin' little club ...
        (DEN TAKES ONE LAST PUFF ON
        HIS CIGAR) Long live the Phoenix.

*DEN takes his cigar out and throws it into
the waste bin. He exits.*

*We cut to a close-up of the waste bin. The
cigar is smouldering on the paper towels.*

CUT TO

39. INT. BACKSTAGE. NIGHT
*JERRY is locking the fire doors. BRIAN
wheels himself along behind him.*

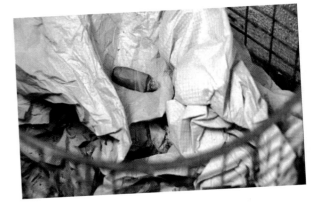

JERRY   I can't believe you did that
tonight.

BRIAN   Did what?

JERRY   You know.

BRIAN   Ahhh, they loved you, Jerry.
They loved you.

JERRY   They'll kill me if they find out.

BRIAN   They'll not find out. You don't trust
me, do you?

JERRY   No.

CUT TO

40. INT. GENT'S TOILET. NIGHT
The waste bin is on fire.

CUT TO

41. INT. MAIN CORRIDOR. NIGHT
*We see the 'disabled boy' money box
and smoke coming through under
the door.*

CUT TO

42. EXT. CAR PARK. NIGHT

BRIAN   You'll be off on your cruise soon.
I suppose I'd better start looking for
a new compere. We'll miss you,
Jerry – you know that, don't you?
Will you miss us?

JERRY   No.

BRIAN   What?

JERRY   I'm not going.

BRIAN   You're not going?

JERRY   I've changed me mind. Well can you
see me on a cruise? I get sea sick. I
threw up on a pedalo once. Besides,
I'd miss this place too much.

BRIAN   Aye, that's right, you know it Jerry:
this is where you belong. This is it,
me and you, and this is just the
start, this is; this is just the
beginning.

JERRY   Aye. Not much, but it's our Caesar's
Palace.

BRIAN   Correct.

CUT TO

43. INT. MAIN CORRIDOR. NIGHT
*Flames are licking round the 'disabled boy'
moneybox in the corridor.*

CUT TO

44. EXT. JERRY'S CAR. NIGHT
We cut to see JERRY's car driving out.

The car pulls out of the car park.

BRIAN   Who won Talent Trek?

JERRY   The ventriloquist.

BRIAN   He didn't! He was moving his
         bloody lips.

JERRY   I booked him.

BRIAN   Oh, Jesus. Jerry, Jerry, Jerry. This is
         supposed to be a new beginning, this
         – a fresh start. How much are we
         paying the monkey?

We pull-focus on the club and see the flames
through the curtains!

CUT TO

END CREDITS

THE END

Series 2

Episode 1

PART ONE

1. INT. GENTS' TOILETS. NIGHT

DEN PERRY is standing looking at himself in the mirror.

PUNTER It's a cracking little club, in't it?

DEN PERRY
       Oh yes, a cracking little club.
       Long live the Phoenix.

DEN throws his cigar into the bin and it starts to smoulder.

CUT TO

2. EXT. THE PHOENIX CAR PARK. NIGHT

BRIAN There she is, Jerry.

JERRY Aye, not much but it's our Caesar's Palace.

BRIAN Correct.

CUT TO

3. INT. GENTS' TOILETS. NIGHT

We cut to the toilets and the bin on fire.

CUT TO

4. EXT. THE PHOENIX CAR PARK. NIGHT

We cut back to the car park, JERRY'S car pulling out. We see the club on fire. The car drives out of shot.

BRIAN Are you hungry, Jerry?

JERRY Aye, I could eat something.

BRIAN (VO) Jerry?

JERRY Yeah?

BRIAN (VO) The club's on fire.

We hear a screech of brakes.

CUT TO

5. EXT. THE PHOENIX CAR PARK. NIGHT

Two fire engines in the car park. A police car. Hoses on the floor and water. BRIAN is mortified – not again!

YOUNG KENNY runs over. We cut to a GROUP OF ONLOOKERS standing eating kebabs. FIREMAN goes over to them.

FIREMAN Can you move right back now, please, right back!

BRIAN   That's my club! That's my fire, that! That's my club burning down!

We cut to KENNY SNR smoking next to a preoccupied FIREMAN.

KENNY SNR
         I don't need a suit. I've got special skin asbestos – the doctors are baffled. I'm a genetic freak, me.

FIREMAN Wanker!

We cut back to JERRY. He puts the 'disabled boy' moneybox in BRIAN's arms.

JERRY   I've got your disabled boy.

BRIAN   (CRYING TO JERRY) My little disabled boy. His face is all melted.

JERRY   My hands have all melted.

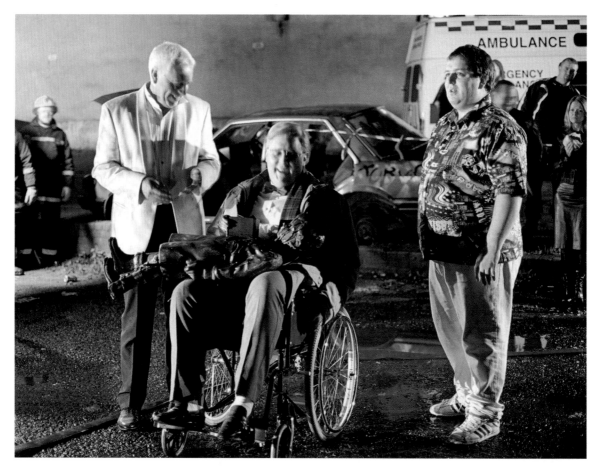

CUT TO

6. EXT. THE PHOENIX CLUB CAR PARK. PASSAGE OF TIME

The fire is nearly out. Smoke still drifts out of the building. FIREMEN bring charred furniture. RAY VON is helping them. JERRY sits with his hands in a bucket of water. He shakes his head. BRIAN is talking to the CHIEF FIREMAN.

CHIEF FIREMAN

 (USING HIS HANDS) Right, well, we've managed to save your big cabaret room. But the fire started very quickly. You've lost your other function room, your office and your games room.

BRIAN groans.

CHIEF FIREMAN (cont.)

 I think you've been very lucky.

BRIAN Lucky? Lucky? How?

CHIEF FIREMAN

 Well, if you'd have had batteries in those smoke alarms … It started in the gents' toilets. (TAKES OFF HIS HELMET) There's your culprit.

We cut to a FIREMAN coming out of the club carrying a burnt wastepaper basket.

BRIAN Him?

CHIEF FIREMAN

 Discarded fag.

JERRY A discarded fag?

LES and ALAN come over.

LES What's happened?

BRIAN (POINTING TO THE FIREMAN) Some queer's burnt my club down.

CHIEF FIREMAN

 It'll be a job for the fire-investigation lads now, but it looks to me like it's been started by a cigar or cigarette.

BRIAN Or cigar?

CHIEF FIREMAN

 Yeah … why?

BRIAN Two words … Den Perry.

CUT TO

OPENING CREDITS

CUT TO

7. EXT. MAGISTRATES' COURT. DAY

Establishing shot. BRIAN is looking up a huge flight of steps.

CUT TO

8. INT. MAGISTRATES' COURT CORRIDOR. DAY

HOLY MARY, RAY VON and KENNY SNR are sitting outside the court with BRIAN's solicitor, who is looking at his watch. He looks relieved when he sees BRIAN.

We cut to BRIAN wheeling himself down the corridor.

BRIAN Ah! You're there!

SOLICITOR

 Where've you been?

BRIAN Where have I been? Have you seen those steps out there? I don't know if you've noticed but I'm disabled.

BRIEF Shh!

BRIAN   Get bent! I'll put you on your back. It's a disgrace, I should sue.

He clocks HOLY MARY and the OTHERS.

SOLICITOR
   Well, you're lucky they're running late.

BRIAN sees RAY VON and the OTHERS.

BRIAN   What do *they* want?

SOLICITOR
   (OUT OF EARSHOT) They're your character witnesses.

BRIAN   Them? Where's Jerry and the others?

SOLICITOR
   I don't know. I phoned them all.

BRIAN   Sweet baby Jesus, Mother Theresa, Billy Liar and Miami Vice! They'll throw the key at me. Hey, er you all right?

CUT TO

9. INT. MAGISTRATES' COURT. DAY
There are a handful of people in the room. BRIAN's with his SOLICITOR.

BRIEF   The court is in session. All rise.

BRIAN   I can't rise. It's not happening.

BRIEF   The court calls Mr Potter's first character witness, Mr Kenny Dalglish Snr.

BRIAN   Dalglish? Dalglish? Where's he got that from?

We cut to KENNY SNR. He rises from his seat and walks to the stand (he is now wearing medals on his jumper). He salutes the JUDGE as he goes past. We cut to BRIAN, who is staring in disbelief.

We cut back to KENNY SNR, who's sitting in the witness stand. He taps his nose and points at BRIAN.

BRIEF   Mr Dalglish, do you swear by almighty gos that the evidence you shall give shall be the truth, the whole truth and nothing but the truth?

KENNY SNR
   Oh, yes.

BRIAN   I'm going down. I'm going down.

CUT TO

10. INT. MAGISTRATES' COURT. DAY
It's the end of the trial and the JUDGE is summing up.

JUDGE   Mr Potter?

BRIAN   Yes?

JUDGE   I've considered all the evidence that has been put before me and taken into account your character testimony, your undercover military

work in Vietnam and your glittering boxing career. However, for the forging of insurance documents and your negligence towards fire and safety equipment, it is the judgment of this court that you are no longer fit to hold a licence to trade alcohol.

BRIAN   What?

JUDGE   Furthermore, I have no choice but to permanently revoke your licence.

BRIAN   No, no, you can't do that! No! No, you can't do that, Your Majesty! You can't take me club off me!

JUDGE   That's all.

BRIAN   I'm nothing without me club, don't do that! Tell him! Get him!

DISSOLVE TO

11. EXT. THE PHOENIX CLUB. DAY
Wide shot of the club. We hear 'DON'T CRY OUT LOUD'. BRIAN sits in the car park staring at the boarded-up, fire-damaged Phoenix Club. The Phoenix sign is hanging down.

DEN PERRY
    Oy, excuse me, son. I'm looking for the Phoenix Club. It used to be round here somewhere.

We cut to see DEN PERRY sitting in the back of a Jaguar (one of his CRONIES is driving).

DEN PERRY
    All right, Brian … I didn't see you down there. I think you need some air in your tyres.

BRIAN   What do you want? Eh, you've got a nerve showing your face round here, after what you've done.

DEN PERRY
    What do you mean?

BRIAN   You know what I mean, you arsonist … you caused all this.

DEN PERRY
    Watch your mouth, Potter. That's slander, that is. You don't want to end up back in court. I heard they took your licence off you. Still, at least your customers are happy: they're all down at my place.

BRIAN   Yeh, just … just keeping them warm, Perry, that's all you're doing, just keeping them warm.

DEN PERRY   They'd rather be warm than well
             done. Oh, yes, business is booming,
             booming! Oh, Brian, just pop inside,
             see if my jacket potato's done, could
             you? (NODS TOWARDS THE CLUB
             AND LAUGHS) Drive on, Terry. Have
             a nice day!

BRIAN   (GIVING HIM THE FINGER) Eh, have
         a bit of that! Eh, go on! Hey!

*DEN drives away. BRIAN is left staring at
the club.*

CUT TO

12. INT. BRIAN'S HOUSE. DAY

*BRIAN, in pyjamas, is sitting flicking
through the channels using the TV remote.*

*Cut to the television. Kilroy-type programme
on with BOB CAROLGEES AND SPIT THE
DOG. He's sitting in the audience. Caption on
screen: 'MUMMY'S BABY, DADDY'S MAYBE'.*

BOB   (TO YOUNG GIRL) Well, we hope
       everything works out for you.
       (TURNS TO CAMERA) A teenage
       pregnancy can have tragic
       circumstances. Louise, how did you
       find out you were pregnant?

GIRL   Well, I went to the doctor's and—

She is interrupted as SPIT gobs on her.

BOB   Don't be disgusting, you bad, bad
       boy! Sorry, Louise, what were you
       saying?

GIRL   Well, I went to the doctor's—

*BRIAN flicks over. Armchair Superstore
(ASS) Shopping Channel is on. A GUEST*

*PRESENTER is wearing an umbrella hat.
GARY, THE ANCHOR PRESENTER, is
pouring water on it with a watering can.
The hat rotates, spinning the water off
onto the floor.*

GUEST PRESENTER
         No, Gary, hat's magic. (GARY
         LAUGHS) The difference with this
         and your more conventional
         umbrella hats is that you simply
         don't get wet.

CUT TO

13. INT. BRIAN'S HOUSE HALLWAY. DAY

*We jump cut to the hallway. BRIAN starts
his answer machine: 'YOU'VE NO NEW
MESSAGES.' BRIAN stares at it. In the
background we hear the TV from the
other room.*

GARY   (VO) The price should be coming
        on the screen now. There it is now.
        And where does this product come
        from again?

GUEST PRESENTER
         South America.

GARY   South America. God bless South
        America!

GUEST PRESENTER
         South America. You need
         something like this and they are
         available in …

CUT TO

14. EXT. THE PHOENIX CLUB. DAY

*It's raining. 'DON'T CRY OUT LOUD'
(reprise). BRIAN is collecting litter. We pan
up with a crisp bag. BRIAN puts it in a*

carrier bag. We cut out to reveal BRIAN
wearing a plaid umbrella hat as seen on ASS
Channel. He's shaking his head.

CUT TO

15. INT. ASDA. DAY
Close-up of JERRY against a black background.
He's singing 'HEAVY DUTY BLACK BIN BAGS,
ON OFFER TILL DECEMBER' to the tune of
'MEN IN BLACK'. We cut out to reveal that he's
at the front of ASDA demonstrating the bin
bags. He's also wearing a huge badge that reads
'HAPPY TO HELP'. ALAN is accompanying him
behind on a small keyboard. The SHOPPERS
pass by, ignoring the entertainment.

JERRY   (SINGING)
      'Come and get your black bin bags.
      They're on offer till December.
      Come and get your black bin bags.
      They're long and black and slender.
      Heavy-duty black bin bags, no
      matter what your gender.
      Heavy-duty black bin bags ...
      whether bi or straight or bender.
      Heavy-duty black bin bags ...
      something to remember.
      Just rip with me, just rip with me
      and tear with me right now.
      Just rip with me and rip with me

and tell me right now. Fill them
up now!'

We cut to see BRIAN at the main entrance
doors. He's staring at JERRY and ALAN
with disbelief.

CUT TO

16. INT. ASDA CAFÉ. DAY
BRIAN, JERRY and ALAN sit round a table
eating: BRIAN with large fish, ALAN with
sandwich, JERRY with a salad and mineral
water. He messes with a small tin that
contains tablets. He takes one and swallows
it with water.

BRIAN   What are you doing?

JERRY   (TAKING TABLETS FROM BOTTLE)
      Herbal medication, them ... for me
      libido. I get early-morning stiffness.

BRIAN   Who doesn't? (NOTICES A COPPER
      BRACELET ON JERRY'S WRIST)
      What's that on your arm?

JERRY   It's a copper bracelet – it aids
      fitness and mobility.

BRIAN   Does it? I'd better get two for
      my legs.

JERRY   Look, have you come here to shop or take the piss?

BRIAN   Bit of both.

BRIAN   To think two of my best pals have ended up like this, yeh … singing in Asda.

JERRY   Right, and where do you suggest we sing? Because thanks to you there is nowhere else, is there?

BRIAN   What do you mean? It wasn't me that burnt the club down.

JERRY   No, you didn't burn the club down, but it was you with your cutting corners, with your dodgy fire equipment, with your forged insurance documents.

BRIAN   I had to cut corners: it were third club. The premiums were sky high. They were through the roof!

JERRY   You could have killed somebody.

BRIAN   Aah! Could've. Would've. Should've. We didn't. Anyway, it'll be different this time.

JERRY   This time. What do you mean, 'this time'?

BRIAN   I'm reopening the Phoenix. (JERRY STARES AT HIM BLANKLY) We're gonna reopen the Phoenix.

JERRY   Are you on some sort of medication?

BRIAN   I am Jerry, two tablespoons of ambition, three times a day!

JERRY   Reopening the Phoenix, what with?

You've no money, you've no licence, you've no brewery. And what's this WE are going to reopen the Phoenix? What's this 'we'?

BRIAN   We – me and you and Alan and the others.

JERRY   There is no 'we'. 'We' has moved on. So has everybody else. It's about time you got off your fat arse and did the same.

BRIAN   Fat? Fat arse? (LOOKING AT HIS ARSE)

TANNOY ANNOUNCEMENT
         Jerry St Clair to customer services, please; Jerry St Clair.

BRIAN   (POINTS TO JERRY'S BADGE) Happy to help?! Happy to help?! Well help me, Jerry … help me. I need you!

JERRY   Help yourself, Brian. Look take my advice: stop living in the past, forget the Phoenix, it's over. Move somewhere else. Start again.

BRIAN   Jerry, Jerry!

ALAN   (DOESN'T KNOW WHAT TO SAY) I better … you know. OK.

We cut to ALAN and JERRY as they walk off.

ALAN   You were a bit hard on him, weren't you?

JERRY   (GLANCING BACK) I suppose … it's for the best.

We cut back to BRIAN. He's scraping JERRY's salad onto his plate.

CUT TO

17. INT. ASDA. DAY

*JERRY is back singing. This time it's
'CORNED BEEF' ('CALL ME' by BLONDIE)
He's standing beside tins of stacked corned
beef. He's opened a can and is cutting into it
as he sings.*

*We cut to BRIAN, who is wheeling himself
towards the main doors. He turns back to
JERRY to give one last pathetic look. We cut
to JERRY. He obviously can see BRIAN but
turns away.*

JERRY   (SINGING)
    'If you're feeling rather hungry, hey
      there's a product you'll remember.
    Eat it hot or cold on Sunday, or you
      can put it in a blender.
    Corned beef with chips or with salad,
    It's corned beef – even Buckingham
      Palace eats corned beef.

Hey, why don't you try corned-beef
hash!'

END OF PART ONE

PART TWO

18. EXT. THE PROMENADE, BLACKPOOL. DAY

*BRIAN wheels himself through the wind
and the rain. He wheels himself across
the tramlines. Tied to a lamppost by the
road is a bunch of flowers, with a message
(in felt tip): 'IN MEMORY OF ALAN'.
BRIAN exits shot. We see an establishing
shot of a hotel, 'LE PONDEROSA'. BRIAN
wheels himself into the shot. His back to
camera. He looks up at the Grand Hotel.
Throughout the scene we hear a reprise
of 'DON'T CRY OUT LOUD' played on a
Wurlitzer organ.*

CUT TO

19. INT. LE PONDEROSA. DAY

BRIAN enters the reception area. There is a Guide Dogs for the Blind collection money box in the shape of a labrador. BRIAN wheels himself past it and pats it. The music fades and we hear the GIRL behind the reception desk.

RECEPTIONIST
    ... and we went for a fish supper. Took me back to his place, drops his trousers, couldn't believe it. Anyway, he's just about to get to the vinegar strokes and his bloody mobile goes off! (SHE SEES BRIAN) Can I call you back, Mum. (SHE HANGS UP) Yes, can I help?

BRIAN   Is Hoss around?

RECEPTIONIST
    Who?

BRIAN   Hoss. Frank, Mr Cartwright, Frank Cartwright?

RECEPTIONIST (SHOUTS)
    Mr Cartwright?

FRANK   (OOV) What?

RECEPTIONIST
    There's someone here to see you.

FRANK   Wha— Who, Where?

FRANK enters shot. He's bears an uncanny resemblance to JIM BOWEN. He's shocked but happy to see BRIAN.

138

FRANK   (cont.) Eh, Brian Potter.

BRIAN   Frank Cartwright.

FRANK   What happened to your legs?

BRIAN   What happened to your head?
        You were bald last time I saw you.

CUT TO

20. INT. LE PONDEROSA. NIGHT

*A busy function room, PENSIONERS and
FAMILIES. TERRY FOY is on stage singing
'LOVE REALLY HURTS WITHOUT YOU'.
BRIAN and FRANK are sitting in front of the
window, overlooking the promenade. The
illuminations are behind them. They laugh as
they reminisce.*

FRANK   (LAUGHING) He was a devil,
        wasn't he?

BRIAN   Who can hit him? Like a frog up
        a pump!

FRANK   (LAUGHS) They were happy days,
        weren't they?

BRIAN   Oh, you can't go back.

FRANK   Well, no, I tell you, I'm glad I'm out
        of clubland now. It's not what it used
        to be. See, that's why I've come
        here, see.

BRIAN   Are you?

FRANK   Oh, aye. Well, look at me now. See,
        I've got this place, I've got sixty-
        nine rooms *en suite*, I'm making a
        fortune here. They don't call this the
        Golden Mile for nothing, you know.
        Do you know, I've got a bar, a bistro,

a children's play area. I've got a
sauna, a solarium, lift to all floors.
If Carole's leg pays out, I'm going to
get a Jacuzzi.

BRIAN   Are you?

FRANK   I am that. Do you know, not only
        that, the future is – I'll tell you
        where the future is. Are you
        listening to me? The future is
        everything under one roof. See,
        that's what it is, look – look on
        there, see. Sunshine indoors.

BRIAN   Sunshine indoors?

FRANK   Aye. You want to forget clubland, get
        yourself out here, get yourself set
        up out here.

BRIAN   Le Ponderosa, sunshine indoors.
        I like that. That's very good, Frank,
        it's catchy.

FRANK   See.

BRIAN   Well, you're forgetting I'm ... I'm
        blacklisted, Frank. I've not got a
        brewery, they won't touch me.

FRANK   It don't matter: you don't need a
        brewery. What have I got here?
        Bottles and cans, that's all I use.
        It's not what they drink, it's where
        they drink it, see, and when you
        make a big success of it on your
        own two feet, well the brewery will
        come crawling back to you.

BRIAN   Frank I've not got a licence.

FRANK   Neither have I. It's Carol's name
        over the door but I call the shots.

BRIAN   What do you mean?

FRANK   What you need Brian is a fall guy,
somebody you can manipulate and
(TWISTS HIS HAND FORWARD AND
MAKES A CLICKING SOUND) He
thinks it's his gaff but it's yours.
You're working him from behind.
There must be somebody. Trust me,
Brian, there's always a way, think
about it …

BRIAN   Yeah.

FRANK   Anyway make yourself at home.
Just enjoy all the facilities. We'll
sort your bill out when you leave,
all right?

CUT TO

21. INT. LE PONDEROSA. DAY
*BRIAN's in his hotel room, overlooking the
sea. He gets out his diary (semiclad woman
on the front). We see a cutaway of the
pages. BRIAN fingers down, two names
(MAX and PADDY) and a mobile number.*

CUT TO

22. INT./EXT. MINIBUS. DAY
*MAX is driving. PADDY beside him.
CHORLEY FM is on the radio. They're both
singing along to theme from TV's MINDER on
the radio. Cutaway of MAX's mobile on the
dash, vibrating and ringing – it says
'IRONSIDE' on the display. They can't hear
it.*

CUT TO

23. INT. LE PONDEROSA. DAY
*BRIAN's frustrated reaction. We jump-cut,
cutaway of the address book. His finger
stops at another name: LES CAMPBELL.*

BRIAN   What are they doing?

CUT TO

24. EXT. FARNWORTH MARKET. DAY
*Mobile meat wagon. LES (BUTCHER) is
putting meat into a carrier bag while doing
his spiel into a headset, which feeds out
through a PA. There's ANOTHER BUTCHER
working behind him.*

LES   There's a bit of brisket already in
there. I'm being good to you. I'll tell
you what, Mo, I'm filling up (HE
FILLS THE BAG UP), and I'll tell you
what we've got today Sir. It's BSE
day, bit of something extra, right. A
full bag there, and I'm not asking
eight quid, I'm not even asking
seven quid… six quid the lot, and I'll
tell you what I'm going to do I'll
throw in a pig's dick for the dog …
(HOLDS IT UP) Bit of a delicacy in
Thailand those, my love. (HIS
MOBILE RINGS. HE ANSWERS IT)
Hang on. Excuse me a minute. Hello?
(THIS, TOO, COMES OVER THE PA)

BRIAN   Hello! Leslie, it's Brian Potter.

LES   Hiya, Brian, how's it going?

CUT TO

25. EXT. CROSSING. DAY

KENNY SNR, dressed as a lollipop man, is standing on the kerb. TWO BOYS (in uniforms) run up the crossing. He quickly lowers his stick and stops them.

KENNY SNR

    Whoa, whoa, stop right there. Hang on a minute, you don't just run out like that...

BOY   There's nothing coming.

KENNY SNR

    Oh, you can't be too careful.

BOY 2   Come on, we're gonna be late.

KENNY SNR

    Better late than dead.

He makes them both wait on the side of the road until a car comes. Then he walks out into the road and stops it. His mobile rings.

BOY   We were late yesterday 'cause you said Jackie Chan was coming to see you about some paint.

KENNY SNR

    He did. You missed him by seconds. He kicked an old woman in the back over there. (PHONE RINGS) That's probably him now.

CUT TO

26. INT./EXT. LE PONDEROSA/CROSSING. DAY

INTERCUT BETWEEN BOTH LOCATIONS. BRIAN looking at the phone, confused.

BRIAN   Kenny? Kenny Senior?

KENNY SNR

    Hello, Jackie ... yeah I got you that paint. One-coat gloss.

BRIAN   Jackie? Who the hell's Jackie?

KENNY SNR

    Chuck Norris wants what? Woodchip? I'll see what I can do.

CUT TO

27. EXT. CROSSING. DAY

Cut back to KENNY SNR. He's in the middle of the road and has stopped the traffic.

BOY   He's a liar.

BOY 2   He sick. (POINTS TO HIS HEAD) He ate his family.

KENNY SNR walks back to his position smiling

KENNY SNR

    Hello, Brian. Sorry about that.

CUT TO

28. INT./EXT. LE PONDEROSA/MINIBUS. DAY.

INTERCUT. MAX and PADDY are singing along to 'AMARILLO' by TONY CHRISTIE on the radio.

MAX AND PADDY
> 'Through the wind and rain.
> Is this the way to Amarillo …'

BRIAN   (PHONE RINGING) Come on, come on, come on. (HE TUTS)

MAX AND PADDY
> (CONTINUING SINGING)
> '… how long I've been holding my pillow,
> Dreaming dreams of Amarillo
> And sweet Marie who waits for me …'

SONG CONTINUES

MAX   (TURNING TO PASSENGERS) Come on, sing along!

MAX and PADDY both turn round and reveal that the minibus is full of ASIAN ELDERS all

looking fed up. We jump-cut to the exterior of the bus. 'ASIAN ELDERS' is written on the side of the bus in big letters.

CUT TO

29. EXT. FUNFAIR. DAY

The waltzers/speedway. The fair is closed. RAY VON is teaching a LAD how to walk backwards while the ride is moving slowly. 'YOU SPIN ME ROUND' playing in background. We hear a voice over the speakers.

RAY VON The longer you scream, the faster the ride. Remember, fun is the key, but keep singing at all times or you may die. Shabba! (HIS PHONE RINGS) … Hello Mr. Potter. Sit down!

CUT TO

30. INT. CHURCH. DAY

Holy communion. HOLY MARY is in the queue. Her mobile rings 'HOT STUFF' by DONNA SUMMER. It shatters the quiet. She answers it … nodding her apologies to those around.

HOLY MARY
> Hello? Oh, Brian, how are ya?
> Sorry, love, I can't talk much: I'm in a church.

CUT TO

31. INT./EXT. MINIBUS. DAY

MAX AND PADDY
 (CONTINUE SINGING AND PRESSING
 HOOTER IN TIME TO SONG)
 'Sha la la, la la la la la …'

MAX Right, here we are, boys (HELPING
 ELDERS OFF MINIBUS). Say one for
 me.

PADDY (LOOKING AT THE MOBILE) Hey,
 have you seen this?

MAX What?

PADDY Eight missed calls off Ironside.

*The OLD ASIAN MAN gives MAX a filthy
look.*

CUT TO

32. EXT. THE PHOENIX CLUB. NIGHT
*It's raining heavily. JERRY and ALAN make
their way towards the club. JERRY stops in
the rain and looks up at the damage,
shaking his head.*

JERRY Look at that. What a bloody shame.

ALAN I know.

CUT TO

33. INT. GAMES ROOM. NIGHT
*The MAIN CHARACTERS are gathered. The
room has no electricity, so they've had to
use an assortment of lanterns and lights
(left over from Half a Shilling).*

JERRY (OOV) What are we doing here,
 anyway?

ALAN You'll see.

JERRY I'm missed my power yoga for
 this … (HE SEES EVERYBODY AND
 IS SURPRISED) Bloody hell! Look
 who's here!

EVERYBODY
 (RANDOMLY) Hello/All right, Jerry.

JERRY They're all here, aren't they? Paddy
 and Kenny … What are you lot
 doing here … don't tell me – Brian?

KENNY SNR
 Yeh …

JERRY I knew he'd have something to do
 with this.

ALAN Let's just hear what he's got to say
 first, eh?

JERRY Aye, well, where is he?

*We hear a clatter followed by the theme
from BLACK BEAUTY. The door by the
side of the bar opens. A bright shaft of
light shines through, the dramatic music
becomes louder.*

BRIAN enters the room. YOUNG KENNY is behind him, holding a powerful torch and a portable stereo.

BRIAN (TO YOUNG KENNY) All right, knock it off. Thank you for coming, everybody. I suppose you're all wondering why I've gathered you here. Well, I'll tell you (HE NODS TO YOUNG KENNY, WHO PRESSES PLAY ON THE STEREO AND WE HEAR THE GRANDSTAND THEME) ... track six, you pillock, track six!

YOUNG KENNY quickly knocks it on a track. We hear the theme from VAN DER VALK.

We cut to JERRY.

JERRY (ASIDE TO ALAN) God forbid he'd be melodramatic.

We cut back to BRIAN.

BRIAN I have a dream, people. I have a dream. If we build it, they will come.

LES Build what?

BRIAN A new Phoenix, bigger, better! Faster, stronger, rising out of the ashes!

JERRY Here we go again!

BRIAN A superclub, a king of clubs. Only this time we'll have it all. A restaurant, a bistro, and we'll serve food ...

JERRY Food, eh?

BRIAN Not just any old food, Jerry, *proper* food: scampi, Chicken Kievs, garlic bread ...

MAX Garlic bread?!

BRIAN Garlic bread. That's right, Max. It's the future – I've tasted it.

JERRY Who's gonna cook it?

BRIAN Cooks, chefs ... us! We'll all cook it. We'll all muck in.

HOLY MARY I can cook.

BRIAN You can cook and you will cook sister. Amen to that. Oh, yes! We'll have a playroom for the kids, 'cause I believe that children are the future ...

YOUNG KENNY I thought garlic bread was the future.

BRIAN Shut up, I'm on a roll. We'll have a solarium, leisure facilities, sunbeds ...

PADDY Go on!

MAX That's it, Brian, eh, I'm up for that!

BRIAN (SMILING, GETTING EXCITED) That's right! Sunshine indoors! Sunshine indoors! They can tan while they drink.

JERRY Drink! Drink what? We've not got a brewery?

We can hear the rain falling hard and the roof is starting to leak heavily now.

BRIAN We don't need a brewery. We can do it. Balls to the brewery. Bottles and cans, that's all we need to run a club.

KENNY SNR
And my home brew ... it's won awards.

LES   It tastes like piss.

KENNY SNR
That was piss.

BRIAN   You see, it don't matter what it drinks, it doesn't care. It's the facilities, it's the surroundings — and they'll have it all here, all under one roof.

LES   But Brian, we haven't got a roof.

BRIAN   Well we'll *build* a friggin' roof, right Ray, we'll build one? Few slates, bit of MDF?

RAY VON   No, you can't use MDF, it'll—

BRIAN   That's right, that's the ticket ... We'll do a *Changing Rooms*, we'll do it in half an hour.

HOLY MARY
Alleluia!

BRIAN   You see this rain? This rain is a baptism for the new Phoenix.

JERRY   But I've told you, Brian: we've all moved on, we've all got new lives.

BRIAN   New lives? You call singing in Asda having a life, eh? (TO LES) You call selling meat from the back of a wagon having a life, eh? (TO KENNY SNR) Lying to kids as they cross the road? That's not living: that's existing ... You deserve better, you deserve this club. You are this club

and this is where you belong. I can't do it without you.

JERRY   You can't do it, Brian, full stop. You've no licence, you've been banned for life.

BRIAN   Ah, ah, Jerry that's right: I have, been banned for life, but you've not. You've not been banned Jerry ... You could be the licensee. Think about it.

Everybody turns and looks at JERRY as one man.

JERRY   Me?

BRIAN   Yeh, you, Jerry, you the licensee of the new Phoenix. I'm not getting any younger Jerry. My running days are over. I'm handing the baton to you. Take it, run wild and run free. There'll be no more cutting corners now you're the gaffer.

JERRY   I don't know what to say.

BRIAN   Say yes, Jerry. Say yes and inherit what's rightfully yours.

JERRY   What do you think?

There is a pause while JERRY thinks about it.

JERRY   (cont.) Yes, all right, yeh ... I'll do it. I'll bloody do it. (EVERYONE CHEERS) I will!

BRIAN   I knew you wouldn't let me down, Jerry.

CUT TO

34. EXT. THE PHOENIX CLUB MAIN ENTRANCE. NIGHT

Licensee plaque over the door in the name of 'JERRY "THE SAINT" ST CLAIR DIGNAN'. We cut to BRIAN. He has all the necessary paperwork resting on YOUNG KENNY's back as he bends over (still holding his torch, he shines it on the plaque as JERRY stares at it in awe). BRIAN deliberately coughs. JERRY snaps out of his trance and BRIAN hands him a pen.

BRIAN   There you are, Jerry. What do you think?

JERRY   Aye, smashing.

BRIAN   If you just sign on there on the dotted line, Mr Licensee. Oh, yes, there you go.

JERRY signs the paperwork.

CUT TO

END CREDITS

35. INT. GALAXY LOUNGE – END CREDITS

Backing music – 'EVERY LITTLE THING SHE DOES IS MAGIC'. BRIAN AND CO are auditioning a FEMALE MAGICIAN. She wears a black leotard, white cuffs, sequined bowler hat. Three doves are already on a perch. She produces another one from a handkerchief. It flies off the stage towards an extractor fan. We cut back to her reaction. We cut to BRIAN and the others. They are covered in dove's innards and blood. A few feathers fall down from the ceiling.

Music stops.

BRIAN   (SPITS OUT A FEATHER) Next!

THE END

Episode 2

PART ONE

**1. INT./EXT. PHOENIX CLUB CAR PARK/
BRIAN'S BEDROOM (INTERCUT). DAY**
*BRIAN's telephone rings – he's wearing an
eye mask.*

BRIAN   (ANSWERS PHONE, FLUSTERED)
      Who's this? Yes?

MAX   *Bonjour*, Mr Potter, *je m'appelle
       Max. Où est le pantalon?*

BRIAN   Who's this?

*We cut to the Phoenix Club car park. MAX,
PADDY and ALAN are standing by the side
of a small box lorry, parked facing the wall
(sweet truck haul on the side – 'IF YOU
THINK I'M DIRTY YOU WANT TO MEET THE
WIFE' written in the dirt on the back.) MAX
is wearing a beret and carrying a big bag.
PADDY, yawning, looks half asleep.*

MAX   It's me: Max. I'm here with Paddy.
       Just letting you know, reporting in.

BRIAN   Yeh … And?

MAX   You told me to ring you.

BRIAN   Yeh, when you get to France …
       (LOOKS AT CLOCK) It's only half
       past six in the pissing morning.

MAX   It's half-seven in France.

BRIAN   Eh?

MAX   It's half-seven in France.

BRIAN   Why, are you there?

MAX   No, I'm at the club with Paddy …
       but they're an hour ahead of us
       in France …

BRIAN slams the phone down.

MAX   (Cont.) (WE HEAR A DIALLING
       TONE) Hello?

*We cut back to BRIAN, rolling over and
replacing his eye mask.*

PADDY   What's he said?

MAX   (LOOKING AT THE PHONE) He's
       hung up!

BRIAN   (IN BED) Oh, I need a piss now.

CUT TO

2. EXT. PHOENIX CLUB CAR PARK. LATER
*We jump-cut to later. MAX and PADDY are
sitting in the lorry. MAX is driving. ALAN is
talking to them through the door.*

ALAN   How much beer are you gonna get?
        I don't want you overloading it or
        anything.

MAX   *Oui, oui, oui.* Fear not, monsieur
       Alan … she's in good hands.

ALAN   Right, well think on … because if
        anything happens to her it'll be me
        who's for it, right?

MAX   I used to drive one like this. (REVS
       UP THE ENGINE) She's safe with
       me. OK, *Viva La France!*

ALAN   *Auf Weidersehen!*

MAX   Off we go!

*MAX alters the mirror slightly, looks over
his shoulder and drives forward into the
wall. ALAN watches. On the back of the
lorry there's a 'HOW AM I DRIVING?' and
a phone number.*

CUT TO

OPENING CREDITS

CUT TO

3. EXT. THE PHOENIX CLUB. DAY
*Establishing shot of car park. Fun day
preparations – lorries being unloaded,
fairground rides and stalls being set up.
'KEEP ON MOVIN'' and local 'What's on
guide' on CHORLEY FM.*

CUT TO

4. INT. THE GAMES ROOM. DAY
*Half-decorated. Dust sheets on most things
(including the snooker tables), tins of paint,
wire, tools, pasting table. REGULARS in
overalls. There follows a montage of people
getting the club ready to the song on
CHORLEY FM.*

*Montage – YOUNG KENNY is on stepladder.
He's placing some canoe oars on a ceiling
shelf. There are other artefacts up there
already: old books, bottles, a couple of wheat
sacks, spinning bobbins, cast irons. It's
theme-pub time again.*

*Montage – FEMALE REGULAR sewing
curtains for the windows.*

*Montage – close-up of somebody wiring a
plug or socket.*

*Montage – YOUNG KENNY up stepladder, now
placing an old black typewriter on the shelf.*

*Montage – KENNY SNR painting the skirting
boards.*

Montage – *YOUNG KENNY wheels an old bike into the room.*

CUT TO

5. INT. GAMES ROOM. DAY

JERRY, KENNY SNR, YOUNG KENNY, LES, ALAN, HOLY MARY, JOYCE all sitting round the snooker table. BRIAN is facing them and facing the window. they're all looking up at the theme pub shelf. The bike is now hanging from the ceiling.

BRIAN   Will somebody please tell me why we've got a bike on the wall?

YOUNG KENNY
>It's a theme pub.

BRIAN   What theme? Hiroshima? Old shite? Hey, is that my good typewriter up there? (STRAINS TO SEE) Get that down, get that down right now!

ALAN   It's all the rage this, Brian – loads of pubs are doing it now.

BRIAN   Well, we're not a pub, we're a club. Get it all down, get it slung. Get it on the jumble sale, will sell it today!

JERRY   No, we won't. I like it …

HOLY MARY
>Oh, I do 'n'all. I think it's fancy.

JERRY   All those in favour of it staying up there say aye.

THE COMMITTEE
>Aye!

BRIAN   Whoa, whoa, whoa! Hey, I say aye.

JERRY   No, Brian, I'm the licensee now. I'm running this meeting … and I say aye.

BRIAN   Right, then, all those in favour of Jerry saying aye, say aye.

THE COMMITTEE
         Aye!

BRIAN   Right, good ... next!

JERRY   (LOOKING AT HIS PAPERWORK) Right, item three ... Er ... what are we going to call our new games room? Now I propose the Sir Steve Redgrave suite.

BRIAN   *Sir* Steve Redgrave? Chreest, they're just giving them out to anybody these days, aren't they?!

JERRY   Come on, Brian, he won five gold medals for rowing.

BRIAN   Oh, big hook!

LES   Oh fair play. You've got to be super fit in that game. You've got to have huge upper-body strength.

BRIAN   Don't talk to me about upper-body strength, Leslie. I wrote the bloody book. My forearms are massive!

LES   Yeah, and we all know why that is, don't we? Too much trumpet polishing.

BRIAN   Hey, toilet mouth. There's a child's bike outside.

JERRY   Can we get on with this meeting?

BRIAN   It were you that brought up Sir Steve Redgrave. I just think chucking knighthoods at boat people's a bit much. I mean, how hard can it be to ride a boat?

YOUNG KENNY
         (CLENCHING FISTS TOGETHER) Ooh, I don't know, it's not easy. They move around a lot. You've got to hold on really tight and persevere.

ALAN   You don't *ride* a boat. You *row* a boat!

YOUNG KENNY
         Oh, 'boat'. I thought you said 'goat'.

CUT TO

6. EXT. PHOENIX CLUB CAR PARK. DAY
RAY VON is overseeing his LADS setting up. A van ('GAMES SANS FRONTIÈRES' on the side) pulls up alongside the window. ERIC and his mate LANCE.

ERIC   Howdy! Where do you want it?

RAY VON What is it?

ERIC   It's an inflatable for Brian Potter.

RAY VON Sounds like a good swap (LAUGHS). Set it up out here.

CUT TO

7. INT. GAMES ROOM. DAY
The meeting continues. JERRY is checking his list. Each member of the group raises his or her hand in acknowledgment.

JERRY   Madam Zelda, fortune teller? Mary?

HOLY MARY
         That's me ...

JERRY   (TICKS HIS LIST) Les and Alan, you're on the lorry with me. Kenny Snr, bouncy castle.

KENNY SNR

> How much should I charge?

JERRY   I don't know ... er ... fifty pee?

BRIAN   Fifty pee? A pound ... for five minutes more like. Get them spending. There are people out there with giros burnin' a hole in their shell suits. Whatever you'd normally charge 'em, bloody double it. Today's all about making money.

JERRY   I thought today was about raising the profile of the club.

BRIAN   Well, Jerry, there'll not be a club till we finish off the decorating, will there?

JERRY   And there'll not be a club till we get something to drink. We've still not sorted that out. I told you, you can't run a club without a brewery.

BRIAN   Balls to the brewery! We don't need no brewery. We can do it ourselves.

JERRY   How?

BRIAN   I've told you how! That bar tonight will be stocked with the finest selection of foreign quality beers known to man. As we sit here wasting time and money, Max and Paddy are on their way to France. (POINTS)

JERRY   To France?

BRIAN   Yes, France! (LOOKS AT WATCH) And if my Casio's on the ball, they should be halfway there by now.

CUT TO

8. EXT./INT. MOTORWAY SERVICES. DAY / ALAN'S LORRY.

MAX has his flask out. PADDY is walking back from the services with an armful of food. He gets in. We hear MOTOWN on the stereo.

MAX   Come on! (PADDY CLIMBS INTO LORRY) What's all that crap you've bought?

PADDY   Necessities ... and a bit of *Gold* for the road. (HOLDS UP A PORN MAG) Dink-dank-doo.

MAX   You're gonna go blind, Patrick!

PADDY   You what? Who ... who said that, Max?

MAX   Funny, aren't you?

PADDY   Ooh, look at them ... she could breastfeed a crèche.

MAX   (SHAKING HIS HEAD) They're not real.

PADDY   And?

MAX   You want to pace yourself, Patrick – you only get a bucket and a half.

PADDY   Is that all?

MAX   That's all I got.

CUT TO

9. EXT. PHOENIX CLUB CAR PARK. DAY

The bouncy castle is being inflated with a compressor. As it rises slowly, we reveal a huge flesh-coloured penis shape protruding from the front of it, with two egglike shapes, one on either side. RAY VON and his LADS are all standing round laughing and pointing at it.

ERIC   You've not seen one like this!

CUT TO

10. INT. GAMES ROOM. DAY
The meeting continues. JERRY's looking at his notes and fumbling with his pills. BRIAN watches him with astonishment.

JERRY   Right, then. Cadillac rides ... what's that?

BRIAN   Rides in a Cadillac.

JERRY   I know. Whose?

BRIAN   Mine.

JERRY   Yeah, and it looks well, doesn't it, us struggling for money and you swanning round in a Cadillac?

BRIAN   Hey, that Cadillac's my pension, Jerry!

LES   Can we just get on? We've got to rehearse.

BRIAN   Don't tell me: tell bloody Keith Moon here with the drugs?

JERRY   They're not drugs: they're herbal medication, I've told you.

BRIAN   Aye you'll be shooting up in the bloody bogs next!

CUT TO

11. EXT. PHOENIX CLUB CAR PARK. DAY
BRIAN, JERRY and the REST OF THE COMMITTEE are gathered around the

inflatable genitals. ERIC is showing it off with pride.

ERIC   He's pleased to see you! How about that! You all want one, don't you! (LAUGHING)

CUT TO

12. INT. GAMES ROOM. DAY

JERRY   Look what it is we're struggling here, right? I've not got enough helpers. I've not got anybody to do the face painting yet!

BRIAN   One of Ray Von's mates is doing it! I've sorted all this out! Right, just relax. You're twisting me melon, man. Eh, everybody knows what they're doing, everything's going to be all right!

BRIAN   (SEEING THE BOUNCY 'CASTLE' INFLATING) Oh my God, sweet Jesus of Nazareth!

CUT TO

13. EXT. PHOENIX CLUB CAR PARK. DAY
BRIAN AND CO. are gathered around ERIC's inflatable cock.

ERIC   Well, what do you think?

BRIAN   It's not a castle.

ERIC   You never said a castle.

JERRY   (IN SHOCK) We're not having that.

BRIAN   I said I wanted an inflatable.

ERIC   It is an inflatable.

BRIAN   It's ... inflatable filth, that's what it is.

KENNY SNR
          It's almost as big as mine, that.

BRIAN   Where did you get it?

ERIC   Big festival in Amsterdam, it's one
          of a set. I've got the other one in the
          van. Do you want to see it?

BRIAN   No, I do not.

JERRY   We're not having that.

BRIAN   You're damn right we're not having
          it, Jerry – it's going back! Go on –
          take it!

ERIC   But Brian ...

BRIAN   It's a family fun day, man!

ERIC   Yeah!

BRIAN   There's kiddies around, they can't
          go jumping up and down on a ...
          love length!

A muffled laugh from everybody, repeating.

ERIC   A what?

YOUNG KENNY
          Can we not disguise it?

BRIAN   Yeah ... we'll put a woolly hat on it
          and say it's you.

ERIC   It's not what it looks, Brian.

BRIAN   Not how it looks? It's a twenty-foot
          cock and balls, man. It doesn't look
          like nothing else! Get me Zantac,
          Kenny. It's not happening ...

ERIC starts laughing.

BRIAN   (cont.) What's so funny?

ERIC   (LAUGHING) Hey, Lance, he thinks
          this is how you have to have it ...
          No, no, Brian, the cock's optional.
          (SMACKING IT) All you do is strap it
          down here ... (HE ACTUALLY DOES
          THIS WHILE HE TELLS BRIAN)
          Whack some tarpaulin over it and –
          hey presto! – Sammy Snake.

BRIAN   Sammy Snake?! He's only got one
          eye.

*ERIC pulls two large velcro eyes out of his
bag and sticks them on either side of the
inflatable.*

ERIC   Oh no he hasn't. Ta-da!

BRIAN   What about the balls?

ERIC   (THINKING) Snake eggs ... kids love
          reptiles, Brian. You'll make a
          fortune.

BRIAN   (THINKS) Well, stick it in the corner.
          We'll have it!

ERIC   Lance!

*As BRIAN speaks, Lance reverses his van,
revealing the Big Pink Paradise at the rear
of the club. JERRY stares at it.*

BRIAN   I tell you what, Jerry, you've got to have eyes in the back of your arse in this business.

JERRY is looking in another direction.

JERRY   What's that?

BRIAN   What's what?

JERRY   That!

We cut to reveal a huge pink portakabin plonked beside the club. 'BRIAN POTTER AND THE BIG PINK PARADISE' written on the front of it in big letters.

BRIAN   Oh, that. That's my big pink paradise ... it's for the kids. Come on, I'll show you. Come on, Jerry, come on, up and at 'em! That's it! What do you think, eh? My big pink paradise.

CUT TO

14. INT. BRIAN POTTER'S PINK PARADISE. DAY

It's a portable toilet. The toilets have been ripped out and the interior painted bright

pink. There's a climbing frame (scaffolding), a slide and a ball pool (filled with tennis balls, footballs). There are also a couple of hand dryers with 'BRIAN POTTER AND THE HURRICANE DRYERS' on them (again, a parody of Harry Potter). A condom machine with Jerry the Berry's Chewy Treats.

JERRY   No, no, no ...

BRIAN   What?

JERRY   It's a portable toilet.

BRIAN   Forget that ... *was* a portable toilet, Jerry, not any more. It's a playroom for the kids. What do you think? Got the climbing frame there, look!

JERRY   What's that?

BRIAN   For the kids, little 'uns!

JERRY   Scaffolding? You gone mad?! Come and feel this (RUNS HIS HAND ALONG THE SCAFFOLDING) that'll take a kids eye out, that!

BRIAN   Bit of bubble wrap. It'll be right as rain – you'll never tell. Got a ball pool there, look. (POINTS)

JERRY   Where did you get those balls from?

BRIAN   Off the roof. Give them a rinse, good as new. Look at these, Jerry, look at these! (POINTS TO HAND DRYERS) Brian Potter and the Hurricane Hand Dryers. Watch this! (HE PRESSES THE BUTTON AND THE HOT AIR BLOWS OUT) They'll love 'em, love anything like that, little 'uns.

JERRY   Why's everything got Potter on it?

BRIAN   Potter's all the rage, Jerry. Kids love Potter. You not go to the pictures?

JERRY   No.

BRIAN   I've not forgot you, though, Jerry, not forgot you. Got you in there. Look at that! ... Jerry the Berry Fruity Penny Chews. (POINTS TO CONDOM MACHINE WITH A DRAWING OF JERRY DRESSED AS A BERRY.)

JERRY   Please God tell me that's not a condom machine.

BRIAN   *Was* a condom machine. Now it does penny chews at ten pence a piece. (LAUGHING) I don't know how I think them up, Jerry – I frighten myself!

JERRY   I'm sorry, Brian, it's not going to happen. I can't let this thing go up, look it's a bloody death trap.

BRIAN   But it's not finished, Jerry, it's not finished!

JERRY   I'm the licensee. They'll shut us down!

BRIAN   It's a bloody good thing this, kids will love it! Everything under one roof, Jerry, that's the future! A playroom for the kids – they'll lap it up!

JERRY   No, no, there's no way, it's not going to happen!

BRIAN   Right fine, I'll tell the papers not to bother coming down.

JERRY   You never said anything about papers.

BRIAN   Newspapers are coming down, TV were coming out, radio – they're all coming down this afternoon ... watch you do the grand official opening.

JERRY   Me? You never said anything about papers ...

BRIAN   Course I didn't Jerry. It was a surprise; it was a thank-you for dragging me out of the shit, helping me with the club.

JERRY   Yeh, well, I'm sure it will be all right for today. I mean ... you know, like you said, a bit of bubble wrap.

BRIAN   All you've got to do now is get into your costume.

JERRY   Costume? What costume?

BRIAN   I've told you, Jerry the Berry. (POINTS AT CONDOM MACHINE)

Cutaway of JERRY THE BERRY caricature on the condom machine.

END OF PART ONE

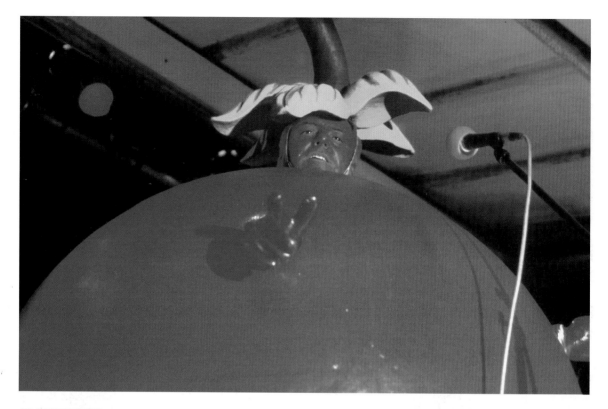

PART TWO

CUT TO

15. EXT. MAIN ROAD TO PHOENIX CLUB. DAY

JERRY   (IN BERRY COSTUME SINGING)
'Oh there'll be lots of laughter here today.
Come and join the fun in our parade.
He-haa! Mums and dads, boys and girls,
Grannies and granddads too –
We've got lots of incredible things for you
At the Phoenix Fun Day. Come and join the gang
At the Phoenix Fun Day, the best in all the land.
What's the place we all love best?
The Phoenix, the Phoenix, forget about all the rest ... oi!'

16. INT. FRENCH HYPERMARKET. DAY
MAX is pushing the trolley, still in his beret. MAX is browsing the shelves. PADDY is pointing out an English product that's written in French.

PADDY   Hey, Max, look at these... Les Cadbury's Fingeres ... Cadbury's Chocolate ... French.

TWO ORIENTAL MEN are browsing too. They bump trolleys with MAX and PADDY and apologise in their language.

ORIENTAL MAN
    Aaaah!

MAX   Sorry!

ORIENTAL MAN
    (IN PIDGIN ENGLISH) You France?

MAX   You what?

ORIENTAL MAN
          You French?

MAX   France? France, oh no, we're not
          France, my friend … no, no. We
          English my friend … (POINTS) We
          English! 'Rule Britannia'!

They go off, speaking and pointing in their
language.

ORIENTAL MAN
          Aah, 'Rule Britannia'!

MAX   Yeah, that's right!

The ORIENTAL MEN mumble to each other in
their own language.

MAX   (cont.) Beautiful language, Patrick,
          beautiful …

PADDY   What are they?

MAX   Haven't got a clue!

CUT TO

17. EXT. PHOENIX CLUB CAR PARK (GENERAL ACTIVITIES). DAY

Montage – establishing shot of fun day in full
swing. The car park is only a quarter full.
General activity shots. PEOPLE eating food.
CHILDREN on rides.

Montage – RAY VON is on the top of a fire
escape with tape player, speakers, lights,
commenting on the day into a radio mic.

RAY VON Shabbaaa! That's my welcome, everyone, to Fun Day at the Phoenix! ... What have we got for you today? We've got a bouncy castle and Sammy the Snake!

KENNY SNR
(SPEAKING TO KIDS AS THEY GET ON THE BOUNCY CASTLE) Take your shoes off the snake!

RAY VON (VO) Don't look at his eggs! You're coming to the rebirth of the Phoenix Club! Come and enjoy yourselves, spend a little bit of money!

CUT TO

18. EXT. PHOENIX CLUB CAR PARK (FACE-PAINTING). DAY
Montage – a gruff, nasty-looking GYPSY is spray-painting children's faces. He's clutching a BOY with one arm and spraying his face with an unmarked can of yellow car spray with the other. The obviously frightened BOY is holding a stencil mask up to his face. He takes the mask down and has the face of a tiger. The GYPSY motions for the next one to come forward. ANOTHER BOY steps forward, scared. Sign by the side: '£3 A FACE'. Collection tin on the table with the paints.

CUT TO

19. EXT. PHOENIX CLUB CAR PARK (MOBO-KARTS). DAY
Montage – we cut to 'THE MOBO-KARTS'. Three differently coloured shop-mobility carts drive round in a coned-off area. There's a (slightly altered) felt-tip sign 'MOBO-KARTS – £3' changed to '£3.60'.

RAY VON (VO) Why don't you try our fabulous Mobo-karts, if you fancy yourself as a bit of a Michael Schumacher? Why should the physically impaired have all the fun! Jump on board, break the speed limit.

CUT TO

20. INT. MADAM ZELDA'S TENT. DAY

It's dark. MARY is sitting behind a table with a crystal ball. She wears a cloak and yashmak affair. There's a collection tin by her side. The MIDDLE-AGED WOMAN peeps into the tent.

RAY VON (VO)

    Why don't you check out your future ... Madam Zelda. Maybe you don't have a future. Who knows? You pay the money you take your choice.

HOLY MARY

    Enter, my child.

The WOMAN enters and sits down.

CUSTOMER

    I wondered—

HOLY MARY

    First, cross my hand with gold.

CUSTOMER

    Gold?

HOLY MARY

    A pound, love.

The WOMAN hands over a pound.

HOLY MARY (cont.)

    Ta. Now, two questions only.

CUSTOMER

    A pound for two questions! Expensive, love, isn't it?

HOLY MARY

    Yes, it is, love. And your second question?

CUT TO

21. EXT. PHOENIX CLUB CAR PARK (CAR BOOT). DAY

Mini car-boot/jumble sale. JOYCE is running it. A MAN is holding up JERRY's jumper and pants. His WIFE nods approvingly. He buys them.

RAY VON (VO)

    A fabulous jumble sale! A selection of books, sporting goods and clothing! Shabba! Go and check them out!

CUT TO

22. EXT. PHOENIX CLUB CAR PARK (PINK PARADISE). DAY

BRIAN   I now declare Brian Potter's Big Pink Paradise open! Hey.

(APPLAUSE) Hey ... there you go! Whoa, whoa ... two quid – two quid a kid! Two quid – two quid a child, come on!

BRIAN is being interviewed by a REPORTER, she is writing.

REPORTER

    Well, what's this fun day in aid of?

BRIAN   Oh, it's the new Phoenix Club. The whole new Phoenix rising from the ashes! We've spearheaded a new campaign. Everything under one roof, that's the future.

REPORTER

    (GLANCES UP) Oh I see ... the new licensee, Jerry St Clair, is he around?

BRIAN He's around somewhere love, if I see him ... There he is! He's ... look at that: he loves getting involved, Jerry. There he is!

We cut to see a GROUP OF CHILDREN rolling JERRY (THE BERRY) at some speed through the car park. We hear him scream as he goes by: 'BRIAN!! BRIAN!'

CUT TO

23. INT. FRENCH HYPERMARKET. DAY

PADDY Who you texting?

MAX What?!

PADDY Who you texting?

MAX Potter ... let him know we're coming home.

As they push the trolleys full of beer across the road, a van almost hits them. It screeches to a halt.

MAX Whoa, whoa, whoa ... le beer for le dickhead! Can't you see?

CUT TO

24. EXT. PHOENIX CLUB CAR PARK. DAY

Montage – BRIAN is at the Bouncy Cock (Sammy The Snake) with KENNY SNR.

KENNY SNR
(OFF CAMERA TO BRIAN) ... yeah, I had to blow one of these up with my mouth once.

BRIAN Did you?

KENNY SNR
Oh, aye.

BRIAN Keep that snake tied up!

BRIAN's mobile beeps. He searches for it.

BRIAN (cont.) Hey up ...

BRIAN *gives him a look and then looks at his mobile. It's a text message. Cutaway of his screen. It reads, 'MISSION ACCOMPLISHED: ON R WAY BACK WITH BOOZE: M & P'.*

CUT TO

25. EXT. FRENCH HYPERMARKET. DAY
MAX *and* PADDY *are wheeling trolleys out through the front door, piled high with booze.*

CUT TO

26. EXT. FRENCH HYPERMARKET CAR PARK. DAY
MAX *and* PADDY *are (halfway) loading up the lorry.* MAX *stops to drink a can of beer.*

MAX	Oh, I tell you, it's beautiful, this!
PADDY	Hey, I've been thinking. We've got a shitload of this. How are we going to get it back through customs?
MAX	Don't worry. Piece of piss. I've got a plan.

CUT TO

27. EXT. PHOENIX CLUB CAR PARK. DAY
BRIAN *and* JERRY *(THE BERRY) walk through the fun day.*

JERRY   I can't believe you did the opening without me.

BRIAN   Well, you were busy, Jerry. You were playing with the children ... look at them, they love you, you're like the Pied Piper.

JERRY   Yeh, followed by rats!

BRIAN   Oh no, don't say that!

JERRY   Well ...

BRIAN   They're the future, Jerry!

JERRY   I look like an idiot.

BRIAN   You don't look like an idiot! You're like a hero, Jerry. Ridicule's nothing to be scared of. (A KID JUMPS ON BRIAN) Hey, will you sod off! I'm not a ride. Bring back the birch, little swines!

A shop-mobility cart drives through shot in front of them both with a YOUNG LAD riding it. BRIAN and JERRY just watch.

CUT TO

28. EXT. PHOENIX CLUB CAR PARK (CADILLAC RIDES). DAY
Montage – BRIAN'S Cadillac is by the road. A QUEUE OF CHILDREN. YOUNG KENNY is taking their money and pushing them into the already overloaded Cadillac. He struggles to shut the door. He bangs on the roof twice and it drives away.

CUT TO

29. EXT. PHOENIX CLUB CAR PARK (DARTS). DAY
Montage – darts game: 'THREE DARTS FOR A POUND, HIT THREE PLAYING CARDS, WIN A PRIZE'. A GYPSY is running the stall. A CUSTOMER (with a LITTLE GIRL pointing at

a cuddly toy) throws a dart. Cutaway as it hits the card. The MAN and the GIRL smile. He's won, the LITTLE GIRL is happy. We cut to the dart, hear a bang and see it fall out of the card and onto the floor.

STALLHOLDER
    Come on, lad, have a go! Oh, unlucky! Ooohhh!

CUSTOMER
    That's bollocks, that!

STALLHOLDER
    Gravity's a bitch. Have another go ...

CUSTOMER
    I'm not having that. I want me three quid back!

We cut to the back of the stall and see ANOTHER GYPSY holding a hammer, waiting to hear the sound of a dart. We hear a thud and he bangs on the wall.

CUT TO

30. EXT. UK DOCKS. DAY
Inside the lorry, MAX and PADDY are dressed as priests (THORN BIRD-style cassocks). PADDY is staring at MAX.

PADDY   Priests?

MAX   Have you never seen *The Cannonball Run*? Dean Martin and Sammy Davis Jnr. It worked for them.

PADDY   Which one am I?

MAX   Never mind which one you are ... shift your porn mag ... and put your rosemary beads on. We'll sail through. They're not going to suspect a couple of priests bringing in altar wine. Trust me.

PADDY   (NODS OUT OF WINDOW) Oh, I don't know, you reckon?

We cut to PADDY's POV. CUSTOMS OFFICERS have pulled a van over. THREE 'PRIESTS' are getting out, one of them smoking. Black shirt, dog collar, jeans and trainers.

We cut back to a CUSTOMS OFFICER. He waves MAX and PADDY's lorry forward. They pull up alongside him. We see (from his POV) MAX and PADDY both naked from the waist up, both sweating. PADDY's hair is stuck up.

CUSTOMS OFFICER
          Everything all right, boys?

They both nod nervously.

MAX   Oh, yeh ... yeh, everything's fine.

CUSTOMS OFFICER
          What have you got in the back?

MAX   Just some ... stuff.

PADDY   (NERVOUS) Stuff ... things ... this and that.

SECOND CUSTOMS OFFICER
          (SHOUTING, OUT OF SHOT) Dave, get here!

We cut back to see that a fight has broken out between the CUSTOMS OFFICERS and the 'PRIESTS'. The CUSTOMS OFFICERS have two of the PRIESTS pinned to the ground, one against the van. Another makes a run for it with tray of beer. We cut back to MAX and PADDY and the CUSTOMS OFFICER.

CUSTOMS OFFICER
          Wait here.

He exits shot and gives chase to one of the PRIESTS, who's making a run for it. MAX and PADDY exchange glances and then MAX puts his foot down.

PADDY   Go on Max, floor it!

MAX   How do we get out of here?

PADDY   I'll give you a clue....look at that sign over there E.X.I.T.

MAX   Excite?

PADDY   Exit!

MAX   Indicate, indicate! And we're out!

PADDY   Go on! Oh yes!

We cut to an exterior shot of the lorry. It screeches out of the line and drives off through the customs checkpoint. A few other vehicles decide to follow them, too. We cut to inside the lorry. MAX and PADDY are both cheering and laughing. They both do a high five. We hear music in the background.

CUT TO

31. EXT. PHOENIX CLUB CAR PARK. NIGHT

The fun day lit up. It's show time on ALAN's lorry. LES and ALAN are backing JERRY (THE BERRY) as he sings 'WALKIN' ON SUNSHINE'. The tables and chairs are now full – FAMILIES and REGULARS. BRIAN (with vase) is also watching.

We cut to BRIAN. DEN PERRY and his CRONIES come up behind him. DEN puffs cigar smoke, which causes him to cough.

BRIAN   (LOOKING ROUND) What do you want?

DEN PERRY
　　　　I've come to congratulate you, Potter, on your new open-air club.

BRIAN   Well, you've no right being here! Sod off, eh! We wouldn't be out here if it weren't for you! It's not an open-air club. It's family fun day!

DEN PERRY
　　　　A family fun day in November? I thought you'd have had a bonfire Brian ... Sorry, I forgot: you've already had one.

We cut to the bouncy penis. It's starting to overinflate. The 'SAMMY SNAKE' is starting to rise and pull tight and break free of the straps that are holding him down.

We cut back to JERRY on stage. We reach the rap bit of the song and JERRY turns to LES, a spotlight goes on him, and he performs the rap.

We cut back to DEN PERRY and BRIAN.

DEN PERRY
>   (REGARDING JERRY) Your lad's let himself go. Is he on steroids?

BRIAN   No, he's a berry, Perry … he's Jerry the Berry.

DEN PERRY
>   Is he? He looks like something Disney forgot to draw.

CUT TO

32. INT. THE PHOENIX CLUB GENTS' TOILETS. NIGHT

Brightly decorated. YOUNG KENNY is trying to wash his panda makeup off. He dips down and scrubs his face with water. Comes up and looks in the mirror: nothing's happened. He does it again, looks again: still nothing. He stares at himself, puzzled.

CUT TO

33. EXT. PHOENIX CLUB CAR PARK. NIGHT

KENNY SNR is watching the show from the front of the stage. He's left the bouncy penis unattended. He occasionally glances back to it but he's enjoying the show. We cut to the bouncy penis. It's lit with security lights and is positioned behind the lorry. A few kids still jumping up and down behind JERRY (THE BERRY). We cut to the compressor for the bouncy cock. TWO BOYS hanging around, they turn a lever on the compressor that increases its power. They laugh and run off.

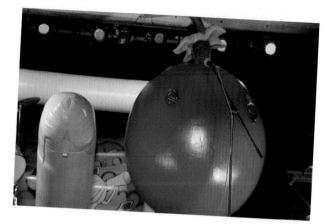

The inflatable cock inflates higher and rises up out of the tarpaulin. We cut to the front of the stage to see it rise up in all its glory. It continues inflating. JERRY is still singing.

We cut to BRIAN, who is taking a drink. He does a double-take and stares at it. DEN PERRY and his CRONIES laugh. The AUDIENCE reaction is mixed: some people laugh and cheer. But a lot of the PARENTS aren't happy – when they realise what it is, they desperately attempt to shield their children's eyes.

BRIAN   Aaaagh! Get it down! Get it down!

We cut to KENNY SNR. He's trying to jump and reach the inflatable cock in order to pull it down.

We cut to DEN PERRY and his POV of KENNY SNR.

DEN PERRY
>   You've excelled yourself this time, Potter, eh?! Family fun day, eh?!

BRIAN   Get it down!

We cut to the front of the stage. KENNY SNR runs round the side of the lorry, waving and shouting.

CUT TO

34. INT. THE PHOENIX CLUB GENTS' TOILETS. NIGHT

YOUNG KENNY is still trying to wash his face but the makeup is clearly not coming off. He's starting to panic and wash it faster.

CUT TO

35. EXT. PHOENIX CLUB CAR PARK. NIGHT

KENNY SNR
 It's gonna blow! Get back! Brian, Brian!

DEN PERRY
 Oh, Christ!

The inflatable cock explodes. We cut back to see the CROWD being showered with the debris from it.

CUT TO

36. INT. THE GAMES ROOM. NIGHT

Collection tins on the snooker table. BRIAN and YOUNG KENNY count the money. The room is dimly lit. Snooker light on.

BRIAN (COUNTING THE MONEY) Come on, bring it on!

YOUNG KENNY
 I've tried everything – I've tried Swarfega, soap and water, everything they've got – it won't come off.

BRIAN Have you tried bleach? Acid … Battery acid, that's a good remover.

YOUNG KENNY
 Everything … nothing, it won't come off, I told you. I've been scrubbing for ages.

BRIAN Well, don't scrub too hard … end up looking like me laddo there … a face like a smacked arse! What's the matter with you, man?!

Cut to JERRY standing in corner. He is wearing a woman's fun-fur coat, no trousers and flip flops. He still has a red face and hair.

JERRY What's the matter with me? I'll tell you what's the matter with me! Me first week as licensee. I'm stood here looking like a … a gay Satan because somebody sold all me clothes as jumble. I've been rolled round car park all day dressed as a hernia … and I've got twelve people in casualty with rubber burns.

BRIAN   Rubber burns ... wasn't he a
         Scottish poet?

JERRY   Very funny.

KENNY SNR comes in.

BRIAN   Have you swept that cock up, you?

KENNY SNR
         Most of it ... one of the balls went
         over a garden and they said we
         can't have it back. (LAUGHS)

BRIAN   Very funny.

KENNY SNR
         Max and Paddy are here with
         your beer.

BRIAN   Oh, good.

CUT TO

37. EXT. PHOENIX CLUB CAR PARK. NIGHT
*The lorry is parked. MAX and PADDY are
opening the back.*

*BRIAN, JERRY (woman's fur coat), KENNY
SNR, YOUNG KENNY (tiger), RAY VON, LES,
ALAN, MADAM ZELDA.*

MAX   Wait till you see this.

BRIAN   Crack it open ... (RUBBING HIS
         HANDS TOGETHER) and let the good
         times roll.

*We cut to the back doors. They open. We see
the TWO ORIENTAL MEN whom we saw
earlier at the French hypermarket. They
stagger to their feet, both holding bottles and
surrounded by empties. They shield their*

eyes from the light ... and then recognise
MAX and PADDY.

ORIENTAL MAN
      (SMILING) 'Rule Blitannia'!!

BRIAN   'Rule Britannia'?

CUT TO

END CREDITS

38. INT. THE PHOENIX CLUB

BRIAN and other CLUB MEMBERS watching
an audition. A scantily clad woman pulls out
some little coloured balls.

BRIAN   A bit of juggling, yeh ... a bit of
          juggling ... Oh, no ... oh, no ...
          What's she doing now? Whoa, whoa,
          whoa!

WOMAN auditioning on her back with her
legs apart.

LES   She's not wearing any—

BRIAN   I know. I can see, Leslie! What's she
          doing?

Ping-pong balls are flying all over the place.

BRIAN   (cont.) Next! No! Next! Next! Oh.
          Ah ... next! Where are they coming
          from?! She only had four!

THE END

Episode 3

PART ONE

1. EXT. JERRY'S OFFICE. DAY
We see JERRY's office door. Brass plate reads, 'JERRY ST CLAIR – LICENSEE'. We can hear BRIAN through the door.

CUT TO

2. INT. JERRY'S OFFICE. DAY
BRIAN's behind his desk, on the phone. The receiver is tucked under his chin. He appears to be masturbating.

BRIAN   ... straight up, keep going, keep going, oh, yeh ... oh, yeh ... That's it as far as you can go. Right up, no, right up, right up as far as you can go ... (PULLS HIS GLASSES OUT FROM UNDER HIS DESK, WHERE HE'S BEEN CLEANING THEM. PUTS THEM ON) That's it we're a hundred yards down on your left love. That's right, just past the dry cleaners. All right.

RAY VON sticks his head round the door.

RAY VON Mr Potter.

BRIAN   Do you not knock?

RAY VON It depends. Have you got a minute? I just want to show you something.

BRIAN   Jesus, I've just sat down.

CUT TO

3. EXT. MAIN ROAD. DAY
RAY's pushing BRIAN. He comes to a stop on the pavement.

BRIAN   Well, what do you want to show me?

RAY VON This ...

BRIAN   A speed trap, who's put that there?

RAY VON (PROUD) Me.

BRIAN   Are you out of your mind?

RAY VON Well you're always saying you want more members.

BRIAN   (CONFUSED) Yeah ... and?

RAY VON What do you do when you see a speed trap?

BRIAN   (THINKS) I'm in a wheelchair, son. It's not a problem.

RAY VON You slow down. We get loads of cars going by the club each day but they go by too fast to notice. With this they see the markings, they hit their brakes, then they hit the pressure pad, which triggers the sign.

BRIAN   What sign?

RAY VON Young Kenny?!

RAY VON points. BRIAN turns.

Cut to reveal a large bus-shelter case by the side of the road. There is a blanket covering it. YOUNG KENNY (with tiger's face) pulls it off.

BRIAN   Oh yes, oh yes, I like that! Oh very good! It's not wired to the lamppost, is it?

RAY VON (QUICKLY) No, now they'll see the sign and pull into the car park! All we've got to do now is wait for a car.

BRIAN   Hmm ... yeh ... yeh.

CUT TO

OPENING CREDITS

CUT TO

4. EXT. MAIN ROAD. DAY
All three of them still waiting for a car. RAY VON's face lights up.

RAY VON Here's one now!

BRIAN   Thank God for that. I'm going away in June.

RAY VON Watch this, watch this ... he'll see the white marks ...

We cut to interior of car and see POV of white lines. Cut to exterior as the car slams on brakes.

RAY VON (cont.) ... now your little pressure pad and bingo!

The car drives over the pressure pad. We cut to the sign. It lights up, flashing bulbs, police lights, the works.

Typical of RAY VON, we hear cheesy music with RAY's voice over the top in a dramatic tone.

BRIAN   (THROUGH SMILING TEETH) In a bit, indicate, son, indicate, indicate!

We see from POV of the sign as the car drives slowly past. We cut back to exterior shot of DRIVER's reaction. We see DRIVER's POV of BRIAN, RAY VON and YOUNG KENNY in a line, smiling, beckoning him in.

DRIVER Jesus Christ!

We cut to exterior as the car screeches away.

We cut to BRIAN's, RAY VON's and YOUNG KENNY's reactions. A few beats of silence.

BRIAN   Well, I don't know how we're gonna fit them all in the car park, Ray, I really don't.

CUT TO

5. INT. SOLARIUM. DAY
MAX and PADDY are in the 'sarolium' on the sun beds. The room is brightly lit with ultraviolet light. We hear 'CLUB TROPICANA' by WHAM!

PADDY   (HALF ASLEEP) This is the life.

MAX   Oh, you know it, my friend.

The song is interrupted by the sound of a tannoy.

HOLY MARY
          Order number two, your food's ready.

MAX   That's us ...

He sits up, sees PADDY with his arse out.

PADDY   Yeh.

MAX   Oh, cover your arse up, man!

CUT TO

6. INT. TONY KNOWLES SUITE. DAY
REGULARS playing snooker. A side door marked 'SAROLIUM' opens. MAX and PADDY exit both wearing 'LE PONDEROSA HOTEL, BLACKPOOL' robes and flip-flops. MAX with goggles on his forehead. (Spill of ultraviolet light) the MEN playing snooker look up.

PADDY   Max ... women like a brown arse.

MAX   I've never had a brown arse.

PADDY   You've never had any women.

We cut to MAX and PADDY. They arrive at the bar area – their food's already there. KENNY SNR sits at the side of them. The TV is on. Few REGULARS. The room is done out like a café.

MAN IN CLUB
          (LAUGHS) Look at these two! (WOLF WHISTLE IN BACKGROUND) Get some clothes on!

MAX   You'll never know how many women I've loved and lost.

PADDY   Where do you take them, back to –
your mum's?

MAX   I've got the Volvo.

*Cut to JOYCE serving behind the bar. She
pretends to pull a pint. We cut behind the
bar and reveal that she's topping up the
man's pint with a bottle of French beer.
She hands it to the CUSTOMER. (There are
other pints ready to be topped
up.) A DELIVERY MAN with
boxes of crisps, an order form
and a pen in his mouth enters
the room.*

JOYCE   There you are, my
darling. (HANDING
MAN HIS PINT) That's
one twenty, please.

MAN IN CLUB
    Thank you.

JOYCE   Thank you, sweetheart
… (ADDRESSING MAX
AND PADDY) Get some
clothes on!

MAX   We're in the sarolium!

KENNY SNR
    (TAKES A BITE OF HIS
FOOD) Urgghhh … that
tastes like horseshit
that – and I've tasted
horseshit.

PADDY   You talk shit.

MAX   Urrrggghhh … they're
stone-cold, these!
What's going on?

CUT TO

7. INT. KITCHEN. DAY
*The STOWAWAYS are stir-frying frozen chips
(slight flash fire). There are baguettes and
salad all ready on the side. HOLY MARY
enters carrying plates of half-eaten food.*

HOLY MARY
    (MOUTHING) No, no, no. No wonder
they're cold. You don't stir-fry chips.
No, no, no!

The STOWAWAYS copy HOLY MARY. 'NO, NO, NO, NO, NO.' They then continue in their own language.

CUT TO

8. INT. BRIAN'S OFFICE. DAY

BRIAN's on the phone. Opening mail. We go to a cutaway of the envelope in his hand, addressed to JERRY ST CLAIR. He rips it open. It reads 'HAFIZ CASH AND CARRY'.

BRIAN   Hello, Frank, it's Brian. How are you, you old bugger? How's Blackpool? Have you still got ... Potter ... Brian Potter ... yeh, yeh. Oh ... oh, yeh ... No, not three bad. No, everything's going, everything's up and running, yeh. Yeh, yeh, we've been open now, everything's ... What? No, I took your advice. Balls to the brewery! Balls to 'em! Yeh, I sent the doormen to France on a booze run. Yeh, oh aye, they got plenty. Eh, they got they got two stowaways 'n'all ... yeh! Fell off the back of a lorry ... so he did ... yeh. I don't know where they're from. No, they can't speak ... speak a word of English. No, have I hell, no. I've ... I've got them working in the kitchens ... earning their keep.

CUT TO

9. INT. BRIAN'S OFFICE. DAY

BRIAN is still on the phone to FRANK. There's a knock at the door.

DELIVERY LAD
    Jerry St Clair?

BRIAN   (CLICKS HIS FINGERS. THE LAD HANDS HIM THE ORDER. BRIAN SIGNS IT) Yes, well, you know what

it is ... well it's not, I mean ... I've got Jerry running the show. Well, he thinks he is.

CUT TO

10. EXT. MAIN ROAD. DAY

We see JERRY's car coming down the road. We cut to interior. JERRY's singing along to 'LOVELY DAY' by BILL WITHERS. He drinks while still steering. He leans over to turn the stereo up, sees the speed trap and brakes. Cutaway of his foot on the brake. He jolts forward, dropping his coffee.

We cut to exterior and hear the car horn beep. We hear the Phoenix Club sign 'CONGRATULATIONS, DRIVER'.

CUT TO

11. INT. TONY KNOWLES SUITE. DAY

JERRY's sitting at the bar – busted nose, bloodstained cotton wool. HOLY MARY is nursing him. BRIAN is there and a FEW REGULARS. JERRY moans in pain.

JERRY   Oooh ... ahh!

HOLY MARY
    Sorry, love ... Oh, Jerry what a shame.

JERRY   Aaaah!

BRIAN   Shut up, you girl! You should have had your seat belt on.

JERRY   I *did* have my seatbelt on! I just weren't expecting a speed trap in the middle of the road? Who put that there?

BRIAN   Ray Von ... he's trying to get more people in.

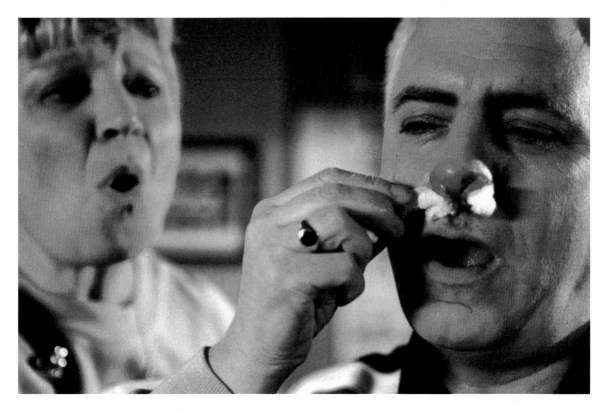

JERRY   In where – casualty?

BRIAN   (SEES JERRY'S WET CROTCH) Have you pissed yourself?

JERRY   No, it's coffee. Why didn't you stop him?

BRIAN   Me stop him? You're the licensee. You stop him.

JERRY   (TAKES A TABLET) Am I? Am I the licensee? I am when it suits you …

BRIAN   What do you mean by that?

JERRY   You know what it means, you know what's going on here, you think I don't know, but I do know. I know what's going on (TAKES SOME TABLETS), you're running this place, not me. I'm just a puppet here.

BRIAN   A puppeteer? Do you do kids' parties? You're paranoid, that's what you are. Look at you, eh! It's those drugs you're on. No wonder your bladder's caved in: you're smacked up to your tits.

JERRY   Herbal medication, Brian, I've told you before. This has knocked me karma out of kilter. I've got to rebalance me yin and yang.

BRIAN   What are they? Singing pigs?

HOLY MARY
          No! That's Pinky and Perky!

JOYCE   Hey, there's a lad here to see you for the bar job.

JERRY   Hey, whoa, whoa, whoa – where are you going?

BRIAN   (MOVES FORWARD) I'm going to see the lad.

JERRY   Oh, it won't take two of us. Remember, Brian, I'm the licensee.

BRIAN   (MIMICKING JERRY) I'm the licensee!

CUT TO

12. INT. GALAXY LOUNGE. DAY
JERRY's interviewing the BAR LAD. Cotton wool up the nose.

JERRY   Right! Come here, son. I'm Jerry St Clair, I'm the licensee.

SPENCER All right.

JERRY   Sit down there. Spencer, isn't it?

SPENCER That's right.

JERRY   I never forget a face.

SPENCER Spencer for hire – and may I suggest that you remove the 'situation vacant' sign in the window and replace it with one that reads 'situation full'? I'm your man.

JERRY   Right good. Tell me, Spencer, have you had any previous experience with bar work?

SPENCER Oh, yes. You name it. Not only have I seen the film *Cocktail* six times, I also once was an innkeeper.

JERRY   Really?

SPENCER Yes.

JERRY   Where was that?

SPENCER In Bethlehem. Er, in St Peter and Paul's groundbreaking production of *The Nativity*. Not only did I give Mary and Joseph room at the inn, I also offered them *en suite* with full English and a lovely view of Galilee.

JERRY   Galilee?

SPENCER Yeh.

JERRY   Right.

CUT TO

13. INT. TONY KNOWLES SUITE. DAY

KENNY SNR takes a pair of women's reading glasses from a mannequin's head on the bar. 'PHOENIX CLUB GLASSES – PLEASE RETURN'. BRIAN watches HOLY MARY polish a framed photograph of TONY KNOWLES on the wall. A plaque underneath reads 'THE TONY KNOWLES SUITE'.

BRIAN   (TO HOLY MARY) That's it! Shine him up ... they don't make men like TK any more. He broke a million hearts – on and off the table.

HOLY MARY
    (WHISPERS) Million and one.

HOLY MARY kisses her hand and touches TONY KNOWLES's face on the photo, then exits. YOUNG KENNY enters the room carrying some stepladders. He climbs up some stepladders and hangs the new stepladders on the ceiling. BRIAN, astonished, watches him.

BRIAN   Jesus wept! Hey, Tiger Woods, what have I told you about using my walls as a skip. Bloody junk!

YOUNG KENNY
    Well, Jerry likes it.

BRIAN   He will: he's a junkie.

KENNY SNR
    Hey, look at this. Den Perry's taken out a full-page ad. (BRINGS IT OVER)

BRIAN   He's what? (LOOKS AT IT) The shithouse ...

Cutaway full-page colour advert. DEN in the corner with a speech bubble coming out of his mouth.

KENNY SNR
    'The Banana Grove. Come and lose yourself in our new Bermuda Triangle suite. Top Jewish tribute act Rabbi Williams.'

SPENCER Yeh, um … 'Dear Mr St Clair, Spencer would be great behind a bar.' That's from my mum, that one. (POINTS) Er, my old woodwork teacher, Mr Haroon, he says, 'Spencer will definitely end up behind a bar.'

JERRY It says 'bars', this … someone's crossed the 's' off.

SPENCER Have they?

JERRY It says 'bars', this.

CUT TO

15. INT. TONY KNOWLES SUITE. DAY
BRIAN, RAY VON, YOUNG KENNY and KENNY SNR sit watching the TV. The TWO STOWAWAYS enter carrying food for BRIAN, speaking their language.

BRIAN Oh, here they go, here they go! Come on, I'm ready for this! (THEY WALK STRAIGHT PAST HIM) Whoa, whoa, whoa! (WHISTLES) Oy, I'm here, come on. (THEY COME BACK WITH BRIAN'S FOOD) Haven't got a clue, haven't got a clue, you know?

YOUNG KENNY
(UP LADDERS) He's good, him …

BRIAN 'Forget the rest … they're second best … The Banana Grove beats the rest'. He's rhymed 'rest' with 'rest' – he's no class.

YOUNG KENNY
Why don't we get one of these?

BRIAN And are you going to pay for it?

We hear a car screech outside, followed by a beep, then the 'IT'S THE PHOENIX CLUB' jingle. RAY VON jumps up and goes to the window.

BRIAN Anything?

RAY VON turns and shakes his head.

CUT TO

14. INT. GALAXY LOUNGE. DAY
JERRY interviewing SPENCER.

JERRY Those are your references, are they?

I'll have a black milkshake and pound of piss ... Hey nothing, nothing. See ... see Ant and Dec, there they go. (TAKES THE TOP OFF THE ROLL AND REVEALS CHARCOAL-BURNT CHIPS UNDERNEATH) Oh, oh, oh, oh, sweet child of mine ... they've cremated my chips!

Cutaway of BRIAN's chips.

BRIAN   (cont.) (WHACKS IT ON THE TABLE) Like mummies dicks.

Advert comes on the TV for CRIMETIME.

TRAILER (VO) Tonight on Crimetime ... the brutal assault of a Birmingham pensioner – have you seen this man? Police probe Leeds girl snatch – can you help? And a violent armed robbery of a high street jeweller's – does any of this ring a bell?

Cut to exterior shot of a jewellery shop. We clearly see the name and telephone number of the shop plus various signs in the window of special offers and price reductions.

RAY VON That's very clever.

We see the reconstruction on screen. A WOMAN ASSISTANT stands back while TWO MEN in bob hats stuff diamond rings on display trays into a holdall.

BRIAN   What?

RAY VON That! Well, it's blatant advertising, isn't it? A jeweller gets robbed. Now he knows the insurance are going to pay him out but he gets *Crimetime* in to film a reconstruction. He gets free publicity on national television

and it hasn't cost him a penny.
TRAILER (VO) Join us tonight, you know the time ... it's *Crimetime*.

A graphic comes on screen displaying the time. 9.00 P.M.

CUT TO

16. INT. GALAXY LOUNGE. DAY

JERRY   And what made you apply for this job?

SPENCER The DSS.

JERRY   And ... and why do you think I should give it to you?

SPENCER Because it'll be the DSS pay me wages and it won't cost you a penny.

JERRY   Really?

SPENCER Yeh.

JERRY   When can you start? Welcome to the Phoenix, Spencer lad! (SPENCER LAUGHS) Welcome aboard!

SPENCER Great!

CUT TO

17. INT. TONY KNOWLES SUITE. DAY
KENNY SNR is telling a story, mapping it out with BRIAN's burnt chips and salad. Only YOUNG KENNY is listening to him. RAY VON is watching TV.

BRIAN   Hang on! That's it? That's bloody it! ... Talk about wood for trees, that's what we'll do ... We'll get the crime team in, the TV boys or whoever they are – they can reconstruct us.

RAY VON Reconstruct what?

BRIAN Us burning down, the club burning down, the night of the fire ... think of the publicity, national television. They must get a hundred million viewers, easy ... That's better than any bloody crappy newspaper ad and it won't cost us a penny ...

RAY VON Look, that's what I said.

BRIAN ... and we can catch Den Perry 'n'all, send him down for arson, the fat pig, two birds, one stone. (LAUGHS)

KENNY SNR
        Why would they want to come here?

BRIAN Cause we're an unsolved crime, Poirot. The Joe Public ... he loves a good mystery blaze ... Oh yes, wait 'til I tell Jerry this, he's going to love this! I don't know how I think them up!

END OF PART ONE

PART TWO

18. EXT. MAIN ROAD/PHOENIX CLUB CAR PARK. NIGHT
A white van approaches the club – 'CRIMETIME – TV'S CRIME CRUSADERS' on the side. It hits the speed trap in the road and sets off the sign. We cut to the 'IT'S THE PHOENIX CLUB' sign.

We cut to see the van pulling onto the packed car park. TV CREW lights/trailers/ catering all camped in the car park. General

hubbub. Few cutaways, lights going on.

CUT TO

19. EXT. THE PHOENIX CLUB. NIGHT

The DIRECTOR (CHRIS) gets out. A CREW MEMBER points him towards BRIAN. We cut to BRIAN (in Sunday best), who is telling a SPARK to angle his light on the Phoenix Club sign.

BRIAN   Turn it up! Put it on the side, pointing to the sign.

CREW MEMBER
    All right, mate.

BRIAN   To the sign ... there you are! What watt is it?

CREW MEMBER
    Two K.

BRIAN   UK? Put it on the sign, that's what you want.

CHRIS   Mr Potter?

BRIAN   Yeh.

CHRIS   I'm Chris, the director. We spoke on the phone.

BRIAN   Are you? I thought you were a girl ... Well, all right ... Well there you go. Here we are, nice to meet you. This is the Phoenix. Burnt but not beaten, singed but not ... Come on I'll show you where they found the first body.

CUT TO

20. INT. FOYER. NIGHT

BRIAN, CHRIS and the first AD walk down the foyer. An ELDERLY MAN, who's dressed like BRIAN, also in a wheelchair, comes towards them down the corridor.

KENNY SNR
    It's been all hands on dick. We've rebuilt her from nothing, you know.

BRIAN   (SEES THE LOOKALIKE) Whoa, whoa, whoa! Who's he?

CHRIS   Oh, that's Tom, an actor, he'll be playing you.

BRIAN   He'll be playing me? I'll be playing me ... Go on, get up, go on, off you go!

CHRIS   But I thought that—

BRIAN   You thought wrong, that's what you thought – you thought nothing!

TOM (THE ACTOR) stands up and walks away. BRIAN watches him.

CHRIS   But Mr Potter, have you ever worked in TV before?

BRIAN   Have I ever worked in TV before? Oooh, Mr TV, pal, eh? You name it, I've done it ... *Band of Gold, Queer* as *Folk* – played one of the folk. You just shout 'cut' and I'll do the rest.

CUT TO

21. INT. PHOENIX CLUB. NIGHT

CHRIS   OK camera rolling and ...

CREW MEMBER
        Slate forty-one, take one ...
        (SOUND FROM CLAPPERBOARD)

CHRIS   And action!

BRIAN   Now?! We were busier than this. We were full! It was Talent Trek, man, the hottest night in clubland. We were jam packed! Cut that!

We jump-cut. Clapperboard claps in shot. In the background now stands RAY VON and the TWO STOWAWAYS (in bright shell suits and wearing flat caps) holding pints. BRIAN wheels himself down the aisle towards RAY VON and the STOWAWAYS.

BRIAN   Good evening ...

They answer BRIAN in CHINESE.

CHRIS   Cut!

BRIAN   What?

CHRIS   Boom in!

BRIAN   Boom in? What's boomin'?

CHRIS   Boom in!

BRIAN   We were booming but you can't tell, can you? There's no frigger in! I keep saying ... where are the extras you promised us?!

See clapperboard ...

BRIAN   (cont.) Say it again, son.

Someone sneezes.

CHRIS   Action!

185

BRIAN   Bless you! You've got a sneeze in here. I'm sorry ... I'm sorry ... cut!

CUT TO

22. EXT. MAIN DOOR. NIGHT

MAX and PADDY in luminous tabards ('TV CREW' written on them), baseball caps ('CRIMETIME – AS SEEN ON TV'). They both have radios.

PADDY   (SHOWING MAX THE WALKIE-TALKIE) Push that in, don't put your thumb over that.

MAX   Can you hear me?

PADDY   I can – I'm stood at the side of you.

MAX   Yeh I know, but can you hear me through this? ... How you doing? Paddy are you there?

PADDY   Yes, yes I'm here!

We cut back to CHRIS in galaxy lounge. He's looking at his radio.

CUT TO

23. INT./EXT. MAIN DOOR/GALAXY LOUNGE (INTERCUT). NIGHT

A FEW EXTRAS in shot. BRIAN is going for a take. JOYCE sitting at table as extra.

CHRIS   (INTO RADIO) OK, quiet, please.

MAX   OK, quiet please.

CHRIS   We're going for a take.

MAX   (INTO RADIO) We're going, we are going for a take.

CHRIS   Who is this?

MAX   Who's this?

CHRIS   What channel are you on?

PADDY   Tell him.

MAX   (OS) ITV ... ITV, I think.

CHRIS   Would somebody sort them out?

We jump-cut again. Clapperboard in shot. BRIAN has just gone past the STOWAWAYS and approaches MARION.

CREW MEMBER
    Slate forty-one, take seven.

Clapperboard.

BRIAN   Thank you.

CHRIS   Action!

BRIAN   Good evening.

COOK   (DRESSED AS CUSTOMER) Heyo ...

RAY VON All right, Mr Potter?

BRIAN   Yes. Good evening, Joyce.

JOYCE   All right, Brian, we're busy tonight ...

BRIAN   (POSH VOICE) Well, we will be, we're the Phoenix Club, the country's premiere entertainment complex ... with a sarolium ...

MAX   (ON WALKIE-TALKIE) Let's get Potter ...

PADDY   Let's do Potter ... Go on!

MAX   Taxi for Potter, taxi for Potter. (LAUGHING)

BRIAN   Oh God!

MAX   Outside ... over!

BRIAN   It's those two tits ... you should go and tell them! A couple of clowns, I had it in the bag then! There was none of this on *Bergerac*!

We cut outside to see MAX and PADDY laughing.

We jump-cut to the clapperboard. BRIAN is in the same position. RAY VON and STOWAWAYS in position. BRIAN is rolling through the club.

CUT TO

24. INT. GALAXY LOUNGE. NIGHT
BRIAN is having his makeup done.

BRIAN   I see ... oh it's very therapeutic. They used to touch me up on *Taggart*, you know. I played a drugs baron ...

FIRST ASSISTANT
    (TO CHRIS) That's understood, thank you ...

CHRIS   Can we go?

FIRST ASSISTANT
    No, still waiting for Mr Perry.

BRIAN   What? What? Wait on who?

FIRST ASSISTANT
    Mr Perry.

BRIAN   *Den* Perry?

FIRST ASSISTANT
    Yeh.

BRIAN   Christ, don't have him down here. He was the one that torched the bloody place.

The door opens and DEN PERRY walks in, cigar in hand.

DEN PERRY
    Right, where do you want me?

CUT TO

25. INT. GALAXY LOUNGE. NIGHT
BRIAN and DEN set ready for shot.

BRIAN   You've got a nerve showing your face round here, Perry! Bloody damn cheek!

DEN PERRY

    Always glad to be of help, Brian,
    you know me. Now do you know
    your lines?

BRIAN   Do I know my lines? Do I ... Yes, you
    just watch, I'll act you off the bloody
    screen.

DEN PERRY

    Ahhh but what's your motivation?

BRIAN   What! I've got plenty of motivation
    fat boy. To see you in jail, biting a
    pillow on D wing.

CHRIS   Camera rolling ... and action.

CREW MEMBER

    Slate forty-three, take one!

BRIAN   He did it! He did it ... He's in there,
    he burnt the club down. That's who
    you want, him ...

DEN PERRY

    I can't work with this. I'll be in my
    trailer.

BRIAN   Trailer? He's got a trailer?

CUT TO

26. INT. GALAXY LOUNGE. NIGHT

*BRIAN has got everybody in a circle. YOUNG
KENNY (foundation face), KENNY SNR,
HOLY MARY, JOYCE, SPENCER, RAY VON
and the TWO STOWAWAYS.*

BRIAN   Right, huddle up ... huddle up ...
    everything's going well, but what ...
    (TIME OUT. SEES YOUNG KENNY)
    What have you got on your face now?

YOUNG KENNY

    It's foundation.

BRIAN   Whose? Michael Jackson's? Right,
    things are going well but we've not
    advertising enough. We've got to
    blatantly advertise, sell, sell, sell
    the Phoenix – this is our big
    chance, right?

TOGETHER

    Right, right!

We cut to CHRIS.

CHRIS   Cut! Get it up!

BRIAN   Get what up? Get what up ...
    what?

CHRIS   The sign, bloody sign!

BRIAN   What sign, what's he on about?

CUT TO

27. INT. GALAXY LOUNGE. NIGHT

*DEN and BRIAN are in their positions.
Behind them at the bar we see SPENCER
and HOLY MARY. SPENCER is a customer
and is drinking a pint of beer.*

CHRIS   Right, remember, you're just
    watching the show and listening to
    the music.

CREW MEMBER

    Slate forty-four, take one.

Clapperboard.

CHRIS   And action!

In the background HOLY MARY is serving SPENCER.

SPENCER And there you go.

HOLY MARY
            Oh, thank you, and that is a lovely
            silky smooth pint.

SPENCER Oh, and here's your change,
            madam.

HOLY MARY
            Oh thank you, oh no you've given
            me too much change, surely that
            can't be right?

SPENCER Well, this is the Phoenix Club,
            madam.

They both turn to camera and smile.

CHRIS   Cut!

BRIAN   But why? That's exactly how it
            happened! That's exactly how it
            happens every night of the week!

CUT TO

28. INT. GALAXY LOUNGE. NIGHT
*JERRY enters the Galaxy Lounge. He is
wearing leather pants and his hair is dyed
dark brown/jet black.*

JERRY   Right, Chris, where do you want me?

BRIAN   Eh, Jerry, look at that, eh, what
            have you got on?! Have you dyed
            your hair or have you gone
            prematurely maroon?

JERRY   Leave it out.

BRIAN   Oh, I like that. Leather pants? Go
            and get your dad, tell him he's on.

CHRIS   If we could just have you on the
            stage, Mr St Clair.

CUT TO

29. INT. GALAXY LOUNGE. NIGHT
*JERRY is on stage singing 'REACH FOR THE
STARS' by S CLUB 7. LES ALANOS backing
him. JERRY turns around to reveal 'JERRY
ST CLAIR, COMPERE FOR HIRE' (and a
mobile). ALAN reacts. He hits the side of his
keyboard, an advert rolls down the front:
'LES ALANOS – THE BEST BACKING IN
CLUBLAND [AND A MOBILE], ANY TUNE,
ANY PLACE, ANYWHERE'. The song reaches
its climax. An enormous banner advertising
the club rolls down, covering almost all the
stage and JERRY. Two flash pots explode.
We cut to CHRIS and the CREW standing
open-mouthed. BRIAN is clapping.*

CUT TO

30. EXT. THE PHOENIX CLUB. NIGHT
*We see a shot of the CRIMETIME van – a
CREW MEMBER loading the last piece of
equipment into it. He slams the doors.*

BRIAN   Eh ... fantastic, eh, put that on your
            TV programme!

*We jump-cut. BRIAN AND CO. wave as the
van screeches off. It hits the speed trap once
again: 'CONGRATULATIONS DRIVER ...'*

BRIAN   (SHOUTING AFTER THEM) See you,
            son ... We'll let you know if we find
            your *Crimetime* lights. All the best.
            Ta-ta!

HOLY MARY

    Aah lovely.

BRIAN   (TO JERRY) Well, Jerry, do you think we exposed the club enough?

JERRY   Oh, aye, a great job. Well done, everybody ...

They all congratulate each other.

CUT TO

31. INT. TONY KNOWLES SUITE. DAY

We see a poster 'SEE THE PHOENIX CLUB LIVE ON TV'S CRIMETIME – HERE!! WEDNESDAY 21ST ONLY £3.50 INCLUDING BUFFET'. We track off the poster with a REGULAR and reveal the room packed. Everyone in front of the television. We cut to the screen – CRIMETIME is on. The

PRESENTER is talking in the studio.

PRESENTER

    Your calls will be treated in the strictest confidence and the lines are open till midnight. We'll bring you an update at eleven after *An Audience with Jockey Wilson*.

RAY VON Is it on?

MAX   Sssshhh!

PRESENTER
    Now we go back to November of
    last year, and to the Phoenix Club
    in Bolton ...

There is a huge cheer.

PRESENTER (Cont.)
    It was the grand final of Talent
    Trek. A night (SOMEONE CLAPS) of
    fun and laughter, but a night that
    was to turn to tragedy. A mysterious
    blaze swept through the Phoenix
    Club, devastating it. The club's
    owner, Brian Potter, now takes up
    the story.

*Cut to shot of the club. There is another
cheer from the REGULARS.*

BRIAN   (VO) (THERE IS A BOO FROM
    EVERYBODY) I'll never forget the
    night of the fire. It wasn't an
    ordinary night. It was the grand
    final of Talent Trek, the most
    prestigious night in clubland,
    that we'd held concurrently for
    three years.

The reconstruction cuts to YOUNG KENNY.

YOUNG KENNY
    Good evening sir, enjoy Talent Trek
    at the Phoenix Club.

PUNTER I'll try to.

*Cut to YOUNG KENNY being interviewed (on
blue screen). Caption reads 'YOUNG KENNY'.
He's wearing a T-shirt that reads 'DEN
PERRY DID IT'.*

YOUNG KENNY
    I'd been working at the club that
    night. I'd been on since six o'clock
    but I hadn't seen anything
    suspicious.

*Cut back to YOUNG KENNY and BRIAN
chatting by the poster advertising the
Phoenix.*

BRIAN   Have you found anything
    suspicious?

YOUNG KENNY
    (SHAKES HIS HEAD) No.

BRIAN   Very good.

*YOUNG KENNY unknowingly covers the
poster. BRIAN discreetly moves him and
points at it.*

BRIAN   (VO) We were packed to the rafters,
    but we're used to that, being the
    most successful club in the region,
    open seven nights a week, coach
    parties and charities welcome.

*The reconstruction cuts to MAX and PADDY
on the door. (There is a cheer in the Tony
Knowles suite.) They're very nervous and
wooden. A few people enter the club.*

MAX   Evening, Pauline ... don't go causing
    any bother.

LADY   Who's Pauline?

*The LADY enters the club. PADDY mimes big
breasts. He's saying something but it cuts off.*

We cut to the Tony Knowles suite.

BRIAN   (VO) It were a cracking night. The
    ventriloquist won ...

PADDY   They've cut my line ...

MAX   That's 'cause you're shit!

Laughter.

*We cut back to the reconstruction. YOUNG
KENNY (with white face) is sitting signing
people in behind a desk in the foyer.*

*Cut back to the reconstruction. KENNY SNR
is outside the gents' toilets reading a
newspaper (wearing Phoenix glasses),
BOLTON INDEPENDENT LEADER. He unfolds
the paper to reveal a mocked-up headline
that reads 'THE PHOENIX CLUB IS THE
BEST' on the back page. The camera pans off
him but he walks back into shot and opens
the paper revealing the front page, which
reads 'DEN PERRY BURNS CLUB DOWN'.*

BRIAN   (VO) Who would have thought while
          we were laughing and singing that
          next door a towering inferno was
          being started deliberately in the
          toilets? I mean it just ... just reducing
          my dreams to ashes you know ...

*Cut to an establishing wide shot of the
Phoenix Club and we hear approaching
sirens.*

*Cut to BRIAN in shot on a blue screen. He's
talking and sitting with the melted plastic
'disabled boy' charity box, with a sign on it
saying 'DEN PERRY DID IT!'.*

BRIAN   It burnt the face on my disabled boy
          – look at him. Can't go back. Ni'
          night son, eh ... oh ... can you turn
          it off, please ... let's have a breather
          for a minute.

Cut to the Galaxy Lounge

CLUB MEMBER
          He's going to cry now ...

CLUB MEMBER 2
          Look at that ... look at that!

Laughter.

*Cut back to the studio and a shot of the
PRESENTER sitting behind a desk.*

PRESENTER
          Well, disturbing scenes ...

BRIAN   (OS) Is that it? Where's the rest of
          it? Eh?!

BRIAN   You've cut it all out!

CLUB MEMBER
          That can't be it!

PRESENTER
          (RAISES HAND TO SHUSH BRIAN)
          We're joined in the studio by
          Detective Inspector Jack Crawford
          and by the club's owner Mr Potter.
          Detective Inspector Crawford if I
          could turn to you first ...? Do you
          have any leads at all as to who could
          have committed this terrible crime?

BRIAN rubs his crotch and sniffs his fingers.

DETECTIVE INSPECTOR
    Well, we've known about Mr Potter
    for quite a while now. He has been
    involved in a number of clubs that
    have all been destroyed and in
    suspicious circumstances …

PRESENTER
    Really …?

BRIAN   Whoa, whoa, whoa, roll that back.
    What do you mean 'suspicious
    circumstances'? What's all that
    about? Eh, I hope you're not
    accusing me! Did you hear that?

*We cut to the Tony Knowles suite. JERRY is
watching the TV through his fingers. The
rest of THE REGULARS are just staring at
the screen.*

BRIAN   (ON TELEVISION) Eh, what's all that
    about?! I tell you who burnt the club
    down and you cut him out the
    bloody film … Den Perry, that's who
    you want – Den Perry!

DETECTIVE INSPECTOR
    Mr Potter, you cannot publicly
    accuse somebody during an ongoing
    investigation.

BRIAN   Well, someone's got to do your job:
    you've done piss all, that's what
    you've done! (THE DETECTIVE
    INSPECTOR TOUCHES BRIAN'S
    ARM) Look at this. Did you see
    that? See – he went for me then.
    That's how it 'appened! See that …
    Two words … Biko.

DETECTIVE INSPECTOR
    Calm down!

BRIAN   Calm … look he's doing it again!
    He's doing it again!

DETECTIVE INSPECTOR
    For crying out loud!

BRIAN   Ooh, I tell you, he fell, Your Honour.
    That's how, that's how it happened,
    you know. You'll have another
    Rodney King on your hands. Tell
    bloody Norman Tebbit here!

DETECTIVE INSPECTOR
    Let me finish!

BRIAN   Like a bull to a red rag!

PRESENTER
    Mr Potter, *please* calm down. And
    could we return to the subject!

BRIAN   No, I've lost my licence! I've come
    on here and he starts accusing me
    and you've cut out …

Everyone's yelling out back in the club.

BRIAN   (cont.) You can stick your show! You
    can't bring me on here and then
    start … You're not treating me like
    one of the bloody Bee Gees.

*BRIAN rips off his radio mic and reverses
out of shot.*

TV PRESENTER

    Mr Potter

BRIAN   Oh, sod you! I'll tell you! No, no!

Laughter and shouting from the club again.

BRIAN   I'll tell you something – I'll catch
    him myself, because you, *you* lot,
    you couldn't ... you couldn't find
    your arse with both hands. I'll tell
    you that! I'm getting out here!

PRESENTER

    Mr Potter if you'd just ...

*The cameras pan left and right trying to find
the correct shot.*

PRESENTER

    (LISTENING TO EARPIECE) Er ...
    thanks to Mr Potter ... and we
    have a rather special *Crimetime*
    appeal of our own, because during
    the filming of ...

BRIAN   No! How do you get out of here?!

PRESENTER

    ... we lost several pieces of rather
    expensive film lighting equipment.
    We'd love to know about their
    whereabouts.

BRIAN   Where's the bloody door, eh?!

PRESENTER

    If you know about it, do let us know.

BRIAN   You, ring me a taxi! Oi, love, ring me
    a taxi!

MAX   (IN CLUB) Call me a taxi!

CUT TO

32. EXT. PHOENIX CLUB CAR PARK. NIGHT

*BRIAN and JERRY looking up. The front of
the club is illuminated by two huge
CRIMETIME lights.*

BRIAN   Come on, Jerry ... turn the
    Crimetime lights off 'n'all.

The lights go out.

BRIAN   (cont.) Did we get any calls on the
    update?

JERRY   Twelve ...

BRIAN   *Crimetime*, bloody *waste* of
    time! I'm gonna stop paying my
    licence fee.

JERRY   You've never paid your licence.

BRIAN   Yes and why? It's all chefs and
    DIY shagging ... don't know why
    I bother.

*We hear a car beep. BRIAN and JERRY both
turn to look.*

*Cut to see a car by the side of the road. A
YOUNG LAD leaning out of the window and a
GIRL PASSENGER.*

BRIAN   Yes?

LAD   (NERVOUS) Are you that bloke off
    Crimetime?

BRIAN   What?!

LAD   Were you on telly tonight?

BRIAN   Yeah. Why? Who wants to know?

LAD   Is this the club that burnt down,
         then?

BRIAN   Yes this is the world-famous
         Phoenix Club ...

The speed trap sign lights up 'IT'S THE
PHOENIX CLUB'.

BRIAN   ... as seen on TV. I'm Brian Potter,
         that's Jerry St Clair ... You must be
         thirsty after your long journey ...
         (ASIDE TO JERRY) Get the bar open
         ... Move forward, pull off into
         paradise, come on!

LAD   Nice one! (PULLS OFF IN CAR)

BRIAN   Come inside. I'll show you where the
         fire started.

CUT TO

END CREDITS

34. INT. PHOENIX CLUB
Audition scene. ELVIS impersonator.

ONE-LEGGED ELVIS
         (SINGING) 'I'm going be your man,
         I'm a one-girl guy ...
         Nobody else will do ...
         No woman ... I'm a one-girl guy,
         I don't want nobody else but you ...
         Play that leg, sugar!'

ONE-LEGGED ELVIS plays the symbols on his
artificial leg.

BRIAN   Go on! Oooh, look at that! He's
         playin' his leg! Very brave, son.

ONE-LEGGED ELVIS
         (CONTINUES SINGING)
         'I'm a one-girl guy,
         I don't want nobody else but you ...
         yeh ...'

BRIAN   Fantastic! Do you do anything else?

ONE-LEGGED ELVIS
         Aye ... 'Blue Suede Shoe'.

THE END

Episode 4

PART ONE

1. INT. PHOENIX CLUB FOYER. DAY

Poster (A2): 'THE WORLD FAMOUS PHOENIX CLUB AS SEEN ON TV'S CRIMETIME. DAILY TOURS OF THE CRIME SCENE AVAILABLE £5 (£7 INCLUDES MEAL VOUCHER). MEET THE STAFF! SEE WHERE THE FIRE STARTED!'

A GROUP OF PEOPLE (including children) pass by the poster and through shot. KENNY SNR leads the tour. He carries a large golfing umbrella and wears a baseball cap with 'THE PHOENIX CLUB – SMOKIN'' on it. Body outline on the floor. 'DISCO INFERNO' playing in the background.

KENNY SNR

> ... come on, keep together, we're getting warmer. Did anyone see the film *Backdraft*? I worked on it. Showing De Niro the ropes. He's a lovely bloke, Bobby. That completes the tour for today. I've been your tour guide, Kenny Senior. Hope you've enjoyed ... hope you've enjoyed the tour today. Hope you've enjoyed the very extensive ...

BRIAN   Thank you, Kenny Senior. This way, ladies and gentleman. This is the part of the tour where you buy your charred souvenir remains. There you go.

CUT TO

2. EXT. PHOENIX CLUB CAR PARK. DAY

RAY VON in front of a brazier, surrounded by broken club furniture and holding an ashtray with a pair of tongs over a flame. YOUNG KENNY (with face still painted as tiger) carries the pre-charred furniture indoors.

YOUNG KENNY

> Potter wants more ashtrays.

RAY VON Hold up ... (GIVES YOUNG KENNY A BIT OF BROKEN CHARRED CHAIR) A bit of chair there.

YOUNG KENNY

> Right.

RAY VON Be careful of that.

CUT TO

3. INT. TONY KNOWLES SUITE. DAY

BRIAN is giving his spiel on the souvenirs to the CUSTOMERS. YOUNG KENNY puts down a tray of ashtrays in the background.

BRIAN   Two pound your charred glasses there … as left on the fire. All this is charred remains, love.

WOMAN   You're just cashing in, aren't you?

BRIAN   Oh no, no … oh no, no, we're not just cashing in, love, no, no. You think that, don't you? But all this … getting rid of this is very therapeutic, it's part of the healing process. Many of us still suffer flashbacks of that painful night. It's like Vietnam, this. The scars are mental as well as physical.

WOMAN   How much are ashtrays?

BRIAN   (TO CUSTOMER) Four quid.

WOMAN   (OS) Go on. I'll have two.

BRIAN   Jerry, two ashtrays please for this lady.

JERRY leans and picks one up. He screams, as it burns his hand, throws the ashtray and runs out of shot screaming.

JERRY   You bastard … shit!

BRIAN   Some of us are still suffering, love.

CUT TO

OPENING CREDITS

CUT TO

4. EXT. CASH-AND-CARRY. DAY
Establishing shot of cash-and-carry.

CUT TO

5. INT. CASH-AND-CARRY. DAY
A trolley seems to be making its own way down an aisle, piled high with alcohol and crisps. We cut to reveal BRIAN pushing it from behind. CHORLEY FM on the radio. Golden hour.

RADIO   (VO) Her Majesty the Queen celebrated her Silver Jubilee this year, the Yorkshire Ripper was still at large and David Soul got to number one in the August of this year. But what was the year? Listen to The Golden Years on Chorley FM – coming in your ears.

Cut to a 'FREE SAMPLE' stand at the top of an aisle. An ORIENTAL WOMAN offers out free drinks. A banner reads 'WIN A YEAR'S SUPPLY OF FREE KAMIKAZE LAGER'. BRIAN's eyes light up.

We jump-cut and BRIAN is now testing his fourth free drink. There are four empty cups.

BRIAN   (TAKES A DRINK) What is it?

LADY   (SAYS IT IN JAPANESE)

BRIAN   She what? (SWIGS AGAIN) Oh, yeh, yeh, yeh. I see, I see, I see. Not a bad drop, is it?

He whistles. A MAN comes over smiling and bows to BRIAN. He is wearing a badge that clearly reads 'REP SAKAMOTO'. BRIAN attempts to bow back.

BRIAN   (cont.) I was just saying to the wife there: not a bad drop.

REP   New premier Japanese lager, Kamikaze.

BRIAN   (TAKES ANOTHER DRINK) They could have done with a drop of this when they were building your railways. Not bad, not bad. (HOLDING FLYER) What's all this about? Win a year's free supply?

LADY   A year's supply ...

REP   Big promotion, for big UK launch – let the British people know.

BRIAN   Oh, right, let the British people know. Well if you want to let the British people know, my son, you've got to get out, you know. You're wasting your time in here, flogging a dead horse. You've got to get out, you know, into the pubs and clubs ... (ASIDE) Take it to the heart of clubland.

REP   Pubs and clubs?

BRIAN   Clubland. Brian Potter, I run the Phoenix Club, world-famous, as seen on TV. You might recognise me.

REP   No.

BRIAN   (SHOWS HIS PROFILE) No? I'm a bit of a celebrity round here. This big UK launch ... have you thought about where you might be having it?

CUT TO

6. INT. TONY KNOWLES SUITE. DAY

A meeting. BRIAN and the others are sitting round the covered snooker table drinking cans of Japanese lager.

HOLY MARY
         (AT LAGER TASTING) What do you think, Joyce?

JOYCE   I'm not raving, Mary.

HOLY MARY
         No.

BRIAN   Well, what do you think?

There is a general chorus of mumbling approval.

LES   It's got a bit of a kick, hasn't it?

BRIAN   Like a Japanese mule, Leslie. What do you think, Jerry?

There is an unopened can in front of JERRY.

JERRY   I can't drink on these tablets.

BRIAN   More? What are these for?

JERRY holds up his bandaged hand.

JERRY   Remember, you burnt me hand?

BRIAN   I didn't burn your hand: you burnt
your own bloody hand! Eh, Christ
look at all these! Druggie, druggie,
druggie – you'll be in the toilets next
snorting Cecil.

JERRY   You mean Charlie!

BRIAN   What?

JERRY   Charlie.

BRIAN   I don't know who he is, I've never
met the man.

MARION Can you get mules in Japan?

KENNY SNR
        (TAPPING NOSE) I can.

BRIAN   Beautiful isn't it, it's good gear.

*In the background the two STOWAWAYS
enter carrying a big pile of Chinese food
and chopsticks. They put some down in
front of HOLY MARY and start to talk in
Chinese loudly.*

ALAN   So what are you going to do then –
sell it?

BRIAN   Oh, we're going to do more than sell
it, Alan: we're gonna launch it.
(CHORUS OF MUMBLINGS) Yeah, I
had a powwow this morning in the
cash-and-carry with the old top
bollocks. He couldn't speak a word

of English but he was fluent in the
language of business. That's it,
that's the main thing, you see. The
upshot being that he wants to have
his grand launch right here.

JERRY   Here, why?

BRIAN   'Cause we're the Phoenix Club, as
seen on TV. We're world-famous!
Once he knew about that he jumped
at the chance. (SNIFFS) Do you
have to eat that muck in here? It
bloody stinks!

HOLY MARY
        Oh, Brian it's beautiful ... Come on,
come on, try a bit, go on!

BRIAN   Get bent. I've got heartburn just
smelling it.

JERRY   This grand launch – what does he
want, then? A big cabaret show?
Dancers, bingo, a raffle?

BRIAN   No, no, no – he wants a quiz, a pub
quiz.

JERRY   A pub quiz?

BRIAN   Oh yes, that's right, a big quiz with
a big prize. Read that.

*He gives JERRY a handful of leaflets. He
hands them out.*

JERRY   (READING LEAFLET) 'Win a year's
supply of Kamikaze Lager'.

BRIAN   Yeh, and we're gonna win it.

JERRY   How?

BRIAN   We're going to cheat.

JERRY   You can't cheat!

BRIAN   We can. Why can't we? Somebody's got to win it. Why can't it be us?

JERRY   I wish you'd discussed this with me, Brian, beforehand. I am the licensee, remember?

BRIAN   What's there to discuss, Jerry? We're losing a fighting battle here, man! That there's the answer to our prayers, my son. A year's supply of free beer for sod all.

JERRY   And when does he want this place?

BRIAN   Wednesday.

JERRY   Wednesday? Not Wednesday, no. That's my night, Wednesday, Free and Easy Night.

BRIAN   Well, if it's that free and easy, shift it.

JERRY   No, I won't, I've built up a following.

BRIAN   Well, tell them they can both come to the quiz.

JERRY   Very funny. Look, Thursday's quiz night – it always has been. Thursday's quiz night; Wednesday's Free and Easy Night. You can't go rearranging days.

BRIAN   I can do what we like – it's your club!

JERRY   Well look, if I'm in charge I say no.

BRIAN   Whoa, whoa, whoa, Adolf! Just roll back, eh? It's a democracy – we'll bloody vote.

JERRY   Right, fine, we'll have a vote on it, then.

BRIAN   Yeh!

JERRY   Right. All those in favour of not having a quiz night on Wednesday say 'aye'.

Silence except for YOUNG KENNY.

YOUNG KENNY
    Aye.

BRIAN gives him a look.

YOUNG KENNY (Cont.)
    I'm sorry. I don't understand the question.

BRIAN   You don't, do you? Would you put your hand down?

JERRY   Right, thanks everybody, thanks for your support. Have your bloody precious quiz, then. Have it.

BRIAN   We will.

JERRY   I tell you something: if you think I'm cancelling my Free and Easy Night next door, you've got another think coming.

BRIAN   Well, good. Have your Free and Easy Night. We'll have our quiz in here.

JERRY   Good.

BRIAN   Yeah.

JERRY   Fine.

BRIAN   OK.

KENNY SNR

    (TO JOYCE) Let me know if you
    want those mules.

CUT TO

7. INT. THE GALAXY LOUNGE. NIGHT

*JERRY is on stage sound-checking. BRIAN
reaches JERRY's CD display at the front of
the stage. He picks one up and reads the
back of it. Cutaway of CD.*

BRIAN   Oh god, eh, frig me, eh! No wonder
    you wanted your Free and Easy
    Night! Jerry St Clair, young at heart!

JERRY   Sorry, did somebody say something
    then? Did you hear anything?

BRIAN   (READING THE BACK OF THE CD)
    'Sex Bomb'? 'She Bangs, She
    Bangs'? Oh, all the hits, eh?
    (LAUGHING) They're all on here!

JERRY   (TAKING TABLETS) Tell him you
    look with your eyes, not your hands.

LES   He said you look with your eyes, not
    with your hands.

BRIAN   I heard what he said, Leslie, all
    right? (READING BACK OF CD) 'The
    drugs don't work'? Christ, they
    should: you've taken enough. Look at
    one of them there. What do these
    ones do? Stop you being an arsehole?

JERRY   It's you that's the bloody arsehole ...

BRIAN   Ahhh! You spoke to me, eh, you
    spoke to me ... Time out, I win. The
    winner. Game over.

JERRY   (SHOUTING) I told you they're for
    stress, all right?

BRIAN   Stress? What do you know about
    stress? You want to try to walk a
    mile in my shoes, boy.

JERRY   Yeh, so do you.

BRIAN   (SHOCKED) Ooo, that was below
    the belt.

JERRY   Well, you wouldn't have felt it, then,
    would you?

BRIAN   That's it, go on, two–nil. While
    you're there why don't you go for
    the hat trick? Go on. Slash my tyres
    while I'm here, go on!

LES   Look for Christ's sake, will you two just pack it in? You're like a couple of bloody kids.

BRIAN   He started it ... Twenty years, twenty years I've known you, Jerry Dignan, for all that time, and, this, this person this past week ... I don't know. Who are you? I don't know you.

JERRY   Do you know why that is? I've realised what you are at last. You're a manipulator, a schemer, that's what you are. You've got your precious quiz next door, haven't you? But you're not happy enough with that, are you? You've got to cheat to win.

BRIAN   I've told you, I'm doing it for the club. (JERRY SAYS IT WITH HIM)

JERRY   I heard it all before, Brian. And what do you think they're going to do when they find out you've cheated?

BRIAN   (SHRUGS) Not my problem. Like you keep saying, you're the licensee.

BRIAN turns and leaves. JERRY takes another pill.

CUT TO

8. EXT. PHOENIX CLUB. NIGHT
MAX and PADDY are eating noodles outside.

MAX   Yeah, noodles, them.

PADDY   Who's made it?

MAX   Lads in back.

PADDY spits out noodles.

CUT TO

9. INT. KITCHEN. NIGHT
The CHINESE STOWAWAYS are singing while stir-frying noodles.

CUT TO

10. INT. TONY KNOWLES SUITE. NIGHT
Samurai merchandise everywhere. The REP and his ASSISTANT are putting answer sheets and pens on each table. BRIAN smiles at the REP as he makes his way to KENNY SNR and SPENCER sitting at a table.

SPENCER (TAKING A SHEET) Yes, please.

KENNY SNR
    Thanks very much.

BRIAN   Here we are, the Phoenix Team.

KENNY SNR nods. We cut to YOUNG KENNY walking back with three lots of Chinese food.

KENNY SNR
    All right?

BRIAN   How are you? I thought there was three of you. Where's Shere Khan?

SPENCER Getting the food.

BRIAN   (WHISPERING) What are those?

YOUNG KENNY
         (WHISPERING) Answers.

BRIAN   (WHISPERING) Do you know the
         questions?

YOUNG KENNY
         (WHISPERING) No … but you never
         know, do you?

BRIAN   Jesus wept!

END OF PART ONE

PART TWO

11. INT. TONY KNOWLES SUITE. NIGHT
*The room is now full, people getting ready
to start.*

RAY VON (OS) The Phoenix Club in
         association with Kamikaze Lager
         presents … the biggest quiz in
         clubland.

CUT TO

12. INT. PHOENIX CLUB FOYER. NIGHT
*We see RAY VON outside the ladies toilets,
doing his spiel.*

RAY VON Please give it up for the one and
         only, the 'mental oriental' Ray Von
         Chong!

CUT TO

13. INT. TONY KNOWLES SUITE. NIGHT
*'TURNING JAPANESE' by the VAPOURS
comes on. RAY enters (Fu Manchu-esque
costume).*

BRIAN   It's a quiz, not a carvery. Christ!
         What colour's your face today?

YOUNG KENNY
         It's false tan.

*YOUNG KENNY pulls his shirt down and
shows him that it stops at the neck.*

BRIAN   False tan? It'd better be. If you've
         been using my sarolium for frig all
         it'll be more than your face that's
         tanned.

KENNY SNR
         (EATING) Hey, it's smashin', this,
         Brian. You want to get some.

BRIAN   It just winked at me. Listen, do you
         know what you're doing?

SPENCER (WHISPERING) Don't worry, we've
         got it all sorted. (TO YOUNG KENNY)
         Go on.

*YOUNG KENNY discreetly rolls his sleeve up
(false tan stops at wrists). He has various
things written on his arm: 'FRANCE, PARIS',
'ENGLAND 4 GERMANY 2', 'PAGANINI',
'HEY JUDE'.*

RAY VON Thank you, thank you. Thank you for that lovely warm welcome, it was lovely. It really did bring a tear to my ... Jap's eye (WIPES HIS EYE, PRESSES KEYBOARD: WE HEAR A COMEDY NOISE OF A KARATE CHOP AND A CYMBAL) Ah so! Fill in your answers on the sheets provided.

CUT TO

14. INT. GALAXY LOUNGE. NIGHT
We see a shot of the room fairly empty. JERRY singing 'A BRIMFUL OF ASHA.'

CUT TO

15. INT. GALAXY LOUNGE BACKSTAGE. NIGHT
Backstage a nervous JERRY tips his tablets bottle. Too many fall out. He puts them back in, goes to fill glass.

JERRY   (THROUGH CURTAIN) Have you seen it out there, have you? Dead, dead. I told him it'd be like this. Where's Dot, and Moira? Cliff and Tony? (DOWNS THE TABLET WITH THE GLASS OF WATER) Wednesday night, Free and Easy Night, eh? Half empty.

CUT TO

16. INT. TONY KNOWLES SUITE. NIGHT
RAY VON is at the mic.

RAY VON OK, let's win that lager. (WE HEAR AN ORIENTAL JINGLE) Your first question. I suffer from pyrophobia, so what am I afraid of?

We cut to YOUNG KENNY, KENNY SNR and SPENCER. They look at each other.

CUT TO

17. EXT. PHOENIX CLUB. NIGHT
MAX and PADDY. We can hear RAY VON repeating the question.

MAX   (CLICKS HIS FINGERS) Pirates!

PADDY   Go on.

He writes it down.

CUT TO

18. INT. TONY KNOWLES SUITE. NIGHT

KENNY SNR
          (GESTURES WITH HANDS) I'm just getting a drink. Do you fancy a drink? (HE STANDS AND LEAVES)

YOUNG KENNY
          I need a slash. (HE STANDS AND LEAVES)

CUT TO

19. INT. GENTS' TOILETS. NIGHT
YOUNG KENNY goes into a toilet cubicle and closes the door.

CUT TO

20. INT. PHOENIX CLUB FOYER. NIGHT
We see KENNY SNR on the payphone.

KENNY SNR
     Hello, Mam, it's Kenny ... Kenny –
     your son ... I know sorry it's been a
     long time ... Yeah I know, I'm sorry
     I missed the funeral ... Don't cry,
     listen: what's pyrophobia a fear of?

CUT TO

21. INT. GENTS' TOILETS. NIGHT
*We cut inside, he's sitting on the seat. We
see a cutaway of the word 'PYROPHOBIA'.*

MAN   (VO) (BREAKING WIND IN NEXT
       TOILET) I'll name that tune in one.

CUT TO

22. INT. THE GALAXY LOUNGE. NIGHT

JERRY   (ON MIC) Thanks very much for
      coming along tonight and supporting
      your Free and Easy Night, not
      bothering with the quiz next door,
      because we've got a great night for
      you here as usual. Will you go wild
      and crazy ... give a lovely Phoenix
      Club welcome to Two's Company!

*(LES ALANOS BACKING.) TWO'S
COMPANY bound on stage. One black,
one white.*

BARBIE QUE
     Put your eyes back in, granddad ...

CANDY I'm Candy Floss.

BARBIE QUE
     And I'm Barbie Que ...

*Go into 'WE ARE FAMILY' by SISTER SLEDGE.
'I'VE GOT MY STEPSISTER WITH ME' ...*

CUT TO

23. INT. GALAXY LOUNGE BACKSTAGE. NIGHT
*We cut to backstage. JERRY comes down the
steps. LES ALANOS are tucking into their
Chinese food.*

ALAN   It's lovely, this. Have you got any of
       them water chestnuts.

LES   Oh, aye, I have yeah. It's good gear
       this. Aye.

*JERRY takes another tablet and guzzles
down what he thinks is LES's water. He
almost chokes, leans forward and can't get
his breath.*

JERRY What's that?

LES   Sake. For God's sake ... drink
       that up ...

JERRY My mouth's on fire.

LES   I'm not surprised: you could strip
       paint with that stuff.

JERRY, with a burning mouth, quickly sucks water from the sink in the corner.

CUT TO

24. INT. TONY KNOWLES SUITE. NIGHT
RAY VON is on the mic.

RAY VON Sport! My balls are black and blue. I've just hit them with a mallet. What game am I playing?

CUT TO

25. EXT. PHOENIX CLUB. NIGHT
We cut to MAX and PADDY outside. MAX gives PADDY a look.

PADDY   He's hit his balls with a mallet?

MAX   That's what he said.

CUT TO

26. INT. TONY KNOWLES SUITE. NIGHT
We cut back inside to SPENCER and KENNY SNR. They both look at YOUNG KENNY (his arm is wet).

RAY VON My balls are black and blue. I've just hit them with a mallet. What game am I playing?

YOUNG KENNY looks at his arm.

YOUNG KENNY
            (ROLLS HIS SLEEVE UP) Oh, shit, no, they've all smudged.

We see DEN PERRY enter with two of his CRONIES.

There is a SCRUFFY-LOOKING LAD at the bar. HOLY MARY hands him his food. He turns with it and bumps into DEN. DEN gives him a threatening look.

WOMAN All right, love?

RAY VON Next question ... (A MOBILE PHONE RINGS). Hang on ... was that a mobile phone I just heard go off? You can't have any kind of phone going off.

We cut to BRIAN. He doesn't look too pleased when he sees DEN PERRY. DEN goes over to BRIAN.

DEN PERRY
            Evening, Potter.

BRIAN   What do you want, Perry? Get out, you're barred.

DEN PERRY
            Now, now, Brian, that's not a very warm welcome! I see you're still attracting the upmarket clientele. (THE LAD SITS DOWN AT A TABLE WITH SOME OTHER SCRUFFY LADS) Christ, I don't know what smells worse: them or the food.

BRIAN   What do you want, Perry?

DEN PERRY
            (NODS AT THE BANNER) I've come for my year's supply of free lager.

BRIAN   Well, you're too late, dickhead, because the quiz has started.

DEN PERRY
            Oh, I know that, Brian. I've just come to see how my team's getting on ... There they are, the Banana Grove's finest, top of the quiz league three years running. Right little Bamber Gascoignes, they are. All right, lads? (HE WAVES; THEY WAVE BACK)

BRIAN   Ringers? You can't do that Perry ... that's cheating.

DEN PERRY

> Well, you tell it to the judge,
> Ironside.

RAY VON The Quiz Ninja's word is final!

CUT TO

27. INT. THE GALAXY LOUNGE. NIGHT
JERRY calling out bingo numbers.

JERRY   One and eight, eighteen. Eight and
         three, eighty-three. Five and nine,
         fifty-nine ... fifty-nine! ... This is on
         its own ...

ALAN   (BACKSTAGE) Something's not
         right ...

CUT TO

28. INT. TONY KNOWLES SUITE. NIGHT
*Oriental version of Who Wants to Be A
Millionaire music in the background.
SPENCER and YOUNG KENNY sit round the
table. KENNY SNR comes back with some
more Chinese food.*

RAY VON Who was I and why did I kill?

KENNY SNR

> (WHISPERS) Hey, Den Perry's got a
> team in ...

YOUNG KENNY

> Where?

KENNY SNR

> Over there ... said they're league
> champions.

SPENCER That's all right.

We cut to RAY VON on the mic.

RAY VON OK, this next question is worth
        seven points ...

AUDIENCE

> Ooohhh!

RAY VON I want you to name the Magnificent
        Seven.

CUT TO

29. EXT. PHOENIX CLUB. NIGHT

MAX   Okay, now you're talking. Here we
         go. Coburn, Yul Brynner.

PADDY   McQueen ...

MAX   McQueen ... Bronson ...

CUT TO

30. INT. TONY KNOWLES SUITE. NIGHT
*YOUNG KENNY and SPENCER counting on
their fingers.*

SPENCER ... Sneezy ... Dopey ... Bashful!
        (LOOKS OVER AT TOP BANANA
        TEAM) We'll shit 'em!

CUT TO

31. INT. THE GALAXY LOUNGE. NIGHT

JERRY is on stage reading the bingo balls very fast. He's a little bit pit bull, chewing and sweating. We cut to the audience – they're finding it hard to keep up.

JERRY   Six and three, sixty-three! Eight and four, eighty-four! Two, two little ducks (MIMICS A DUCK), quack, quack, quack! ... You'll do it, hey, what ... Have a look. Twenty-two ... twenty-two ...

AUDIENCE MEMBER
    Slow it down!

JERRY   ... four and one, forty-one ... Never mind, you'll catch up ... You're going to catch up!

CUT TO

32. INT. GALAXY LOUNGE BACKSTAGE. NIGHT

ALAN is looking through the curtain and shaking his head. LES is looking through JERRY's tablets on the side.

ALAN   Have you seen him? He's off his head.

LES   I'm not surprised. Have you seen all this here? What's this – Co-drydomol, Pro Plus, echinacea, ginkgo bilbao ... He's eight miles high, this lad, he's gangsta-trippin'.

CUT TO

33. INT. THE GALAXY LOUNGE. NIGHT

After he calls the number, he crushes the balls in his hand and throws them over his shoulder. We cut to a few already on the floor. Somebody shouts out 'HOUSE'.

JERRY   There we go ... one and five, fifteen, thirteen ... *Shut up! Shut up!* There are balls left in here, are you blind woman? *You don't own me*, you don't own me, you lot! (THIRSTY, SWALLOWS HARD)

CUT TO

34. INT. TONY KNOWLES SUITE. NIGHT

We cut to a table. A WOMAN is chatting to her HUSBAND.

WIFE   What's fourteen?

HUSBAND Basil Brush.

WIFE   What about twenty-one?

HUSBAND (UNINTERESTED IN HER) The Great Wall of China.

WIFE   Oh were it, you're right clever you. I won't be a minute.

HUSBAND Get us some crisps.

She leaves.

CUT TO

35. EXT. PHOENIX CLUB. NIGHT

MAX and PADDY. The WOMAN is outside giving them the answer.

WIFE   (LOOKING AT THEIR ANSWER SHEET) Syphilis, Basil Brush ... and that's the Great Wall of China.

PADDY   (POINTS AT PAPER) What's that?

WIFE   That?! Haa! That's my mobile.

PADDY   (WITH DIRTY LAUGH) Oh, yeah?! You naughty girl. You'll do for me, go on. Hey! Hey!

The WOMAN giggles and rushes back in.
MAX watches blankly. PADDY slaps her arse.

MAX   I'll tell you, Patrick, you're gonna get nowhere in life doing that.

PADDY   I don't know – it got me my eleven-plus.

CUT TO

36. INT. THE GALAXY LOUNGE. NIGHT
TWO'S COMPANY on stage singing.

We cut backstage. JERRY's watching the show, chewing like a pit bull. LES and ALAN look at each other. JERRY tips his tablets into his hand – there's only one left.

JERRY   (CHEWING FRANTICALLY) I'm cold. Are you cold? It's gone cold, yeh, it's really gone cold, but it's a nice cold, it's a warm cold it's … it's all right, don't worry, it's a warm cold. You know what I mean … I love you, I love you … (GOES TO HUG ALAN AND TAKES HIS PINT. HE DOWNS IT IN ONE)

LES   Hey, pack it in! I thought you weren't supposed to drink on those tablets, Jerry?

JERRY   Gobi Desert. Desert. Going to catch the moon … going to catch the moon. Come on, I'm going to catch the moon. Get the moon now, bring it down, bring it down. No. Can you moonwalk? Look at that. The moon's down here … Can't you, eh?!

He runs out on stage.

CUT TO

37. INT. TONY KNOWLES SUITE. NIGHT
RAY VON is on the mic.

RAY VON Here we go. I'm going to play you a song now. I want the title of the song – not the artist, okay remember the title of the song, not the artist. Here we go …

We hear the opening lyrics to 'IT'S A KIND OF MAGIC'. RAY VON, quickly realising, knocks it off.

MAX   (OS) Put it down!

RAY VON Whoa, whoa, whoa!

There's a moan from everybody.

RAY VON (cont.) Here we go. Now remember: I want the name of the song, not the artist. Here we go, try this on for size (WE HEAR THE OPENING TO 'YOUNG AT HEART') Hang on, whoa, whoa!

Another moan.

YOUNG KENNY
    Oh, not again.

CUT TO

38. EXT. PHOENIX CLUB. NIGHT
We cut outside to MAX and PADDY looking at each other in disbelief.

MAX   (SHOUTING) Look at the programme, dickhead ... Going to win some lager!

CUT TO

39. INT. GALAXY LOUNGE BACKSTAGE. NIGHT

JERRY   Hey, do your teeth itch? Do your teeth itch? Teeth ... your teeth. Give us that! Teeth, teeth, teeth. Give us that ... Good, good for your teeth. Come on!

ALAN   Sit down a minute, Jerry. Just five minutes.

JERRY   Don't sit down. Catch the moon ... catch the moon ... Bring it down, come on! I can't see the moon! Can't see the moon! We've got a bloody plane to catch!

CUT TO

40. INT. TONY KNOWLES SUITE. NIGHT
RAY VON'S playing 'TAKE MY BREATH AWAY' by BERLIN. Everybody listening hard.

Song continues '... AS YOU TURN TO ME AND SAY, MY LOVE ... ' RAY VON fades it down.

We cut to the room and everybody sings it to themselves, mumbled, as they write it.

CUT TO

41. EXT. PHOENIX CLUB. NIGHT
We cut outside to MAX and PADDY. MAX singing what he's just heard, mumbling the lyrics ...

MAX   (SINGING 'TAKE MY BREATH AWAY') As you turn to me and say, my love ... walking on the moon, walking on the moon, haa haa haaaa ...

PADDY scribbles it down.

CUT TO

42. INT. THE GALAXY LOUNGE. NIGHT
We see a close-up of JERRY singing. We cut out to reveal him walking across the tables. Singing 'CHITTY CHITTY BANG BANG' and trying to get the audience to join in. LES and ALAN are trying to keep up.

CUT TO

43. INT. TONY KNOWLES SUITE. NIGHT
RAY VON is reading out the answers. We hear mixed moans from the room: 'THAT'S IT', 'NO WAY', 'I SAID THAT ... I SAID THAT'.

RAY VON ... and the answer was ... (PAUSE) ... The shroud of Turin.

SPENCER Aaah! What did we have?

KENNY SNR   (looking at sheet) Lisa Stansfield.

RAY VON Number twenty-six: the answer was he died in a plane crash.

YOUNG KENNY   (JUMPS TO HIS FEET, VICTORIOUS, ARMS RAISED) *Yeesss!! Yeesss!!* Get in there!

The whole room stops and looks at him. He sits back down, embarrassed.

CUT TO

44. INT. THE GALAXY LOUNGE. NIGHT
JERRY is karate-chopping wood.

JERRY Hmmm ... hold it up, I've told you, hold it up. Sit down, you. Give us a drum roll.

CUT TO

45. INT. TONY KNOWLES SUITE. NIGHT
RAY VON is on the mic, reading the results. Oriental millionnaire.

RAY VON In third place, Lord Love Rocket and his mongy mate Max.

CUT TO

46. EXT. PHOENIX CLUB. NIGHT
We cut outside to MAX and PADDY.

MAX Mongy mate Max, eh? You mean me! I'll rip your bastard head off.

CUT TO

47. INT. TONY KNOWLES SUITE. NIGHT
We cut back inside.

RAY VON In second place with thirty-six points ... Top Banana.

Cut to see the team. They look put out.

We cut to the Phoenix Club team, looking hopeful. SPENCER, YOUNG KENNY and KENNY SNR do a high five.

RAY VON (cont.) ... and the winners in first place ... taking away a year's supply of Kamikaze Lager ... (RAY PLAYS A DRUM ROLL ON HIS KEYBOARD; IT HAS TO STOP WHILE HE TURNS THE QUESTION PAPER ... CONTINUES) with thirty-nine points, the Gypsy Kings!

There is a cheer. We cut to the team at the back. It's the table of SCRUFFY LADS sitting near BRIAN. We cut to the Phoenix Club team. They look confused.

KENNY SNR
Who?!

SPENCER Ray ... there must have been a mistake ... because you didn't call us out.

RAY VON (shuffling through papers) Kenny Snr, Spencer and Young Kenny ... Is that you?

SPENCER Yeah.

RAY VON You came twelfth.

SPENCER Out of how many?

RAY VON Twelve.

CUT TO

48. INT. TONY KNOWLES SUITE. NIGHT
We cut to BRIAN at the back, near the bar, all smiles. DEN PERRY comes over.

BRIAN Well, Denzel, I didn't think much of your Top Banana. What happened there?

DEN PERRY At least they beat your lads ... that's all that matters.

BRIAN My lads? What do you mean? I won. I backed the winning team. Them's my boys over there!

DEN PERRY Yeh, but I thought ...

BRIAN Ah, you see, that's your problem, Denzel: you think too much. You think I'd back that shower of shit of mine? (CUT TO A SHOT OF THE PHOENIX CLUB TEAM STILL LOOKING SHOCKED) No way, no way, not a chance. I took out a bit of extra insurance ... them's my boys over there, the Gypsy Kings, the winning team ... standing over there with the gypsy quizmaster. (LAUGHS)

We cut to RAY VON and REP standing with the GYPSY KINGS. They're all raising a toast.

DEN PERRY You're a snake, Potter ... they had the answers, didn't they?

BRIAN Who knows? Maybe they did, maybe they didn't. You'll never know!

BRIAN shrugs. The door bangs open and they all turn to look. We cut to see JERRY, wearing BARBIE QUE's lime-green leotard, lipstick on his cheek, an afro wig, LES and ALAN behind. JERRY walks over to the bar.

JERRY All right, Brian, how did we do? Did we win? Did we win tonight. How did we do?! (HE LIFTS UP HIS LEOTARD, FOLLOWED BY THE SOUND OF HIS URINATING)

BRIAN Jerry, Jerry, Jerry ... What are you doing?

JERRY I've no idea.

JERRY, glazed-over eyes, falls straight back out of shot and hits the floor.

JERRY   Jerry! Get up, man!

DEN PERRY
(LAUGHING) Well, if that's what your Kamikaze Lager does, you can shove it!

REP   No ... no ... that is not Kamikaze Lager ... Kamikaze is ... (HE SAYS 'NON-ALCOHOLIC' IN JAPANESE)

BRIAN   It's what?

REP   Non-alcoholic.

BRIAN stares at him in disbelief.

DEN PERRY
(LAUGHING) Cheers, Potter, another winner!

DEN PERRY laughs, BRIAN puts his head in his hands.

Fountain of pee in bottom of shot.

CUT TO

END CREDITS

49. INT. PHOENIX CLUB
MAN auditioning with clockwork bear with 'HERE COMES SANTA CLAUS' playing.

BRIAN   Next!

THE END

Episode 5

PART ONE

1. INT. BRIAN'S HOUSE. NIGHT

Front room. We hear the sound of the midweek lottery starting on TV. We see overloaded plugs by the side of the TV. We pull out to reveal the lottery on the TV. The front room is full of Kamikaze lager.

BALLSY (ON TV)
    It's number fourteen. Seventh appearance in the National Lottery. Third ball tonight is number twenty-five. Nine times out for the main ball ...

We cut to the hallway and see BRIAN coming downstairs on his Schindler's stairlift. He's holding his lottery ticket when there's a power cut. The lights go off on the stairs and the stairlift stops.

BRIAN   It's the midweek lottery, the midweek lottery ... Come on!

BALLSY (ON TV)
    It's number forty-one for the second week running ... It's been out nine times now.

BRIAN   Come on, you friggin' thing (BANGS ARM OF STAIRLIFT) Here we go ...

BALLSY (ON TV)
    It's number ten ...

We cut to the front room to see the television and then the lights go out. Darkness. We see the outline of BRIAN sitting on the stairlift in the moon/street light.

BRIAN   Oh, whoa, whoa! Aaaah! Shit ... shit ... shit ... and shitter ... All right, keep calm, keep calm ... Right now – what would Thora Hird do?

CUT TO

OPENING CREDITS

CUT TO

2. INT. BRIAN'S HOUSE. DAY
BRIAN is slumped in the stairlift, asleep. Spit in the corner of his mouth. He wakes and looks around. His face says it all. He's been there all night, sniffs fingers.

BRIAN   Oh shit ... help!

CUT TO

3. EXT. BRIAN'S HOUSE. DAY
Establishing shot of the house.

CUT TO

4. INT. TONY KNOWLES SUITE. DAY
MAX and KENNY SNR. Poster in the background advertising the 'LADIES' NIGHT'. PADDY is reading a catalogue, shaking his head. SPENCER is cleaning glasses.

We cut into the catalogue.

PADDY   This is naughty, this, eh? Have
         you seen some of the gear in
         here? I didn't think Potter would
         have a Ladies' Night ... Look at that
         (FLICKS THROUGH) ... whips,
         chains, dildos. Roll on tonight eh.
         Are you working?

SPENCER No ... it's women only.

PADDY I bet it is. Hey, and you know what goes on at these Ladies' Nights, don't you? (HE LAUGHS KNOWINGLY AND SO DOES SPENCER)

SPENCER No.

PADDY Come on, Spence, you must have had your fair share (LOOKS UP AT HIM) ... Then again ... Well, let me tell you, my friend, the wine's not the only thing that flows ... All those bored housewives, they'll be gagging for it.

SPENCER My mum's a housewife ...

PADDY (NOT LOOKING UP) Is she? (HE HOLDS UP A PICTURE OF A SEMICLAD MODEL IN BLACK BONDAGE GEAR) Does she look like that? (SPENCER DROPS HIS GLASS)

We cut to MAX and KENNY SNR. They're looking at a catalogue.

MAX (SHAKING HIS HEAD) She's beautiful.

KENNY SNR
Hmmmm ...

MAX Look at that!

KENNY SNR
Lovely body.

We see a cut to a catalogue. Pictures of motor homes and caravans with prices underneath.

MAX I'd love one of them. It's always been a dream of mine: get one of them things and take off across country like Easy Rider ...

KENNY SNR
He had a bike!

MAX You know what I mean ... same thing.

KENNY SNR
A mate of mine had a Jacuzzi in his.

MAX Did he ... just the one?

KENNY SNR
Hey, look at these here ... half-price, reconditioned.

MAX How much is that one? I've not got me readers.

KENNY SNR
(READING) Three, nine, nine, five.

MAX Three, nine, nine, five! Ho, ho! Stick with the Volvo, Max, keep dreaming.

We cut to see JERRY enter.

JERRY Has anyone seen Brian?

They all shake their heads and mumble 'NO'.

CUT TO

5. INT. BRIAN'S HOUSE. DAY
BRIAN has unravelled the wool from his jumper to make a length of cord. We can see his T-shirt underneath with a happy yellow face on (rave symbol). We jump-cut to BRIAN's POV of the telephone. He's trying to hoop the phone on the table. It misses. (Umbrella stand at the bottom of the stairs)

BRIAN Go on ... ooohh ... come on, Potter, come on, Potter! Ooohh, this is the one ... this is the one! Come on! Go on! That's it, that's it, come to Daddy! Oooh ...

CUT TO

6. INT. PHOENIX CLUB. DAY
JERRY is on the phone trying to get hold of BRIAN.

CUT TO

7. INT./EXT. BRIAN'S HOUSE. DAY
BRIAN's now got an umbrella jammed between his legs, trying to loosen the mechanics. He's tiredly shouting for help. We hear the sound of a car approach. BRIAN reacts. We hear a car door slam and then JERRY appears through the frosted glass. He rings the doorbell: 'TEARS OF A CLOWN' by SMOKEY ROBINSON.

BRIAN   Jerry! Jerry, is that you?!

JERRY   Brian? Is that you?

We cut to exterior. JERRY looks through the letterbox.

BRIAN   I'm trapped man, I'm trapped, I'm trapped on the stairs! Kick the door in ...

JERRY   What with my back?

BRIAN   No, with your foot, you tool. Kick it in!

JERRY tries to kick the door in and puts his foot through a panel.

BRIAN   What are you doing? You broke my door! Shoulder it, you big dick.

JERRY tries again and shoulders it open.

JERRY   Aaah, come on!

JERRY breaks through the door.

BRIAN   Aah! You broke me door, you broke me door!

JERRY   (MOANING IN PAIN) I broke my foot!

BRIAN   Shut up, you girl. Get me down...

JERRY   What's that smell?

BRIAN   Never you mind what that smell is ... just get me down.

JERRY   What happened?

BRIAN   Bloody power cut, that's what's happened! I've been up here all night. Go on, get me down!

JERRY   Where's your fuse box?

BRIAN   Under the stairs. Under there, go on.

JERRY   What's this thing? Ah, it's just tripped out.

JERRY goes into the power box and flicks the switch. We cut to BRIAN.

BRIAN   Jerry!

He slides violently out of shot. We hear a crash as BRIAN hits the floor. He groans.

BRIAN   (Cont.) ... aaah, friggin' hell!

JERRY   What are you doing down there?

CUT TO

8. INT. GOLDEN PHOENIX SUITE. NIGHT

The room decor is any odd oriental tat that they could get. A big 'GOLDEN EAGLE' on the wall. JERRY wheels BRIAN into the room.

JERRY   Keep your eyes closed ... tight closed, right? Are they closed?

BRIAN's eyes are open.

BRIAN   Yeh.

JERRY   Open them.

BRIAN   (READS SIGN) 'The Golden Phoenix'?

JERRY   Hmmm.

BRIAN   Have you gone mad, man?

JERRY   Do you like it?

BRIAN   No, I do not like it! It looks like a Chinese brothel ...

JERRY   No, it doesn't.

BRIAN   We'll be a laughing stock. We're a working men's club, not a Chinese restaurant!

JERRY   Yeh, but, Brian, listen, I've had this idea. We can be both. We could be a *wok*-ing men's club!

BRIAN   Oh, Jerry, no, no. Jerry, people round here, they don't want chicken chop suet and sweets sold separately, they don't!

JERRY   Yeh, but they do, Brian – you're missing it all. They do. They can't get enough of it! Trust me. They can't make it fast enough, the lads. I'm telling you: this could be just what we need. Let's just give it a try. This food's worth a fortune!

BRIAN   Don't you think I'm traumatised enough without you showing me this? Don't you think that, what I've been through?

RAY VON Yeah, I heard about that. Are you all right?

BRIAN   It's just a blur Ray, it's just a blur ... well, till Chairman Mao here kicked me front door in.

RAY VON You must have shit yourself.

BRIAN   (LOOKS AT JERRY) Oh, thank you, big mouth ... Didn't take long, did it?

CUT TO

9. INT. GALAXY LOUNGE. NIGHT

HOLY MARY is browsing the table full of assorted sex toys. She picks up a package. DONNA is putting tickets on the toys: 'IF IT ENDS IN A FIVE, YOU WIN A NAUGHTY PRIZE'.

HOLY MARY

    (READING PACKAGING) Love eggs?

DONNA   That's right, just pop 'em up your flue before you go to work and I guarantee you'll come before the bus does.

HOLY MARY reads some more.

CUT TO

10. EXT. PHOENIX CLUB MAIN DOOR. NIGHT
PADDY and MAX on the door.

PADDY   Evening, ladies, have a nice night ...

LADY   We will.

PADDY   'We will!' Did you hear that! 'We will'. They're gagging for it. (LOOKS AT WATCH) It's not even kicked off yet! 'We will' ... ooh ... got to get in there ...

CUT TO

11. INT. GALAXY LOUNGE. NIGHT
Busy Galaxy Lounge. HOLY MARY's behind the bar. She's orgasmic now, sweating, banging on the bar, gasping her breath. JOYCE watches her, puzzled. WOMEN with sex name badges on. 'LADIES' NIGHT' by KOOL AND THE GANG. Batteries for sale behind the bar.

JOYCE   Are you OK? Do you want to sit down for a minute?

HOLY MARY
        No ... I'm all right ...

CUT TO

12. EXT. PHOENIX CLUB MAIN DOOR. NIGHT
MAX and PADDY are on the main door.

PADDY   They'll just be getting going in there now.

MAX   Have you farted?

PADDY   Yeh, I can't help it ...

Some WOMEN approach the club. PADDY sees them and ducks inside. MAX is embarrassed. He opens the door for them.

MAX   That stinks! You animal.

PADDY   Oooh ... I won't be long.

MAX   (POINTING) Hey, whoa, whoa ... Evening, ladies, sorry about the drains, sorry about the drains, love!

PAULA   That's all right.

The WOMEN enter. One of them (PAULA) lets her glance linger on MAX.

CUT TO

13. INT. GALAXY LOUNGE. NIGHT
The WOMEN are sitting around and DONNA is doing her spiel.

DONNA   Now, ladies, OK, now in your sexy starter kit ... we've got a whip! (CHEERS) Some handcuffs, (CHEERS) and a blindfold because

you don't want to look at him while he's doing it do you? (LAUGHTER) There you go! And also ... (HOLDS UP JAR) I can never get my tongue round this one ... let me think now ... choc, chip, dick, lick. (CHEERS) This has got to be an improvement, hasn't it?! ... No, no, don't taste that, love, it's a lubricant.

We cut to a shot of a women about to dip her tongue into a jar of lubricant. We hear HOLY MARY screaming 'SWEET JESUS' as she orgasms.

Cut to see her behind the bar.

DONNA   ... another satisfied customer!

All the WOMEN laugh.

CUT TO

14. EXT. PHOENIX CLUB MAIN DOOR. NIGHT
MAX and FANNY TICKLER.

MAX   All right, love?

PAULA   Yeah, just havin' a breather.

She takes out a cigarette.

MAX   (JUMPS TO IT, PULLS OUT A LIGHTER AND LIGHTS HER CIGARETTE) Yeh? Do you want a light?

PAULA   Oh, thanks ... oh, sorry ... cheers.

MAX   You here for the ladies' night ... Fanny?

PAULA   (LAUGHS) Fanny?! That's not me name... no, she give us them in there, these badges ... It was either this or Brenda Blowjob.

MAX   Good choice.

PAULA   Have you been bouncing long?

223

MAX   Too long.

PAULA   I bet you see a lot of violence and that, don't you?

MAX   Oh, aye ... oh, aye you get the odd knobhead, you know, but nothing I can't handle.

PAULA   So you can handle yourself, can you?

MAX   Oh, aye, you've got to be able to in this game love, you know – goes with the territory.

CUT TO

15. INT. GALAXY LOUNGE. NIGHT
DONNA is still doing her spiel.

DONNA   Did you know that your nose is the second most sensitive part of your body? There you go ...

We cut to the LADIES putting the vibrators to their noses and laughing.

DONNA   (cont.) That's nineteen ninety-nine, that one. It sucks, pumps and fits all car lighters ... and don't forget your Vibe 'n' shine for keeping them fresh ...

CUT TO

16. EXT. PHOENIX CLUB MAIN DOOR. NIGHT
MAX and PAULA are still chatting.

MAX   One time ... this guy came at me, he had a knife. Well, I say one 'guy' – there was four of them, four of them, you see. Gets me at the back entry. And if someone comes at you with a knife, and they're tooled up, you've got to do a bit, a bit of split-second thinking, Fanny, you see. It was either him or me.

PAULA   And?

MAX   I'm still here. They don't mess with the Daddy. Kiss, kiss, bang, bang! Eh? Meet K and O (SHOWS HER HIS FISTS).

PAULA   Do you ever do any private work?

MAX   What do you mean? Like pointing?

PAULA   (ANOTHER CIGARETTE. MAX LIGHTS IT) No, I've got ... I need someone taking out.

MAX   What, you mean like an escort service, yeh ... yeh ...

PAULA   No, no, it's my husband.

MAX   Your husband?

PAULA   I want someone to finger him.

MAX   I beg your pardon?

PAULA   I want him bumped off, I want him rubbed out. I want him dead.

MAX   You want him what, love? Oh aye ... oh aye, I get it. Where's Beadle (LOOKING AROUND) ... eh, eh? I know, aye, yeh. Get inside, love, get inside, you've had too much to drink. You're taking the piss!

PAULA   I'm not taking the piss. I want it done. I want him dead!

MAX   You want your husband dead?

PAULA   I've got money, I can pay you. I can pay whatever it costs.

MAX looks at her. She thinks 'FUCK YOU' and turns.

PAULA   Forget it, right ... just forget I said it. I'm going to get it done. If you don't want to do it, fine, but I'm going to get it done.

MAX   Whoa, whoa ... hey, hey, hey ... hey, love! You're serious, aren't you? Something like this, it's, er ... not cheap, you know ...

PAULA   How much?

MAX   Three, nine, nine, five? Call it four grand, four grand.

PAULA   Right, fine. When can you do it?

MAX   I don't know ... er ... I'll have to make a few calls, you know. Put a few feelers out.

PAULA hands him a piece of paper.

MAX   (cont.) What's that?

PAULA   My mobile ... Give me a ring when you've sorted it.

She goes back inside.

END OF PART ONE

PART TWO

17. INT. GALAXY LOUNGE/FOYER. NIGHT
DONNA doing her spiel.

DONNA   Ladies have I got a treat for you tonight! It's cabaret time! Would you please welcome on stage, he's here at very short notice, the lord of love, Lord Love Rocket.

We hear 'LET'S GET READY TO RUMBLE' by ANT and DEC. Spotlight on a bare arse (G-string). We tilt up, reveal it's PADDY. He turns and starts to dance erotically. Wearing

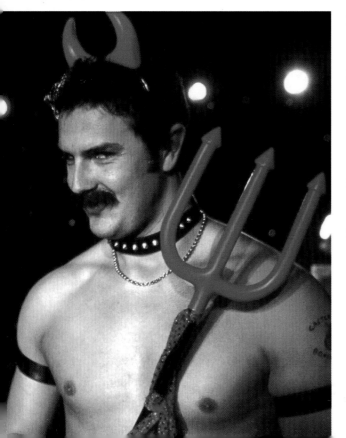

devil's horns and carrying a three-pronged devil's fork, a droopy moustache. Tattoo of boxing gloves on his shoulder. The WOMEN scream and go wild.

CUT TO

18. EXT. PHOENIX CLUB MAIN DOOR. NIGHT
MAX chats to PAULA.

MAX   I've made a few calls and ... it's going to cost you eight grand.

PAULA   Eight grand ... you said it was four.

MAX   Eight grand.

PAULA   Well, why has it doubled?

MAX   Well, this is a two-man job, love. If it were a one-man job ... four. I can't do it on my own, so it's a two-man job.

PAULA   Yeh, I'm just thinking. It's a lot of money to me, that.

MAX   Well, if you want it done, you've got to do it properly – and that's everything. It's a full service: disposal of the body, petrol – it's all in.

PAULA   So this other bloke ... I mean, is he any good or what?

MAX   Oh ... oh, yeh, he's one of the best.

CUT TO

18. INT. GALAXY LOUNGE. NIGHT
We cut back. A WOMAN is now lying on her back on stage while PADDY does press-ups over her.

CUT TO

20. EXT. PHOENIX CLUB MAIN DOOR. NIGHT

MAX   The price on the streets is eight grand.

PAULA   Right.

We hear a scream from inside the club.

MAX   Just hang on love ...

MAX goes in the club.

CUT TO

21. INT. GALAXY LOUNGE. NIGHT.
MAX comes running into the room and sees chaos. The WOMEN have charged the stage. PADDY is in the corner trying to fight them back with an inflatable penis.

CUT TO

22. INT. GENTS' TOILETS. NIGHT
PADDY is delicately nursing his cuts and scratches.

PADDY   Bitches! I tell you what: if I hadn't have farted ... they'd have ripped me head off ... Ow!!

MAX   So what do you reckon?

PADDY   She wants us to kill her husband? Is she a mental?

MAX   She doesn't seem it and she's offered us a thousand pounds.

PADDY   A thousand pounds? (STARES BLANKLY AND THEN SMILES)

MAX   Each!

PADDY   I'll blow his head off.

CUT TO

23. EXT. COUNTRYSIDE. DAY
*MAX's car pulls into shot and stops. We cut
inside MAX's Volvo. MAX is driving, TERRY,
his brother, in the back and PADDY in the
passenger seat. PADDY yawns.*

MAX   Right. We're having a little field
         trip today.

PADDY   Well, we're in the right place.
         (YAWNS AGAIN. TO TERRY) I'm
         frigged. You know, he made me
         watch *Léon* four times last night,
         him ... Then we had to sleep sitting
         up. I only got about an hour's kip.

MAX   It's all part of the training. Look
         at this.

*MAX is slowly unwrapping a piece of velvet
material.*

PADDY   Have you done us a packed lunch?

MAX   Have I! (PULLS OUT A GUN)

PADDY   What's that?

MAX   That, my friend, is a Broomhandle
         Mauser.

PADDY   I'm not using that ...

MAX   Why, what's wrong with it?

PADDY   It's an antique ...

MAX   It's not an antique. There's nothing
         wrong with that. It was my

granddad's, this. He shot a German
with this.

PADDY   What, in the war?

MAX   No, Benidorm, they had a row over
         a sun lounger.

TERRY   He didn't do things by half,
         Granddad.

MAX   He gave me this you know ... for my
         thirteenth birthday.

PADDY   Thoughtful.

TERRY   Bollocks ... you never told me.

MAX   I never told no one.

TERRY   All I got was a Spacehopper ...
         that burst!

MAX   (UNDER BREATH) I know ...
         I shot it.

CUT TO

24. EXT. FIELD. DAY
*TERRY is nervously placing an empty bottle
(of French beer) on the fence. As he puts it
down it explodes.*

TERRY   Bollocks ... hey! Hey! You nearly killed me!

We cut to MAX holding the gun. He and PADDY are laughing.

MAX   Shut up, you soft bastard. Put 'em on the wall!

We cut to TERRY. He's wiping glass off himself. He starts to put another bottle on the fence. PADDY is holding the gun. He's taking aim. MAX holds his arm.

MAX   Here ... gently does it, just hold it ... I know what I'm doing ... it's like a lady.

PADDY   Yes, I know.

MAX   Just hold it right. Relax your wrist.

PADDY   Max! I know how to shoot a gun.

MAX   It's a Broomhandle Mauser, it's not a gun!

PADDY   Max! I know what I'm doing!

MAX   Right, OK. Go on.

PADDY relaxes and fires the gun. We hear TERRY scream out of shot.

CUT TO

25. INT. MAX'S CAR. NIGHT
MAX (behind the wheel) and PADDY sit across from an Indian restaurant.

MAX   I can't believe you shot my brother ...

PADDY   He'll live. It was only a flesh wound ...

MAX   Casualty for four hours. Mum's gonna go up the wall ...

PADDY   He'll be all right.

MAX   He was s'posed to be shifting her fridge tonight.

PADDY   It'll be right. (MAX GIVES HIM A LOOK) So what's the crack here anyhow?

MAX   She's in there with him now. They're gonna have a meal. She's gonna get him pissed, then she's going to drive him out into the sticks for a shag ... That's when we take over.

PADDY   I'm not shaggin' him ... not for a grand.

MAX   Not shag him, shoot him, you prick.

PADDY   (LOOKS AT WATCH) Having something to eat? They'll be ages ... I've got to work tonight: Potter's opening up the restaurant tonight, you know.

CUT TO

26. INT. GOLDEN PHOENIX SUITE. NIGHT
All MAIN CAST and the REGULAR who played the nonce (in false tan and nappy). A few REPORTERS and PHOTOGRAPHERS. There's a countdown from five.

JERRY/BRIAN
    Three, two, one ...

JERRY   I honourably declare the Golden Phoenix ... open!

The NONCE in the nappy hits a huge gong. JERRY pulls the string and unveils the gold dragon with 'THE GOLDEN PHOENIX' underneath. There are flashbulbs and a small round of applause.

BRIAN   This is Jerry St Clair, the licensee. If you'd like to put any of your questions to him, do feel free.

FEMALE REPORTER
    Mr St Clair ... Jane Crossley, *Bolton Independent Leader*. Where did you get the idea?

JERRY   Well ... what happened was—

BRIAN   It just came to me ... in a flash. Like St Paul on the road to Domestos. Talk about wood for trees! We're selling food behind the bar today! I said let's open a restaurant. Next thing you know Jed's a millionaire. Things are going to change now, love. It's gonna be out with the sausage roll and in with the spring ...

ANOTHER REPORTER
    ... where did you find the chefs?

BRIAN looks at JERRY nervously.

BRIAN   There they are, Ant and Dec ... Our Barbara's lads, God rest her soul. (THEY BOTH WAVE) Look at them, fresh out of cooking college. Happy as sand boys the pair of them. They can't speak a word of the Queen's but they can knock the shit out of an Egg Chow Mein quicker than you can say 'Triad'.

FEMALE REPORTER
      ... Mr St Clair, what do you think the rival clubs will make of all this?

JERRY   Well, to be honest what I hope—

BRIAN   Balls to 'em and Den Perry ... they can go and whistle. Something like this'll kick clubland up the arse. They better shape up or ship out. We'll make a fortune ... cookie. (LAUGHS)! Here, we've got some of them there: homemade fortune cookies ... Just crack one off, son ... (WE CUT TO THE REPORTER, WHO BREAKS A FORTUNE COOKIE) What's it say?

REPORTER
      Piss flaps.

KENNY SNR, SPENCER and YOUNG KENNY giggle.

BRIAN   (LOOKING AROUND EMBARRASSED) Piss flaps? Piss flaps? What the hell's that about? Piss flaps? Excuse me ...

CUT TO

27. INT. MAX'S CAR. NIGHT
MAX and PADDY are still on their stakeout.

MAX   This'd make a good film. This is a good story ... what we're doing now.

PADDY   Who'd play you?

MAX   Steven Segal ... he's the only one, he's got the hand speed.

PADDY   I was thinking more Danny DeVito.

MAX   Cheeky bastard! Danny DeVito – he's about four foot! (SEES PAULA AND HUSBAND LEAVING THE TANDOORI) Oh, this is them, this is them. Here we go ...

MAX starts the engine. We cut to see PAULA outside the pub getting into a car with her HUSBAND.

MAX   (Cont.) Put me tape in, put me tape in.

MAX pushes a tape into the car stereo. 'IN THE AIR TONIGHT' by PHIL COLLINS comes on.

MAX   (Cont.) That's her there and that's him ... that's ... that's him with her ... that's it ... there they go.

CUT TO

28. EXT. MAIN ROAD. NIGHT
PAULA drives off. MAX indicates in the Volvo and turns out of the side road and follows.

CUT TO

29. EXT. MAIN ROAD. NIGHT

PAULA *drives down the main street. We*
jump-cut to MAX and PADDY – they drive
about four hundred yards behind her.

CUT TO

30. EXT. COUNTRYSIDE. NIGHT

Dirt track. PAULA's *car is pulled over. We*
hear her laughter and muffled talk from
them both. We cut to PAULA *kneeling on a*
blanket. Her HUSBAND *is in front of her*
(we'll call him PAUL*).*

PAUL   Move up a bit!

PAULA   Hang on ... I'm moving! Hang on a
        minute!

PAUL   We've not done this for a long time,
        have we love. Right you want to see
        him, do you?

PAULA   Well, we're not here for a picnic,
        are we?

PAUL   Say please, then.

PAULA   Oh, here, come on.

PAUL   Come on, you know you want it.

PAULA   Oh ... God ... pretty please, get him
        out!

PAUL   Hang on ...

PAULA   Get on with it.

PAUL   (HE LOOKS DOWN TO HIS FLY AND
        GETS HIS PENIS OUT, OUT OF SHOT)
        There you are, there he is, the little
        pork soldier out on parade. 'Tention!
        There you are, grab him, come on!

MAX *jams the gun into* PAUL's *neck.*

PAUL   Aye, aye, what's going on? Who are
        you?

MAX   We're your worst nightmare, flower.
        You know what that is in the back
        of your head?

PAUL   What is it?

MAX   It's a Broomhandle Mauser.
        (LOOKING AT HIS PENIS) Do you
        want to put that away son?

PAUL   Yeh, yeh, yeh ... calm down, lads.
        Calm down.

MAX   We don't want any heroes.

PAUL   OK.

MAX   Right. Now get up slowly.

PAUL   Yeh, yeh.

MAX   Slowly, do you hear me?

PAUL   Calm down, lads, calm down ...
        yeh, yeh ...

MAX	It's a gun, get up!
PAUL	What is it you want, money? She's got money, she's loaded. (SHOUTING TO PAULA) Give him your bag … go get help, phone my mam.

They both drag him off.

CUT TO

31. EXT. COUNTRYSIDE. NIGHT

MAX and PADDY are leading PAUL through a field. PADDY gripping his arm, MAX the other whilst pointing the gun at him. PADDY stumbles.

MAX	Get up, will you!
PADDY	I'm getting mud all over me Armani copies …
MAX	Shut up!
PADDY	Jesus, Max, get him down there!
MAX	(ASIDE TO PADDY) Whoa, don't tell him my name, dickhead …
PADDY	We're gonna kill him anyway.

There's a moan from PAUL.

PAUL	Please, lads, come on. Look, I'll do anything, I'll get you anything … I can get you proper Armanis, you know …
MAX	Shut up!
PADDY	Can you get Versace?
PAUL	Hey, yeah anything!
MAX	Hey, you'll be able to get as many Versaces you want when you get your money!

PAUL	Money? Is it money? Look, whatever it is they're paying you I'll double it, I'll treble it … you can have my car.
PADDY	What sort of car is it?
MAX	Look, it's not friggin' *Swap Shop*.
PAUL	Oh, please!
MAX	(TO PADDY – LOOKS ROUND) Right, here'll do.

PAUL moans. MAX pushes him down.

PAUL	Oh, God, please. Please.
MAX	(HE HOLDS THE GUN OUT) Right, go on, kill him.
PADDY	You what?
MAX	Go on, shoot him!
PAUL	Please … no … no … please …
MAX	Shut up!
PADDY	Shoot him now?

MAX   Yes!

PAUL   Help me, I don't want to die please
        ... Oh, no, please ... No, no, no ... I
        don't want to die ... Please ... No ...
        Please ...

PADDY   (SWEATING) I can't.

MAX   What do you mean you can't?

PADDY   I can't do it.

MAX   You didn't have a problem with
        our Terry when you blew his back
        leg off.

PADDY   (SWEATING) I can't ... I can't do it,
        Max ... here. (HANDS GUN TO MAX)

PAUL   No please ... don't kill me please ...
        oh no ... no please ... please ...
        no ... no ...

*We cut to PAULA sitting in the driver's side
of her car nervously smoking. There is the
sound of a single gunshot. She jumps.*

*We cut to the field. We see PAUL lying on
the floor with his eyes shut. We cut to
PADDY. He turns around and looks
nervously at the body. We cut to the body.
PAUL opens one eye and then the other.*

PADDY   You missed ... How could you miss
        him from there?

MAX   I've not missed ... See this, son?
        (MAX LEANS DOWN TO PAUL AND
        TAKES AN ENVELOPE FROM HIS
        INSIDE POCKET) There's three
        thousand pounds here.

PADDY   What? Three grand? Where's that
        gun?

MAX   Get off, you! You've had your
        chance. Take it, go abroad, don't
        come back. Do you hear me? If you
        come back we will find you and we
        will kill you, right?

PAUL   Yes, Max.

MAX   Right, now get out of here ... before
        I change my mind. Go on!

*PAUL staggers to his feet and runs off into
the field and the night.*

PADDY   Three grand?

MAX   Think about it: he's gone, he won't
        come back. She's happy: she thinks
        he's dead. We're happy: we've got
        our money. Think about it, Patrick.

PADDY   (THINKING) You'll do for me.

MAX   Right! Let's finish it.

*We cut to PAULA sitting in her car (headlights
on) still smoking. Her expression drops when
she sees MAX and PADDY walk out of a
clearing and up to the dirt track. They walk
to MAX's car.*

PAULA   Is it over? I heard the gunshot ...

MAX   It's done, love.

PAULA   (CRYING) Oh, God, do you think I've
        done the right thing?

MAX   Well, it's a bit late now ... go on,
        get out of here. You haven't seen
        us alright?

*PAULA starts her engine and drives off. MAX
and PADDY watch as the car drives off.*

PADDY   (STARTS TO SMILE) One thousand pounds. Dink, dank, do ...

MAX   Stick with your uncle Max, Patrick. You won't go far wrong.

CUT TO

EPILOGUE

32. EXT. MOBILE/CARAVAN SHOWROOM. DAY

MAX is looking at the trailer home: £3,995.

We cut to see MAX counting the money out into the MAN's hand.

We cut to see MAX driving out of the showroom in his new reconditioned trailer home, past a sign at the entrance that reads 'BIG JO'S, KINGS OF THE ROAD – TRAILERS FOR SALE OR RENT'. We hear 'BORN TO BE WILD' by STEPPENWOLF.

TO BE CONTINUED.

CUT TO

END CREDITS

33. INT. PHOENIX CLUB.

MAN auditioning at Phoenix Club – only a small gorilla-like toy moving about to the music.

BRIAN   (OOV) I don't believe it! It's him again. It's him look!

We see BRIAN'S's reaction.

BRIAN   Is that it? Do you do anything else?

MAN AT AUDITION
   No, there's no more.

BRIAN   Right then ... well fuck off!

LAUGHTER.

THE END

Episode 6

PART ONE

1. EXT. THE PHOENIX CLUB/MAIN ROAD. NIGHT

YOUNG KENNY is driving down the road towards the club on his scooter (Courier carrier on the back). A GROUP OF PEOPLE walking down the road turn to enter the club. We follow them down the steps. We cut in on a sign over the door: 'ENTERTAINMENT COMPLEX AND CHINESE RESTAURANT'.

MAX   Evening, boys.

CUT TO

2. INT. KITCHEN. NIGHT

ANT and DEC are busy cooking. HOLY MARY, in kimono, is on the phone taking orders looking through a big book. YOUNG KENNY enters the room.

HOLY MARY
     I'm sorry, love, no, we're fully booked, love ... We've nothing Thursday, Friday or Saturday ... Not Sunday, love, no, no ... Sunday's a day of rest, love!

CUT TO

3. INT. JERRY'S OFFICE. NIGHT

BRIAN is counting the night's takings. JERRY enters.

JERRY   Brian! Hey!

BRIAN   Look at this, Jerry. Hand over fist, we're raking it in!

JERRY   Hey, I've just had the brewery on the phone.

BRIAN   Have you? What did they want?

JERRY   They wanted to congratulate us on our success.

BRIAN   Did they, now?

JERRY   They did, and said they wouldn't mind coming down and that they might have a proposition for us.

BRIAN   I said, I said they would come crawling back. About time, too!

JERRY   You said we didn't need the brewery.

BRIAN   Well, that was then. This is now. Now we're a success, with the brewery's money behind us, who knows? We could open a chain. Two words, Jerry: investment. We'll get 'em down, give them a good night, a night they'll never forget. Wheel out the big guns, Jerry.

JERRY   What have you got in mind?

BRIAN   A big birthday bash.

JERRY   Why? Whose birthday is it?

BRIAN   It'll be ours ... if we get that brewery money.

CUT TO

4. EXT. THE BANANA GROVE. DAY
Establishing shot. A grey winter's day, a dilapidated palm tree.

We cut in on YOUNG KENNY, putting up a poster for 'STARS IN THEIR EYES' NIGHT.

CUT TO

5. INT. DEN PERRY'S OFFICE. DAY
DEN reading a newspaper. Cutaway of a picture of BRIAN and JERRY smiling. Headline 'THE GOLDEN PHOENIX STILL RISING'.

DEN PERRY
         (READING PAPER) Have you seen this? Have you seen it?! 'Punters today want something more and that's what we're giving them. The future's bright, the future's Phoenix ...' (DEN THROWS THE PAPER DOWN) 'The future's Phoenix'! Prick! He's ruining us all with this Chinese restaurant crap. Nobody in last night, empty again tonight ...

ANOTHER CRONY of Den's enters carrying a ripped-down poster. He hands it to DEN.

CRONY   Have you seen this?

We cut to the poster: 'DUGGY HAYES PRESENTS "STARS IN THEIR EYES" GRAND BIRTHDAY BASH (PROCEEDS GO TO A

POORLY BOY) AT THE PHOENIX CLUB. £15 A TICKET (INCLUDES CHINESE STARTER.)'

CRONY   I just caught that tiger of Potter's putting them up outside ... He said they've got the brewery coming down.

DEN PERRY
    (PICKING UP THE PHONE) Did he? Well they'll be the only ones there when I've finished ... (DIALS) Duggy Hayes please. (PAUSE) Hello, Duggy, it's Jerry St Clair here from the Phoenix Club ... Listen, Duggy, the 'Stars in Their Eyes' night on the twenty-first ... I'm going to have to pull it ... We've hardly sold a ticket ... Den Perry's got a big night on down the Banana Grove. We can't— Yeh, he is a fat bastard, yes ... I understand that, Duggy, we'll pay for any inconvenience. And you ... OK, thanks old son. Ciao.

DEN chuckles to himself and opens his cigar box, he has only one cigar left.

DEN PERRY (cont.)
    Looks like I'm gonna need some more cigars, boys! Ha Haa Haah!

He takes the old cigar stub and smoulders it through the newspaper picture of BRIAN and JERRY.

CUT TO

OPENING CREDITS

CUT TO

6. EXT. PHOENIX CLUB CAR PARK. DAY
We see a close-up of YOUNG KENNY, carefully painting a yellow line on the ground, his tongue hanging out. We hear BRIAN and JERRY talking.

We cut to them as they turn the corner. KENNY SNR is pushing BRIAN.

JERRY   Who are the brewery sending? Mark Brennan or somebody? Never heard of him!

BRIAN   I don't care, Jerry, we should give the five-star treatment tonight. Pull out all the stops.

BRIAN   (HE SEES YOUNG KENNY ON THE FLOOR) Whoa, whoa, whoa, what's that?

YOUNG KENNY

It's your disabled-parking space.

BRIAN   I know what it is. What's that in his
         hand?

YOUNG KENNY

It's your vase. It's you!

BRIAN   Get it off ... get it off now ...
         Do you hear me? I'll roll over
         your fingers!

*BRIAN's distracted by the noise of a door
slamming. We cut to MAX's motor home
in the corner of the car park. MAX is
emptying a bucket of water into a grid.
PADDY is with him.*

BRIAN   Oy, Petrocelli? Are you shifting that
         thing or what?! I've got a full house
         tonight! You're taking up three
         parking spaces with that frigger!

MAX   I'm moving it.

BRIAN   You've been saying that for three
         weeks. They'll start charging you
         council tax.(TO YOUNG KENNY)
         Move, move, move!

CUT TO

7. EXT. MAIN ROAD OUTSIDE RICE AND EASY. DAY

PADDY eating chips, leaning on a bin.

*We jump-cut. PADDY sees PAUL (PAULA's
HUSBAND from Episode 5) walking towards
him. Tanned, Hawaiian shirt, slightly drunk.
He walks past PADDY, oblivious of him.
PADDY stares at him in shock.*

*We cut as MAX comes out of the baker's
with a paper bag.*

MAX   I got you an egg custard ... What's
         up with you?

PADDY   He's back.

MAX   Who's back?

PADDY   The husband ... the one we gave the
         money to, to disappear. He's back!

MAX stares at him blankly.

MAX   What husband?

PADDY   The one we were supposed to shoot
         ... but didn't! He's back!

MAX   Back where? He's supposed to be
         abroad.

PADDY   Well, he's just gone in the bookie's.

CUT TO

8. EXT. MAIN ROAD. DAY

*Outside the bookie's. PAUL is just on his way
out through the door when he bumps into
MAX and PADDY. He instantly recognises
them. MAX throws him up against the door.*

PAUL   Oooh, shit! Er ... all right, boys?
         No ... no!

*MAX and PADDY exchange a look and then
drag PAUL off.*

CUT TO

9. EXT. PHOENIX CLUB MAIN DOOR. NIGHT

MAX and PADDY on the door. 'STARS IN THEIR EYES – SOLD OUT' posters behind them. We start on a shot of TWO MIDDLE-AGED WOMEN walking down the steps into the club.

MAX   Evening, ladies.

PADDY   Nice legs. What time do they open?

GIRL   Oh, piss off!

The GIRLS enter.

PADDY   Oh, yes, I'm on there. Jesus, man, snap out of it! What's up with you?!

MAX   I've things on my mind.

PADDY   Don't worry ... he's gone! We put the frighteners on him! He won't be coming back ... Forget it!

PAULA   (GETTING OUT OF CAB) *Oy!*

MAX and PADDY turn to look. We cut to see PAULA standing in front of the taxi.

MAX   Oh, shit, it's his wife. Leave this to me ... don't you say a word!

PAULA   Well, if it isn't the Hit Man and Her.

MAX   All right, Fanny?

PAULA   I'll give you 'Fanny'! He's alive, back from the bloody dead.

MAX   Who?

PAULA   You bloody well know who: my husband.

MAX   Well, he was dead when we left him.

PAULA   Was he, now? Was he now? Well he's just kicked my back door down and asked what's for tea.

MAX   I can explain.

PAULA   I don't want anything explained. I want my eight thousand pounds back.

PADDY   Eight thousand pounds? You gave me a grand.

PAULA   Looks like he's ripped us both off love. Where's it gone?

PADDY   I'll tell you where it's gone, flower: luxurious motor home.

PAULA   Well, you'd better get it sold and quick 'cause I want it back – all of it.

MAX   Now hang on – a deal's a deal love.

PADDY   Eight grand?

PAULA   No, *you* hang on ... Now listen to me: I came to you for help, you lied to me but you took my money. Well, I've been to see some people tonight, some real villains, not ten-a-penny jokers like you two. And guess what. This time, I'm going to get the job done much cheaper.

MAX   I've told you, killing him is not the answer, love!

PAULA   Who said anything about killing *him*?

She walks off and gets back into the taxi, it drives away.

MAX   Hey!

She walks back to the taxi and flicks the V sign to MAX and PADDY. MAX and PADDY watch her leave in the taxi.

PADDY   *Eight grand?!*

CUT TO

10. INT. GOLDEN PHOENIX SUITE. NIGHT
There's a sign on the door saying 'SMITHILLS BREWERY, PRIVATE PARTY.' BRIAN is at the bar with brewery reps.

BRIAN   And is this the wife?

MARK   No.

BRIAN   Oh, I see ... I see ... cat's away and all that ...

MARK   No, this is my fiancée, Dawn.

BRIAN   Is it?! Dawn! Pleased to meet you, Dawn.

DAWN   Nice to meet you.

BRIAN   Yeh, I'm Brian Potter ... yeh ... yeh ... Do you like what we've done with the place?

DAWN   Yeh, yeh, it's really nice. Mark told me about the fire.

BRIAN   Oh, yeh, talk about a kick in the balls ... Oh, you wouldn't know. Well, you wouldn't, would you? I hope! (LAUGHS) Yeh ... they laughed at me when I said I wanted to rebuild this place, but if you look through history they've always laughed at life's pioneers, you know: Sir Walter Raleigh ... I bet they

pissed themselves when he brought tobacco over ... Look at him now ... he's made a fortune on the fags and ... bikes.

CUT TO

11. EXT. PHOENIX CLUB MAIN DOOR. NIGHT
MAX and PADDY

PADDY   Eight grand!

MAX   I was going to give you some more, you know.

PADDY   Yeah, when?

MAX   When I got ... sorted. In time, I was going to give you some. I just ...

PADDY   Eight grand!

CUT TO

12. INT. GOLDEN PHOENIX SUITE. NIGHT

DAWN   (TO BRIAN) What's that like?

BRIAN   Twenty? Oh it's bootylicious, bootylicious, love. (LOOKS AT MENU) Leeches?

SPENCER Lychees. It's a pudding.

BRIAN   I know what it is, mouth!

SPENCER OK.

CUT TO

13. EXT. PHOENIX CLUB MAIN DOOR. NIGHT
MAX and PADDY

PADDY   Hey, do you think she's got, you know, got somebody to kill us, do you?

MAX   Why not? She hired us to kill somebody, didn't she?

PADDY   Eight grand, though.

CUT TO

14. INT. GOLDEN PHOENIX SUITE. NIGHT

MARK   So how's 'Stars in Their Eyes'? What have you got lined up for us, then?

BRIAN   (MOUTHFUL OF FOOD) Oh, you're in for a treat tonight. These kids, they look and sound like the real thing. It's uncanny. I tell you something, I were sat in the bloody office this afternoon and I heard them practising, and I shouted, 'Turn that radio down!' Eh, that's how good they ... You can't tell the difference!

JERRY comes over.

JERRY   Brian!

BRIAN   Yeh? Oh this is Jerry St Clair – now licensee and my left foot. This is Mark Brennan, Smithills Brewery, and Dawn his ... bit on the si—

JERRY   (ON EDGE) Brian, could I have a word?

BRIAN   What?

JERRY   A word ...

BRIAN   I'm schmoozing now, Jerry ... if you don't mind ... Oh, hang on!

JERRY   (HE STARTS TO WHEEL BRIAN OUT) Sorry about this. It's just, you know, he's needed – with show business and, you know, that sort of stuff.

CUT TO

15. INT. THE PHOENIX CLUB FOYER. NIGHT
BRIAN, LES, ALAN and JERRY are gathered. EXTRAS go through.

BRIAN   What ... what ... Bloody hell, Jerry, I'm on there with the brewery, I'm in there! Drag me—

JERRY   Sssshhhh!

BRIAN   What's happened?

JERRY   What's happened? Listen ... The acts for 'Stars in Their Eyes', they're not coming.

BRIAN   They what?

JERRY   They're not coming.

BRIAN   What do you mean they're not coming?

JERRY   Well, you know they were coming; well now, they're not.

BRIAN   Don't start getting sarcastic, Jerry! Have you phoned Duggy Hayes?

JERRY   Yes, he said I phoned up and cancelled the whole show.

BRIAN   What did you do that for?

JERRY   Well, I didn't. I haven't spoken to Duggy Hayes for weeks. Somebody must have rung him pretending to be me.

ALAN   Who'd do that?

BRIAN   I'll tell you who'd do that ... Den Perry ... that's who'd do that.

LES   Well, what are we going to do now?

END OF PART ONE

PART TWO

16. INT. GALAXY LOUNGE. NIGHT
Packed out. BREWERY REPS/REGULARS.
We cut to BRIAN joining the BREWERY REP
and his WIFE at the back of the room.

JERRY   Good evening, ladies and gentlemen.
        I'm Jerry St Clair, your host and
        compere and licensee of the Phoenix
        Club, welcoming you to our 'Stars in
        Their Eyes' night! Apologies for the
        late start ...

BRIAN   All right?!

MARK   (LOOKS AT WATCH) Everything all
        right, Brian?

BRIAN   Yeh, why?

MARK   Late starting ...

BRIAN   You know the drill: the longer you
        wait, the more they'll sup.

We cut back to JERRY.

JERRY   So let's get the show on the road
        with our first act tonight, singing
        live it's ... Lu Lu!

Applause. HOLY MARY walks nervously
to centre stage, silence. Few cutaways of
AUDIENCE. Worried BRIAN. She looks over
to JERRY, he nods for her to start.

HOLY MARY
        (SINGING) 'Weeeeellllll, (THE
        AUDIENCE JUMP) you know you
        make me want to shout ...'

LES and ALAN back her – she really goes
for it.

CUT TO

17. INT. TONY KNOWLES SUITE. NIGHT
SPENCER and KENNY SENIOR are looking
through a costume hamper.

SPENCER I don't know who I can be.

KENNY SNR
        Just keep looking – there's got to be
        something in there. What do you
        think of this?

KENNY SNR pulls out a green wig and a
cowboy hat and puts them on.

SPENCER Who are you?

KENNY SNR
        I don't know. I was hoping you
        would.

CUT TO

18 INT. GALAXY LOUNGE. NIGHT
HOLY MARY (LU LU) – her confidence grown – is singing fast. LES ALANOS are struggling to keep up. She's flinging herself around.

CUT TO

19 INT. KITCHEN. NIGHT
ANT and DEC are washing pots and are singing along to 'LULU'.

CUT TO

20. INT. GALAXY LOUNGE. NIGHT
HOLY MARY (LU LU) is really going for it.

The AUDIENCE and BRIAN are cheering and applauding.

CUT TO

21. EXT. PHOENIX CLUB MAIN DOOR. NIGHT

PADDY   Did you phone her? What did she say?

MAX   Answer machine …

PADDY   Did you leave a message?

MAX   Did I balls! Saying what? 'Please don't kill us'?

PADDY   I've been thinking you know, maybe we could reason with them, you know, whoever's going to do it?

MAX   I doubt it. Once they've been given the target they won't deviate … This type of beast only speaks one language, Patrick – violence.

CUT TO

22. INT. GALAXY LOUNGE. NIGHT
LES and ALAN backing.

JERRY   Ladies and gentlemen … tonight singing live it's … (READS PAPER) Adam and the Ants.

We hear the opening drums to 'PRINCE CHARMING'. Spotlight hits the stage. RAY VON, LES and ALAN come through the smoke dressed as the band. We cut to BRIAN singing along. He looks at the BREWERY REP.

CUT TO

23. INT. TONY KNOWLES SUITE. NIGHT
SPENCER is searching through the props hamper. He starts to pull out a huge pair of boots. Smiles.

SPENCER   Now you're talking!

CUT TO

24. INT. GALAXY LOUNGE. NIGHT
RAY VON, LES and ALAN (ADAM AND THE
ANTS) are still performing on stage.

CUT TO

25. EXT. PHOENIX CLUB CAR PARK. NIGHT
MAX comes out of of his motor home with
some baking trays. Looks around.

CUT TO

26. EXT. PHOENIX CLUB MAIN DOOR.
NIGHT
MAX hides the baking tray down the front of
his jacket.

PADDY   What's that?

MAX   It's a baking tray ... (HANDS HIM A
CAKE ONE) Here.

PADDY   Is it bulletproof?

MAX   It's nonstick.

CUT TO

27. INT. GALAXY LOUNGE. NIGHT
JERRY is on stage dressed as EMINEM –
hockey mask, dungarees, hedge strimmer –
singing (plug hanging) 'THE REAL SLIM
SHADY' ('WILL THE REAL SLIM SHADY
PLEASE STAND UP, PLEASE STAND UP ...').
Cut to see CONFUSED PENSIONERS
standing up.

CUT TO

28. INT. TONY KNOWLES SUITE. NIGHT
YOUNG KENNY is tarting up his scooter.

CUT TO

29. INT. GALAXY LOUNGE. NIGHT

SPENCER as GARY GLITTER. Huge boots and suit covered in tin foil. Hair combed out. He's having trouble walking in his huge foil shoes. 'DO YOU WANT TO BE IN MY GANG?' SHOCKED AUDIENCE. SPENCER loses his balance and topples off the stage. This causes the AUDIENCE to go wild and cheer. Feedback from mic.

CUT TO

30. EXT. PHOENIX CLUB MAIN DOOR. NIGHT

MAX IS LOOKING ROUND NERVOUSLY. PADDY comes up behind him with a cup of tea.

PADDY   Hey!

MAX   Hey, you pillock! What's that?

PADDY   A cup of tea.

MAX   Who made it?

PADDY   Me!

MAX   Did you leave the room?

PADDY   I had a piss while kettle boiled.

MAX tips it on the floor.

PADDY   (cont.) What are you doing?

MAX   It could have been poisoned, man!

CUT TO

31. INT. GALAXY LOUNGE. NIGHT

JERRY on stage.

JERRY   Tonight singing live ... it's Meatloaf.

We hear the opening of 'BAT OUT OF HELL'. Side doors open, smoke and light pour in.

CUT TO

32. INT./EXT. PHOENIX CLUB MAIN DOOR/FOYER. NIGHT

We cut to MAX and PADDY. YOUNG KENNY drives through the foyer on his scooter (dressed as MEATLOAF). They both turn but he's gone.

MAX   I'm telling you, Paddy, you've got to have eyes in the back of your head.

CUT TO

33. INT. GALAXY LOUNGE. NIGHT
*YOUNG KENNY drives his scooter
(disguised as a Harley) onto the stage.
We cut to BRIAN, in shock, But when
MARK and DAWN turn to him, smiling, he
hypocritically smiles, too. YOUNG KENNY
starts to sing, holding a red tea towel.*

CUT TO

34. EXT. PHOENIX CLUB MAIN DOOR. NIGHT
*MAX and PADDY are putting the frighteners
on each other.*

PADDY   What about Finchy? They gave
him a Burnley wallet (MIMES IT).
Strapped him to the back of a Jag
and drove round the estate. His belt
buckle got caught in a grid. They

only found his top half. The coffin
was yay big. (MIMES WITH HANDS)

MAX   Shut up Patrick. Whatever they do,
I hope it's quick.

CUT TO

35. INT. GALAXY LOUNGE. NIGHT
*We cut back to YOUNG KENNY in full flight
as MEATLOAF.*

CUT TO

36. EXT. PHOENIX CLUB MAIN DOOR. NIGHT
Cut back to MAX and PADDY.

PADDY   Hey, what about Tommy Dickfingers?
(HOLDS OUT HIS HANDS) They
found him in a wheelie bin, two
snooker balls for eyes.

MAX   Leave it. Leave it!

CUT TO

37. INT. GALAXY LOUNGE. NIGHT

*JERRY on stage as GEORGE MICHAEL
singing 'DON'T LET THE SUN GO DOWN ON
ME'. JERRY introduces: 'LADIES AND
GENTLEMEN, MR ELTON JOHN'. A spotlight
hits BRIAN in the corner of the stage dressed
as ELTON JOHN. (Gap in teeth, big red
glasses over his own glasses.)*

CUT TO

**38. EXT. PHOENIX CLUB MAIN DOOR.
NIGHT**

MAX   Oh, it's not fair, Paddy. (CRYING)
        If only I'd have met the right
        woman.

PADDY   If only you'd have met a woman?

MAX   You know I always wanted children! Little Maxes and Maxines running around (PRETENDING TO PLAY WITH THEM) ... Don't worry, it's all right ... it's alright, your daddy's here ... Come here! (STARTS TO BREAK DOWN)

PADDY   Calm down, you're losing it!

MAX is still crying.

CUT TO

39. EXT. PHOENIX CLUB MAIN DOOR. NIGHT
DEN PERRY's Jag pulls into shot. We cut to MAX and PADDY.

PADDY   Max, they're here. (POINTS)

MAX   (DISTRACTED) This is it ... this is it, Patrick.

We cut to DEN PERRY's Jag. His TWO CRONIES get out of the car. Paddy runs off.

MAX   (Cont.) Come here, give me a hug, you big soft ... shithouse.

MAX runs off.

We cut back to the Jag. The CRONY opens the door for DEN PERRY.

DEN PERRY
    I'm looking forward to this. Let's go and see Brian Potter talking to himself. (LAUGHS)

CUT TO

40. INT. GALAXY LOUNGE. NIGHT
We cut to spotlight on BRITNEY (schoolgirl outfit), her back to the AUDIENCE. We hear

a few wolf whistles. She sings the opening line to 'HIT ME BABY ONE MORE TIME', then turns on the beat ... it's KENNY SNR. We cut to a mixed reaction from the AUDIENCE: disgust from the men, laughter from the women.

We cut to SPENCER at the side (still as GARY GLITTER).

SPENCER (TO RAY VON AS ADAM ANT) That wasn't in the hamper.

CUT TO

41. INT. THE PHOENIX CLUB FOYER/GALAXY LOUNGE. NIGHT
DEN PERRY walking smugly down the corridor. Laughing.

DEN PERRY
    Hey lads, what do you call a show with no acts?

He opens the door to the Galaxy Lounge. We cut to interior, see his reaction. It's full. BRITNEY on stage, the AUDIENCE watching. DEN isn't happy. He turns on his heel and knocks his CRONIES out of the way. Exits shot. His CRONIES follow.

CUT TO

42. INT. BRIAN'S OFFICE. NIGHT
BRIAN (still ELTON JOHN) is counting money (notes).

DEN PERRY
    Enjoy it while you can.

BRIAN looks up, startled.

BRIAN   Perry? What do you want?

DEN PERRY
    I've got some unfinished business, Brian ... You!

One of DEN's CRONIES shuts the door behind him.

BRIAN   (SHOUTS) Jerry! Jerry!

DEN PERRY
    Save your breath – they can't hear you. They're all watching the show.

BRIAN   Yeah, I'm lucky I've got a bloody show after the little stunt you pulled today ... Hey, cancelling the acts – oh, very original, Perry. Not in the same league, though, not in the same league as burning us down.

DEN PERRY
    Brian, Brian, Brian, what am I going to do with you, eh?

BRIAN   Nothing, nothing. You're too late, Perry: we're back. The Phoenix has risen! They're queuing round the bloody block to get in here. We're packed to the rafters ... yeh. Not like your club. I think it's gone down the shit pan. All you deserve, you fat pig! (DEN'S HEAVY LUNGES FOR BRIAN) Whoa, whoa, whoa, get back ... get back ... I'll head butt you in the groin.

DEN PERRY
    You're forgetting something, Brian: we've been here before! Do you remember? Last year, Talent Trek, everything hunky-dory ... and then ... (LIGHTS HIS LIGHTER) Be awful if that were to happen again.

BRIAN   No, no, you're making a big mistake, Denzel.

DEN PERRY
    The only mistake I made were setting fire to this place while you weren't inside. Eh?! Come on boys. I wouldn't bother with a coat tonight, Brian. I think you'll be warm enough!

He exits with his CRONIES leaving BRIAN shaken up.

CUT TO

43. INT. THE PHOENIX CLUB FOYER. NIGHT
DEN and CRONIES walk towards the Galaxy Lounge.

CUT TO

44. INT. GALAXY LOUNGE. NIGHT
DEN opens the door of the Galaxy Lounge and walks in, he stops, shocked. We cut to reveal the whole AUDIENCE staring at him in stony silence. BREWERY REPS, JERRY on the stage, with LES and ALAN either side. We hear feedback and the noise of a mic being hit.

BRIAN   (OS) … two-one-two. Did you get all that Jerry?

JERRY   Every word.

DEN PERRY awkwardly turns to leave. But the STAFF (in costume) are blocking the doorway. The STAFF part as BRIAN enters the room. He's holding a radio mic.

BRIAN   All right, Perry, have you got one of these radio mics at your club? Eh, I tell you something: they pick up everything. Cost a few bob, like, but I think this one's just paid for itself.

DEN PERRY
    (TURNS TO BREWERY REP) A mic. You don't think we would, eh … We're old mates … me and Potter … having a laugh eh?! Having a laugh!

BRIAN   I don't think so.

DEN PERRY
    I knew … I knew …

CUT TO

45. EXT. PHOENIX CLUB CAR PARK. NIGHT

Floor shot of MAX's motor home.

We cut to interior, MAX in driver's seat, sweating. He's about to turn the ignition key. He closes his eyes. We hear a loud thud. MAX jumps. We cut to see PADDY banging on the window.

MAX   You daft bastard! What are you trying to do?!

PADDY   What are you doing?

MAX winds down the window.

MAX   Having a pissin' heart attack is what I'm doing! I'm lying low, getting out of here, till the heat's off me!

PADDY   Well, hang on ... I'm coming with you ...

MAX   What?

PADDY   Eight grand, remember? Half of this belongs to me.

CUT TO

46. INT. GALAXY LOUNGE. NIGHT

Cutaway of the opening of a champagne bottle exploding. They all cheer. Cut out to reveal BRIAN and the rest of the STAFF (all still in costume) having a celebratory drink.

ALAN   So we managed to fool the brewery, then?

BRIAN   Did we balls! They knew what we were up to straightaway. They knew it were us but they loved it! Mark Brennan, he wanted Britney's phone number.

KENNY SNR
    Why, does he want to book me?

BRIAN   Well, it sounded like book ... Close your legs, you little slut!

JERRY   Did he say how much they are going to give us?

BRIAN   He didn't, Jerry. No, he didn't specify. He said he was going to come down tomorrow to discuss a deal.

JERRY   Well, at least Den Perry's not going to get anything.

LES   Did you see him? He was crying when they put him in the back of the police van ... sobbing his eyes out, he was.

BRIAN   Good I'm glad.

RAY VON Hey, you know what this means, Brian? They'll have to give you your licence back, now you're in the clear.

BRIAN   Oh, aye, bloody hell! I am, aren't I?
         I'm in the clear!

HOLY MARY
         See, God loves you, Brian.

BRIAN   (THINKS) No, no ... I don't think I
         want my licence back. I think
         Jerry's done us proud. I think we
         should leave things the way they
         are. (THEY ALL SAY AYE) A toast to
         Jerry St Clair, Phoenix licensee ...

*They all repeat the line and toast JERRY
together.*

JERRY   Thanks, everybody, I'd just like to
         say— (GOES TO STAND UP)

BRIAN   Sit down Jerry!

CUT TO

47. EXT. PHOENIX CLUB CAR PARK. NIGHT
*MAX and PADDY sat in motor home. MAX is
still about to turn the ignition.*

MAX   Here goes ... (WE HEAR INTRUDER
         2000 CAR ALARM: 'GET BACK, YOU
         BASTARD – I'LL BREAK YOUR
         LEGS') Oooh, right, off we go! Hey ...
         look! Oi!

*We cut to see it driving out. YOUNG KENNY
(MEATLOAF) is outside.*

YOUNG KENNY
         Come on, lads, come and have a
         drink – we're celebrating!

MAX   Oy, Mandy Dingle ... tell Potter
         we're off.

YOUNG KENNY
         Off where?

MAX   Hey ... who knows? We don't know
         but we'll know when we get there.

YOUNG KENNY
         So how will you know?

MAX   We just will ... all right?!

YOUNG KENNY
         Yeah, but how will you know if you
         don't know where you're going?

PADDY   Just drive over him.

MAX   I'm gonna! Move, penguin, we'll
         flatten you!

YOUNG KENNY
         All right, OK, OK.

*The motor home pulls out of the car park
and off down the road.*

CUT TO

END CREDITS

**48. EXT. PHOENIX CLUB MAIN DOOR.
NIGHT**
*We tilt up the DOORMEN, feet to head, to
reveal the TWO STOWAWAYS in black-and-*

whites. A FEW GIRLS walk towards the club.

ANT   (pidgin English) Evening, ladies ...

DEC   Nice legs ... what time do they open?!

They enter the club. One of the STOWAWAYs motions with his hands the size of their breasts.

THE END

Series 1

Brian Potter/Max/Keith Lard – Peter Kay
Jerry St. Clair – Dave Spikey
Ray Von – Neil Fitzmaurice
Paddy – Patrick McGuinness
Les – Toby Foster
Alan – Steve Edge
Kenny Senior – Archie Kelly
Young Kenny – Justin Moorhouse
Holy Mary – Janice Connolly
Marion – Beatrice Kelley
Den Perry – Ted Robbins
Mary – Sian Foulkes

With

Episode 1
Roy Walker, Ced Beaumont, Tim Healy,
Daniel Kitson, Tony Skip, Jayne Tunnicliffe,
Tony Xu

Episode 2
Ced Beaumont, Rodney Litchfield,
Ron Harrison, Bernard Wrigley

Episode 3
Joe O'Byrne, Helen Moon, Lorraine Cheshire,
Alex Lowe, John Axon, Lynne Roden

Episode 4
Dave Law, Jo Enright, Sally Lindsay

Episode 5
Johnny Leeze, Toby Hadoke, Mark Attwood,
Andy Wilkinson

Episode 6
Alison Burrows, Damian Moore,
Danny Martelli, Daniel Kitson

Series 2

Brian Potter/Max – Peter Kay
Jerry St Clair – Dave Spikey
Ray Von – Neil Fitzmaurice
Paddy – Patrick McGuinness
Les – Toby Foster
Alan – Steve Edge
Kenny Senior – Archie Kelly
Young Kenny – Justin Moorhouse
Holy Mary – Janice Connolly
Joyce – Enid Dunn
Den Perry – Ted Robbins
Spencer – Daniel Kitson
Ant – Julian Sua
Dec – Wai Kee Chan

With

Episode 1
Jim Bowen, David Prosho, James Duke,
Vincent Peters, Paul Crone, Peter Slater,
Orla Cunningham

Episode 2
Bernard Wrigley, Joanne Sidwell,
Patsy Ghadie, Peter Oliver, Phil Brockbank,
Michael Neary, Brian Fearn

Episode 3
Stewart Maconie, Martin Reeve, Billy Boden,
Jack Hudson

Episode 4
Kanako Morishita, Ryozo Kohira,
Jakki Perkins, Soni Walker, Sue Kelly,
Tim Paley

Episode 5
Kate Robbins, Joanne Knowles, Patsy Ghadie,
Penny Lindley, Tim Beasley, Steve Money

Episode 6
Joanne Knowles, Steve Money,
Jason Furnival, Ruth Lawrence